The Final War

The Final War
A Fantastic Story

by
Barillet-Lagargousse

translated, annotated and introduced by
Brian Stableford

A Black Coat Press Book

Edited by Peter Gabbani

Visit our website at www.blackcoatpress.com

TABLE OF CONTENTS

Introduction

La Guerre finale, histoire fantastique, here translated as *The Final War: A Fantastic Story*, was first published in Paris by Berger-Levrault et Cie in 1885, although the company in question was originally based in Nancy, in Lorraine. It bore the sardonic by-line *Barillet-Lagargousse, Ingénieur destructeur, Membre de plusieurs societés philanthropique et savantes* [Barillet-Lagargousse, Engineer of Destruction, Member of Several Philanthropic (i.e. Reformist) and Scientific Societies]; *Barillet* can mean gun barrel, and a *gargousse* is a kind of cartridge. No information is available as to who the person behind the pseudonym might have been, although the content of the text seems to support—superficially, at least—the byline's contention that he was a military engineer by profession with radical political interests, specifically in the co-operative movement.

There is no obvious clue to the possible authorship of the text in the "extracts from the catalogue" that the publisher appends to the text, which, with one conspicuous exception, are books on military matters, but are mostly concerned with naval warfare and weaponry, and "Barillet-Lagargousse" was certainly uninterested in that aspect of modern warfare. The conspicuous exception is *Ignis* (1883) by Comte Didier de Chousy,[1] which presumably heads the list because it is the only other book published by Berger-Levrault in the same genre of futur-

---

[1] tr. as *Ignis: The Central Fire,* Black Coat Press, ISBN 978-1-934543-88-7.

istic fiction as *La Guerre finale*. Even bolder in its speculations, and far more surreal, the earlier book obviously originated from a very different hand and mind, but the publisher's decision to issue both of them, at a time when futuristic fiction was still rare and outré, is an interesting one.

The historical importance of *La Guerre finale*, as a work of speculative fiction, is neatly summed up by its title. The idea of a "final war" or a "war to end war" was to gain considerable ground over the subsequent thirty years, prior to the outbreak of actual Great War, but in 1885, it was still a novel idea. Barillet-Lagargousse's novel is by no means the first literary mention of the idea, but it is the first elaborate extrapolation of the notion and the first to flesh it out with abundant detail.

Future war fiction as such was not new at the time, and the embryo of a genre had been created in England by a brief glut of such stories produced in the wake of George Chesney's anonymous account of *The Battle of Dorking* published in *Blackwood's Magazine* in 1871, inspired by the idea of what might happen if the Prussian armies that had devastated France in the previous year turned their attention to England. That novelette had been rapidly reprinted as a pamphlet and translated into several other languages, including French, where *Bataille de Dorking: invasion des Prussiens en Angleterre* (1871), with a preface by Charles Ynarte, went through several editions. It was swiftly followed up in France by Édouard Dangin's account of *Le Bataille de Berlin en 1875* (1871), which references the battle of Dorking alongside the battle of Sedan as if it were a real occurrence.

Most exercises in a similar vein to *The Battle of Dorking*, however, in France as in England, followed

Chesney's example in focusing on the deployment of contemporary weaponry and strategy, featuring battles that might take place tomorrow or the day after. There was intense interest in the possibilities inherent in the new weapons that were being continually developed in the wake of the Franco-Prussian war, as evidenced by the non-fiction titles included in Berger-Levrault's list, but attempts to imagine their future development in anything more than the most elementary terms were scarce.

French literary dealings with future warfare had, however, deviated from the standard English pattern by courtesy of the endeavors of Albert Robida, who followed up the humorous descriptions of technological warfare contained in his Vernian parody *Voyages très extraordinaire de Saturnin Farandoul* (1879)[2] with the broadly satirical *La Guerre au Vingtième siècle* (1883; different book version 1887; tr. as "War in the Twentieth Century"), in which he provided relatively brief texts to accompany caricaturish illustrations of monstrous engines of war. Both versions of the text describe wars displaced into a sufficiently distant future for technology to have transformed the mechanics of mass murder, each depicting a conflict on a considerably larger scale than a squabble between neighboring nations: a conflict embracing the whole of Europe, and hence (by virtue of colonial expansion) the whole world, although not in any sense "final."

Robida, as a committed pacifist, took the view that any such conflict would be catastrophic because of the scale of the slaughter enabled by technologically advanced weaponry, but not everyone had taken that view

---

[2] tr. as *The Adventures of Saturnin Farandoul*, Black Coat Press, ISBN 978-1-934543-61-0.

of the possible net effect of technology on future warfare. Some futuristic writers associated with the Romantic Movement, including Joseph Méry, in "Les Ruines de Paris" (c.1844)[3] and Théophile Gautier, in "Paris Futur" (1851)[4] proposed, in passing, that a time would surely come when a weapon would be invented that would have such enormous killing power that war would become impractical, because it would lead to the mutual devastation of the contending parties. That notion had become commonplace, although it was rarely foregrounded, in the series of stories that followed in the tracks of those two brief exercises in the latter half of the century, which eventually elaborated their themes with sufficient enthusiasm and continuity to form a virtual subgenre of carefully contrasted visions of future Paris as a splendid utopia or a relic of defunct glory.

Barillet-Lagargousse is obviously aware of both those prior sets of images, although he is not a satirist of Robida's stripe, nor is he preoccupied with Paris as a key symbol of civilization, as the heirs of Méry and Gautier tended to be. Indeed, for much of his text, he seems hardly to be a satirist at all, in spite of occasional scathing sarcastic asides, although he is careful to plant a clue to the possible unreliability of his narrative voice in the brief prologue that precedes the text. Memory of that clue might well serve to prompt readers to wonder exactly how deep the sarcasm really cuts as they are presented with the mind-boggling depiction of a utopian state in the form of a vast armaments factory, whose inventive

---

[3] tr. as "The Ruins of Paris" in *The Tower of Destiny*, Black Coat Press, ISBN 978-1-61227-101-9.

[4] tr. as "Future Paris" in *Investigations of the Future*, Black Coat Press, ISBN 978-1-61227-106-4.

founder eventually comes up with weapons sufficiently powerful for him to take on the world and bend it to his pacifist will.

It is worth noting that the brevity and enigmatic quality of the preface is itself noteworthy, given that very few immersive fantasies set in the future had been produced in 1885, and that almost all of them came with far more cumbersome prefaces explaining the nature of the exercise in advance to readers, who were then assumed to be quite unready to confront the idea of a story of the future told as if written from a viewpoint in the further future rather than being represented as a prophetic dream. That was, however, to become the natural style of future war stories, which were soon able to abandon expository prologues altogether, as in Jules Lermina's *La Bataille de Strasbourg* (1891-92)[5], which was one of the first novels following in the wake of Barillet-Lagargousse's to take up the notion of a "final war" that would settle the fate of the world by means of new powers of technological destruction.

The most interesting feature of *La Guerre finale* from the modern viewpoint, however, is not its narrative strategy, pioneering as that was, but the specific nature of its advanced weaponry, which represents very starkly by virtue of its tactics of exaggeration the narrow horizons of the imagination in 1885. The passage of time has given modern readers a very elaborate education in that regard, and we can now see very clearly that the "ultimate weapons" imagined by Méry and his successors are very tame indeed by the standards of the weapons that were actually deployed in the Great War, let alone

---

[5] tr. as *The Battle of Strasbourg,* Black Coat Press, ISBN 978-1-61227-324-2.

World War II. We now know that the scale and nature of the massacres that actually became feasible did not have the slightest deterrent effect on the willingness of any nation to go to war, and that the first impulse of any nation possessed of a "weapon too dreadful to use" would be to use it before the opposition acquired it too.

The rapid development of future war fiction in the last few decades of the 19th century provides a striking illustration of the adaptation of the imagination to the prospect of future destruction. By the end of the century, the more imaginative future wars were being fought with submarines and aircraft, and the bombardments carried out by the latter, making no distinction between military and civilian targets, employed incendiary bombs and chemical weapons as well as new high explosives of unprecedented force. The most advanced visions also took inspiration from the discovery of X-rays and radium in the late 1890s to envisage weapons involving exotic radiations and atomic disintegration. None of that, however, had been on the imaginative horizon in 1885—except for submarines, whose problematic actual history, extending back to the seventeenth century, hardly lent confidence to the notion that they would become vital instruments of war any time soon, and Albert Robida's employment of them must have seemed to many of his readers, in spite of the literary precedent provided by Jules Verne's *Nautilus*, to be a joke. "Hertzian waves" had not yet been discovered, so the possibility of wireless telegraphy seemed equally fanciful to the hard-headed.

By 1891, when Jules Lermina wrote *Le Bataille de Strasbourg*, the situation was a little further advanced, although Lermina's use of "radiation" in that novel is based on an analogy that now seems all the more absurd because we have much better applications available to our thinking. Barillet-Lagargousse, however, had not the slightest inkling of such eventualities, and his superweapons are much more modest in their imagined mechanisms—although that arguably makes the conception of their destructive force even more extraordinary. Although the weapons that permit the five-hundred-strong army of Canonenstadt to obliterate a German army of several hundred thousand men in a matter of minutes might have stepped (literally) straight out of the pages of Robida's *La Guerre au Vingtième siècle*, the fact that they are not represented as caricatures but as plausible war machines lends them a unique historical interest in the annals of future war fiction.

Similarly, when the bombs employed in the novel's climax produce casualty figures similar to those of the atomic bombs eventually dropped on Hiroshima and Nagasaki, the fact that they do so by means of "conventional weaponry" makes them, in their fashion, very striking in their imaginative quality. It is perhaps significant that although Jules Lermina used extraordinary (and blatantly absurd) technology to facilitate the flying machine and the "blaster" featured in *La Bataille de Strasbourg*, the weapon he used to bring about the climax of his unfortunately-truncated saga is a sketchy copy of the one used by Barillet-Lagargousse to destroy Coblentz.

Although *La Guerre finale* cannot really qualify as a prophetic novel, for several perfectly understandable reasons, it is worth noting that some of its cynical insights do seem, with the aid of hindsight, to have a certain acuity. Like *La Bataille de Strasbourg*, *La Guerre finale* imagines a European war fought in the 1890s that serves as a preliminary to their different versions of the "ultimate war," but whereas Lermina's simply has the

French getting retribution for 1870 and recovering Alsace-Lorraine from Germany—a common theme of French future war fiction of the 1890s—Barillet-Lagargousse has the war of 1896 lurching to a stalemate because of the immense economic cost to all the contending parties, and dying of exhaustion in an armistice signed without any of the issues at stake being genuinely settled. In his future history, the economic woes of the near-bankrupt European nations then continue because of the necessity of maintaining their armies in order to sustain that stalemate, which means continually updating their weaponry to keep up with technological advances, and with, all the while, a further war looming on the horizon. As nineteenth-century speculative histories of the twentieth century go, that is far from being the widest of the mark, no matter how preposterous it now seems that the world might have been saved in 1934 by the heir to the Krupp cannon factories, partly as a result of his re-organizing them as a workers' co-operative.

The novel's literary style is more than a trifle stilted, as might be expected if it really was the work of an military engineer with no literary experience—although it relaxes somewhat as the author warms to his task and lets out the rein on his wit—but the lack of conventional "human interest" and the near-absence of dialogue does help him to cover his narrative ground at a gallop rather than a trot. All in all, the novel remains readable and fascinating, and is entitled to be considered something more than a mere museum piece.

By way of comparison, and to fill out the book, I have added a more conventional future war story by another author who wrote for Berger-Levrault et Cie in the 1880s, although the piece in question is a feuilleton not previously reprinted in book form. The author is the naval officer and mathematician Maurice Loir (1852-1924), whose first book, the oft-reprinted *L'Escadre de l'amiral Courbet: notes et souvenirs* [Admiral Courbet's Squadron: Notes and Memoirs] was initially issued by the Nancy-based publisher a year after *La Guerre finale*, in 1886. Loir went on to write a dozen more books on naval warfare and naval history, with several of the others being similarly based on his own experiences in the "Tonkin campaign" of 1883-86—material that, coincidentally, provided the basis for a tongue-in-cheek fictitious memoir by Jules Lermina published in the same periodical as the feuilleton version of *La Bataille de Strasbourg*.

Loir's most thoughtful futurological essay was *La Marine et progrès, les luttes de l'avenir par la science, par les millions* [The Navy and Progress: The Warfare of the Future, by Science and Millions] (1900, in collaboration with Gaston de Caqueray), but some years prior to that he had transfigured his own memories of life as a midshipman in naval battle into a futuristic anticipation of "Batailles navales de l'avenir," here translated as "Naval Battles of the Future," published as a 22-part feuilleton in *La Science Illustrée* in 1895. Unfortunately, the editor of *La Science Illustrée*, Louis Figuier, evidently confused Loir with the contemporary illustrator Maurice Leloir, and the first three episodes of the serial appeared with the latter signature; although the error was corrected thereafter, the story is still occasionally misattributed in indices and bibliographies.

Another of Barillet-Lagargousse's anticipatory triumphs in *La Guerre finale* is that in his war of 1896 ironclad battleships play no significant part, shunning any actual engagement with the enemy because of their vulnerability to torpedoes. In Loir's imminent-future war, which is probably also set in 1896, that anxiety does not stop the heroic mariners from taking their ponderous ironclads into battle—with the result that their up-to-date weapons inflict enormous damage on one another and rack up horrendous casualty figures.

Although Loir never gives the slightest indication that his own narrator should not be taken entirely seriously, the objective rhetoric of the story he tells, seen with a clinical eye—especially one aided by hindsight—is that patriotism and heroism are very costly follies in the era of modern weaponry. The engineer who signed himself Barillet-Lagargousse, whether or not he really imagined utopia as a gigantic armaments factory, would certainly not have disagreed with that judgment.

The following translation of *La Guerre Finale* was made from the copy of the Berger-Levrault edition reproduced on the Bibliothèque Nationale's *gallica* website. The translation of "Batailles navales de l'avenir" was made from the serial version contained in the relevant volume of *La Science Illustrée* reproduced on the same website.

Brian Stableford

THE FINAL WAR:
A FANTASTIC STORY

The earth is bleak and desiccated,
but it will be verdant again;
the breath of the wicked will not pass over it
eternally like a burning wind.
Prepare your souls for that time,
for it is not far off: it is nigh.
Lammenais: *Paroles d'un croyant.*[6]

---

[6] Hugues-Félicié Robert de Lammenais (1782-1854) was a priest, philosopher and political theorist whose views became famous, as much for their dramatic shift as the radicalism of their eventual content. *Paroles d'un croyant* (1834; tr. as *Words of a Believer*) is a collection of aphorisms published after his desertion of the Church, denouncing the established social order, which it views as an evil conspiracy of monarchs and religious leaders against the people; it was inspired by the incendiary writing of the leading light of the Polish Romantic Movement, Adam Mickiewicz, and was condemned by the pope as an exceedingly wicked book. Its choice as the source of a head-quote for *La Guerre finale* is significant in more ways than one.

PROLOGUE

X***, 29 April 1934

The hour has sounded when the earth must no longer be the permanent battlefield of contrary interests and passions.

The tiger will no longer devour the lamb, or the strong oppress the weak; concord will reign between humans. How will this prodigy be brought about? Open this book, reader, and you will learn.

Your skeptical smile is already profaning these pages consecrated to the memory of the most illustrious of the sons of Adam. But know that his mission down here was revealed to me several thousand centuries ago. Science was then in its swaddling clothes; mathematics had not yet engendered ballistics, and ballistics had not engendered artillery; I had not yet been born. That is why I never prophesied the events that have led to this transformation of humanity.

Today, when the events are accomplished and they are entering into the domain of history, I want at least to recount them, and, strong in the authority of my revelation, I implore you, in the name of enlightenment, to believe in the truth of my story. You will see how an immortal genius has shone over our planet, and how the regime of enforced peace and obligatory labor imposed by him over the entire extent of the continents has modified human intellectual faculties, to the point of extin-

guishing in hearts the burning fire of passions and causing to reflourish among us the celestial bliss of the terrestrial paradise.

Read in peace, my brother.

I

"Now, Messieurs, if we cast a retrospective glance over the twenty years that have just gone by, we will feel a legitimate satisfaction at the sight of the results obtained and the progress realized during that period. The metallurgical establishments of the entire world, once our rivals, have been obliged to cease their competition before the crushing superiority of our cannon-metal. Many of them have been ruined by fruitless research attempting to penetrate our secret or to discover an analogous product that might permit them to continue the struggle. All of them are presently reduced to manufacturing objects of a distinctly secondary importance, such as steam engines, railway equipment and other metallic constructions for which the old steel can still suffice.

"In the not-very-distant future we shall also take away those last and feeble resources, but we can already say today that our laborious efforts have assured us the most brilliant and the most envied of monopolies, that of artillery. We have not only given cannons a perfection in lightness and resistance that has astonished connoisseurs; our projectiles possess such powers of explosion that their prodigious effect on troops has aroused general enthusiasm every time they have been called upon to resolve the grave questions that sometimes divide peoples.

"Thanks to the intelligent and indefatigable zeal of our agents in all parts of the world, the negroes of Africa, the inhabitants of South America, and even the islanders of Polynesia have no hesitation in imposing the heaviest sacrifices upon themselves in order to procure our products, and are now indebted to us for the same benefits as the Europeans powers.

"Thus provided, they too have been able to constitute those superb armies that are the glory of the century, by means of which their fragmented territories will soon be covered by vast and powerful empires. Better than the Spekes, the Burkes and the Livingstones, our commercial travelers have been able to bring these young peoples nearer to old Europe by giving birth among them to the fecund sentiment of national grandeur, and initiating them into the latest discoveries of modern industry.

"We have thus contributed, in large measure, to the acceleration of the march of civilization. A few more efforts, and the world, disrupted so many times by revolutions, drawn into the path of progress by the impulsion that we have been able to impart to it, will surely move in the direction of utilitarian reform, and end up finding the equilibrium and the stability that philosophies and religions have been impotent thus far to bring about.

"However, above that brilliant horizon, I can see the threat of tempest surging forth. A black dot today, it will perhaps be a cloud tomorrow capable of obscuring with its giant shadow the gleam of our success.

"I fear that our riches, so legitimately acquired, might attract the attention of our neighbors, particularly that of the great empire that surrounds us. There, jealous eyes are following the progress of our influence, which is increasing incessantly, to the determinant of some, it is true, but assuredly to the profit of the greatest number. Dazzled by its power, that State seems to have forgotten that it owes its most efficacious means of action to us. Although the ingrate is scornful of us because of the limited extent of our territory, and hates us for our treasures, we shall nevertheless pursue the goal to which we aspire!

"But our security must not be compromised; our duty is to seek to adopt at great haste measures against the unfortunate eventualities that might be produced. I believe, in addition, that I have already found them, and I propose to reveal them to you in an imminent session."

Such is the essence of the remarkable speech of 1 February 1923 in which the eminent engineer Lichtmann, the President of the Cooperative State of Canonenstadt, had revealed to the Government Council the brilliant industrial situation of the country, and also the anxieties inspired in him by external politics.

An extraordinary engineer and an accomplished economist, the man in question combined with his many virtues and many faults an audacity capable of any enterprise and an energy capable of carrying it through. Still young, he had fathomed the abyss in the depths of which terrible social questions stirred, lifted up like black smoke by the irresistible current of our old civilization toward luxury and pleasures. As active as he was indefatigable, he had confronted those somber problems resolutely, analyzed them coldly and recognized fearfully the impossibility of opposing a dam to the ever-increasing overflow of human misery.

But from the violent impact of an elite intelligence against a reef in which so many strong wills had already broken, a powerful idea sprang forth one day, a spark that was to illuminate those depths and serve as a beacon light to society in the sheer paths that it was necessary to climb in order to arrive at the serene heights of universal peace. He set to work without delay and founded, in the final years of the 19th century, in the midst of Europe, a free and respected State, armed to the teeth, whose surface area was less than that of a medium-sized French département.

All the causes of inequality, and hence of jealousy, between the citizens were carefully set aside there by the wisest of institutions. Thus, the constitution dictated by the engineer gave rise to the admiration of other peoples, who would all have liked to be ruled by it. For reformers, it was a model that it would be necessary, sooner or later, to imitate.

That man of genius had nothing particular about his appearance, which greatly astonished his contemporaries. His description was easy to make. He was not one of those men whose cerebral development or profundity of gaze causes people to say, on seeing them: "There goes an intellectual!" No, he could only be judged by his actions, and the examination of his skull would not have revealed any particular protrusion.

It was probably that perfect balance of all the elements of his personality and faculties that had permitted him to assimilate all human knowledge and master the most dissimilar sciences. That universality, which made him simultaneously the greatest chemist, the greatest technologist and the greatest philosopher of the era, had allowed him to discover the true path of progress, which so many others had only glimpsed.

Essentially practical, he had not allowed himself to be dazzled, while studying the religions and philosophies of all eras, by theories that are admittedly seductive, but solely for the usage of educated minds. No system had, in his opinion, preoccupied itself sufficiently with the material interests of the multitude. The liberty that some people thought they had achieved and which others envied was only a deceptive lure, a shadow always on the brink of vanishing, for the turbulent and hungry crowds always dreamed of other destinies and became more irritated every day with the obstacles raised by the constitutions and laws in place. Experience began to demonstrate their insufficiency and even their complete lack of utility. Liberty had been painted by the popular imagination in attractive colors, but with disillusionment had come lofty demands in favor of the absolute equality that, by suppressing unhealthy comparison, was the only means of suppressing completely any seed of revolt.

Lichtmann resolved to give satisfaction to the masses; labor, the source of all wealth, the conqueror of the spirit of independence as well as oppression and tyranny, would unite in the same momentum all the classes of society, and in that leveling of conditions and fortunes, humans would find the remedy for their ills and the pledge of a boundless felicity.

Thus distinguishing the goal with a marvelous lucidity, he had immediately thought about the means of attaining it. We should say, in his praise, that he did not think for a moment of having recourse to the polemics of the press or the podium, the results of which could only be uncertain, and the effects very slow. Those instruments had, moreover, the inconvenience of being in the hands of malevolent wills and paltry interests, which would certainly join up in opposition to him. That century of money and weapons had to furnish him with a more rapid and more reliable means.

In his view, suspicions and hatreds between neighbors, carefully maintained and envenomed, were being aroused by governments at bay in order to deflect attention away from burning questions. For love of peace, peoples were ruining themselves with the expenses of war, and those great deployments of force, that redoubtable military power, hid a fundamental and complete exhaustion. The regime of excessive armaments further exaggerated the evil by opposing a better utilization of human effort.

He therefore promised himself to exploit it, to push it to extreme exaggeration by demanding of it the resources that he lacked in order to arrive at the realization of his ideas. To do that, it would simply be sufficient to bring to the apparatus of war improvements, sufficiently considerable and repeated, to make it absolutely obligatory for the nations that were ready to cut one another's throats to renew frequently their armaments by recourse to him. In that fashion, the greater part of the heavy budgets of war would pass into his coffers, bringing him the omnipotence that he wanted to acquire.

In 1892 he entered as an engineer into the Krupp organization, so celebrated for the quantity, if not the quality, of the cannons that it manufactured. Although still very young, he was bound to attract attention by virtue of his exceptional ability, but in the beginning he had to contend with the attentions and jealousies of his colleagues. His unknown origin gave rise to the most slanderous suppositions and the most extravagant rumors. He was concealing his real name, whispered his detractors; born in Russia, he had prudently quit his native land after having been involved in several nihilist conspiracies. For those absurd rumors, inflated by public gossip, one would have searched in vain for any other foundation than a profound knowledge of explosive materials; but merit is always twisted when a stupid person denigrates it.

His voluminous correspondence with unknown individuals in the most distant countries was also interpreted as being suspicious. It was, however, nothing but the result of connections he had made with a number of enlightened individuals during his numerous voyages, and which he maintained carefully in order always to be up to date with the principal discoveries and the movement of ideas throughout the surface of the globe.

Finally, the malevolence gradually wearied, his modesty and his politeness disarming the most obstinate; everyone was obliged to bow down before his indisputable superiority and the unlimited confidence to which the owner of the factory testified in his regard. The latter, on his death a few years later, could not have made a better choice in designating him as his successor.

At that moment, the prosperity of the establishment was beginning to decrease. It was competing without any marked advantage against foreign competition, especially against Armstrong & Co.,[7] in England and Creusot in France.[8]

Was that not a marvelous opportunity to deploy the extraordinary talents that had earned our hero the first place among so many men remarkable for their knowledge and business intelligence? His fortune was assured, but his ambition was left unfulfilled. The honor of the company to restore, a great reputation to justify, a noble enterprise to pursue—such were still his tasks, and he did not fail in them.

---

[7] The Tyneside operation in question was actually Armstrong, Mitchell & Co. after 1882, when its original armaments manufacturing company merged with Charles Mitchell's shipbuilding company, and before it became Armstrong Whitworth in 1897 after merging with Joseph Whitworth's engineering company, when it also began to produce cars, trucks and, eventually, aircraft.

[8] The armaments factory based in Le Creusot was actually Schneider et Cie, sometimes known as Schneider-Creusot.

Shut away day and night in a laboratory, where only a few disciples had the privilege of accompanying him, he interrogated with an anxious eye the heated crucibles in which unknown mixtures agitated in horrible reactions. Thus, on the eve of battle, the ancient diviners sought in the entrails of victims the prophetic signs of events to come and the fate of human beings. But antiquity only had haruspices, the Middle Ages astrologers and sorcerers; the nineteenth century possessed true chemists, and although Lichtmann, like Basile Valentin, Raymond Lull and many others, did not find the philosopher's stone, a new substance emerged from his scientific research, an alloy of copper, steel and aluminum.

That metal, by virtue of its resistance in limited thickness, left far behind its analogues thus far employed in the construction of cannons. In order to found it he invented a furnace whose temperature was unattainable in rival factories. In a short time, those two well-guarded secrets were to ensure him the preference for the supply of cannons to the military powers.

II

In 1896, having established a new model of campaign cannon, Lichtmann invited the competent artillery experts of all nations to witness the trials; they responded to his summons with enthusiasm.

They examined the gun barrel with interest, which was elliptical in section and whose principal axis was horizontal. By virtue of its restricted thickness, it was reminiscent of a flattened stove pipe. Underneath, a cylinder a few centimeters in diameter, founded along with the first, gave the section of the ensemble the form of an inverted figure 8. The inferior cavity was designed to hold the cartridge, the other a lenticular projectile.

The cartridge was a long cylinder of compressed powder with a varnished surface; it was ignited at the rear via the breech and burned in successive stages as the shell was displaced within the cannon. The internal pressure of the gases and, in consequence, the acceleration imparted to the projectile, being thus continuously rendered, meant that the barrel did not have to support too great a stress, even though the muzzle velocity was about fifteen hundred meters per second.

On the left-hand generator of the elliptical cylinder, the cavity had a series of teeth. These projections, engaging with a copper crown surrounding the shell, forced the latter to adopt an axial rotation, whose circumferential speed was consequentially equal to that of the forward motion—which is to say, thirty times that acquired in an ordinary canon. That would have been unrealizable with a metal less resistant than the new compressed alloy, because the enormous centrifugal force would certainly have caused the projectile to explode, if not within the barrel, at least on its emergence. But that was precisely what would ensure it its unique explosion and procure for it an enormous useful effect. Those advantages were explained by the inventor himself to the elite artillerists he had assembled.

"My shell," he said, "weighing about forty kilograms, can be projected as far as twenty kilometers. That range might seem to you to be exaggerated, and would be, in fact, with your present systems, since one cannot perceive the enemy at that distance and therefore does not know where to direct one's fire. Henceforth, however, it will be sufficient to know their approximate position, and accuracy will only play a secondary role, for the projectile covers two square kilometers with shrapnel, which skims the ground less than one meter fifty from its surface.

"To obtain the latter result, an inferior stopper is unscrewed by inertia in mid-air during the first moments of the trajectory. One then sees emerge, impelled by a spring, a thin stalk about a meter and a half long, which is folded up in the interior like the units of a collapsible telescope. When, at the end of its course, the shell arrives at that distance from the ground and touches it with the extremity of the stalk, the latter transmits the shock to a fulminating capsule, which ignites the interior charge and determines the explosion.

"Now you know, Messieurs, that in the air, speeds of rotation are conserved almost integrally. It will, therefore, be with an average speed of fifteen hundred meters per second, augmented in a forward direction by the residual velocity—still a thousand meters per second at a range of ten kilometers—and diminished from whence it came, that the fragments will be projected in all directions. They will travel horizontally above ground for distances varying from five hundred meters to fifteen hundred meters from the point of explosion, over a breadth of a kilometer. That gives the surface area indicated. The fragments, about two thousand in number and with an average weight of twenty grams, are disposed in the projectile in horizontal layers subdivided into sectors.

"You can see that by this method, none of them will be, as in your present apparatus, launched into the air uselessly to fall back devoid of force, while others will be immediately buried, devoid of useful effect. Instead, they will all furnish a kind of blast footprint. It is easy to calculate, and the trial will demonstrate, that approximately five pieces of shrapnel will pass over each square meter of surface. In such conditions, any troop that is within several hundred meters of the location of the explosion will be literally scythed down.

"These remarkable properties of a unique projectile will permit a small number to be transported on campaign, and, in consequence, a considerable reduction in weight, which has caused serious difficulties in the past.

"I shall only tell you briefly about the gun carriage, which, like the gun, only weighs two hundred kilograms. Thanks to its metal and mode of construction, it supports without fatigue the enormous effort of the shock transmitted to it. Cupel springs that link it to the cannon diminish the recoil, and can even deaden it completely if one supports the butt against any obstacle, without there being any risk of the rupture of any component. That's another advantage that you'll doubtless appreciate.

"In a few days, I shall introduce you to another kind of gun designed to attack fortifications and the armor of ships. In that case, accuracy is absolutely necessary, since one cannot have recourse to the fragmentation of the missile. Thanks to an enormous initial velocity, I've succeeded in achieving a perfect regularity of fire. The weight launched is scarcely fifty kilograms, and yet the projectile, whose anterior part is made of a mixture of molten quartz and steel, a substance of extreme hardness and tenacity, will pierce the thickest armor plating as easily as a needle penetrates into a soft material.

"One can therefore consider as finished the already-old contest of projectiles and armor, for no State will be able to bear the expense necessary to fortify big ships or bunkers with the quartz-metal compound."

In the following days, the engineer carried out before his guests a series of trials designed to convince them that he had not overstated the capacities of his invention.

To render the results more tangible, he disposed a veritable army of mannequins depicting squadrons and battalions grouped in accordance with the principles of modern strategy. After a few cannon shots, those phantom soldiers, without exception, had been afflicted with wounds that would almost all have been mortal.

It was a surprise and a phenomenon before which all the prophets of contemporary artillery bowed down. Oh, illustrious ignoramuses, you all believed that you had made some contribution to the art of destruction during the last thirty years! What were your ridiculous conceptions and innocent ballistic dreams worth by comparison with that gigantic hecatomb, that marvelous butchery!

So, the members of the audience congratulated Lichtmann warmly, proclaiming him their master. When the enthusiasm had died down somewhat, they began to reflect on the new consequences that were about to flow from the introduction of such materiel into armies. They looked at one another suspiciously, wondering who would be the first to take advantage of the discovery. Torn between the desire to get ahead of their competitors and the desire to conceal their intentions, they strove to dissimulate with great care the impressions that their patriotism and the awareness of their responsibility aroused within them.

Colonel von Holzenkopf of the German foot artillery had made a rapid decision. He was already calculating whether the indemnity once paid by France would be sufficient for the acquisition of the large number of the new cannons necessary to endow the subjects of His Imperial Majesty with such precious instruments of labor as soon as possible.

The French envoy, General Rognard, had requested immediate instructions. In the meantime, he was astonished not to have discovered such a simple system a long time ago. As for the others, they were deeply plunged in their reflections and seemed very perplexed, but they kept the thoughts that were agitating them secret.

Only Major Fumistello, the head of the Italian mission, was unable to hide his disquiet on the subject of the projectile designed to pierce the hulls of ships. It was necessary to admit that there was good cause for apprehension, for such a weapon would render useless the gigantic, ponderous and heavily armored vessels that were the pride of the young peninsular navy, likely by virtue of their cost. An immense sadness invaded him at the thought that their inadequacy had been demonstrated even before they had encountered an opportunity to do battle. He therefore awaited with anguish the moment when he could be assured of the reality of the famous projectile's effects, striving to hope that the engineer was mistaken.

He was obliged to remain in uncertainty, for the date of the trials had not yet been fixed when the delegates learned that European diplomatic relations, already compromised when they departed, had deteriorated completely. They all received orders to rejoin their respective armies as soon as possible. The great war anticipated for several years was about to break out before the new cannons could be called upon to take part in it.

III

Without going into detail regarding that memorable conflict, we shall only recall its causes, its principal events and its consequences.

For a long time, the nations had been buckling under the burden of their permanent armies, the maintenance of which threatened to bring them to imminent ruin. On frontiers bristling with fortresses, the number of which was increasing every year, the means of attack and defense had mounted. The roads were cluttered with convoys, the railways and canals appeared only to be made for the transport of arms and ammunition, which were piled up in fortified locations. Agriculture, commerce and industry were dying, and the millions extracted in taxes continued to be swallowed up in the ever-yawning gulf of national debt. In spite of the most astonishing schemes of official finance, the loans multiplied and new excise duties were imposed every year. Crushing taxes were exacted on the most fundamental necessities of life, as it had been necessary to renounce any legitimate desire to balance the budgets.

The malaise was universal, but it was felt most of all in Germany, where the poor populations of several provinces were surfing more particularly from the high cost of objects of consumption, whose prices had hitherto been maintained at moderate levels. The great man who had rendered the country so powerful[9] was carrying

---

[9] Otto von Bismarck (1815-1898); in our history he was dismissed from office by Wilhelm II in 1890.

out a lamentable experiment in popular ingratitude, and his last days were going by in profound sadness.

As at the worst moments of the Germanic Confederation, Parliament was inclined to oppose the energetic measures that circumstances demanded, by refusing to sanction further duties on foodstuffs that were particularly dear to the inhabitants. The taxes having been decreed without the assent of the representatives of the country, serious rebellions broke out, and it was necessary to task a part of the army with assuring the exercise of the law by the forced sale of the merchandise in question. Public opinion then demanded loudly a general disarmament in which even Prussia was to participate.

That would have suppressed the principal branch of national industry, the one that, in a single year—the best, admittedly—had produced a profit of five billions. The taxpayers objected that they had not been included in the distribution of dividends, but that was bad reasoning; they had been amply paid by the glory that had been reflected on every one of them.

It therefore became necessary, as is customary is such cases, to strike a great blow in order to distract the malcontents, and, above all, to secure a few billion more, if possible. Then again, they could not break the superb machine of ransoms and annexations without making use of it one last time.

They therefore made sure of the good dispositions of their allies, the Austrians and the Italians, and made it understood at the Sublime Gate that if Russia took part in the conflict, as was probable, the moment would be propitious to re-establish supremacy over the Danubian states.

When these arrangements were terminated, it was perceived that the security of the Empire's frontiers necessitated the occupation of Luxembourg, because it was evident that France was thinking seriously about taking possession of it.

Without wasting any time, an army corps penetrated into the Duchy, which was added to the Imperial territory of Alsace-Lorraine.

France dared to protest; Russia, which could not allow the power of her dangerous neighbor to increase, joined in. War followed.

The principal French army was concentrated between Toul and Épinal, two others at Verdun and Belfort, while a fourth was held in reserve at Langres. Three corps immediately entered Italy, in spite of the local resistance of the Alpine battalions, and beat the first troops concentrated in the Po valley, thus compromising the already slow and difficult mobilization of the Italian army. In addition, one corps kept watch in the Pyrenees, and four new formations were assembled in Paris.

The Germans combined three armies on the French frontier and two on the Russian frontier, while three hundred thousand Austrians headed awkwardly toward Galicia. Russia committed the greater part of its forces to them, and sent the rest to the Danube, which was threatened by the Turks and the Austrian troops who had just invaded Serbia.

In the west, the French, who had the numerical superiority, were able to take the offensive, but all the hypotheses had been studied for so long and anticipated so carefully that it was difficult to find any tactical flaw on the adversary's part. The operations were therefore expertly managed, and a victorious general was often prevented from following up his success by the checks suffered by a less fortunate colleague.

Every foot of terrain was disputed, with the result that, six months after the opening of hostilities, in spite of eleven major battles, six of which went to the advantage of the French, and thirty-nine combats in which everyone covered themselves in glory, the French armies, entered in a single line, only found themselves along the Rhine between Coblentz and Strasbourg. They laid siege to the latter city, while two corps observed and immobilized the garrison of Metz.

Winter had come and the exhaustion of men and finance was complete on both sides; they sensed the impossibility of continuing the conflict, although no decisive blow had yet been struck.

In the east, the Austrians and the Germans had tried to isolate Poland and to cut off a Russian army concentrated in Warsaw, but their junction was incomplete when a second Russian army coming from the interior defeated the Austrians near Lublin, driving them back beyond their own frontier.

Combined thereafter, the Tsar's troops turned toward the Prussians facing northwest. Driven back in the first encounters, they had been forced to retreat behind the Niemen, where their enemies, harassed by the innumerable Cossack cavalry, dared not follow them. There too they were incapable of a further effort.

The rigors of the temperature ended up demoralizing the soldiers, exhausted by daily skirmishes to which they could see no end.

On the Danube, the Austrian army, having entered Serbia, found itself immobilized by a new uprising in Bosnia, Herzegovina and the neighboring provinces, having been whipped up by the influence of Saint Petersburg. It fought with difficulty, and the Danubian peoples joined forces, hoping to take advantage of the general torment and finally group together into a single state, realizing in part the pan-Slavic dream.

As for the Russians, on that front they had crossed the river and won a few victories over the Turks, but their progress was halted by the recall of a part of their forces to the north.

In Italy, the French corps, soon six in number, had succeeded completely in driving the Italians back into the peninsula, into which they had penetrated themselves, when the appearance in Venetia of an Austrian army prevented further incursion. They were obliged to content themselves with maintaining the positions they had conquered and establishing themselves solidly in the valley of the Po, observing their adversaries. Hoping soon to be supported, a fleet had left Toulon to disembark troops on the coasts of Tuscany, and there was talk—not without the idea giving rise to strong protests—of re-establishing the Papal States. It was necessary to renounce that operation.

At sea, the employment of torpedoes—which had become general—rendered the squadrons very circumspect. They limited themselves to protecting their coasts from enemy enterprises, and the largest and most beautiful battleships were often seen reduced to inaction for fear of minuscule torpedo boats, those invisible enemies against which they could do almost nothing. By the end of the campaign, several of those giants had been sunk or seriously damaged by their tiny adversaries, and yet there had not been any naval combat significant enough to have had any influence on the outcome of the war.

Belgium and Holland had not been threatened and had kept to one side.

England too remained inactive and in the general conflagration had not departed for an instant from her inviolable attachment to the traditions of prudence and composure that had won her a worldwide empire. Combats and bloody conquests were for others! It is all very well to be able to vanquish, but to be able to wait, to obtain a form of belated mediation between exhausted enemies, this would accrue advantages that arms would be impotent to overcome, and is a rarer and more worthy virtue.

The faithful subjects of His Britannic Majesty had, however, been unable to resist the pleasure of settling a few small scores and taking possession of various islands in several seas at their convenience. Those secondary events passed unnoticed, or, rather, the frustrated powers were too busy to raise protests.

Nevertheless, one thing saddened the English, which was the manifest impotence of fleets and the scant importance of maritime operations. Would that not result in a considerable diminution of their influence on continental affairs? It would be necessary, then, in order for them to re-establish themselves, to resolve to maintain a numerous army; there was no lack of capital, but where would they find the men?

Finally, when the belligerents, none of whom wanted to admit defeat, ground to a halt, exhausted, the cabinet of St. James's decided to intervene to settle the dispute. An armistice was proposed while a conference was organized in London.

All the interested parties welcomed the truce gladly and sent plenipotentiaries to settle the terms of the peace. After long and delicate negotiations, in the course of which the war would have flared up again if anyone had still been in a condition to fight, it was eventually stipulated that Germany would hand back to France the provinces ceded in 1871, and that Italy would pay an indemnity of two billion. Between Russia and Prussia everything would remain in the antebellum *status quo*.

As for Austria, which was still fighting against the Slavs and the inhabitants of Bohemia, who had risen up in response to the voices of their southern brethren, they were left at liberty to make their own arrangements with the rebels. Prussia profited from that embarrassment to offer help in return for the cession of what remained of Silesia. It was necessary to accept.

Then the Sublime Gate was constrained to recognize the annexations that the Austrians were about to make along the Danube, founding a Slavic kingdom that would be part of their Estates, thus designated by the name of the Austro-Hungarian-Slavic Empire.

Russia was dissatisfied with that final clause; indeed, as always happens after conventions of this sort, no one was content, which rendered disarmament difficult. A proposal made in that regard by Denmark was very poorly received, especially by the generals who represented Germany at the conferences. The latter had confidence in the future, thinking about the famous cannons to which Colonel von Holzenkopf had given such pompous praise. They had tried hard during the campaign to procure some of them, but that did not enter into the engineer's plans; under various pretexts, he had delayed their delivery indefinitely.

The Italians had been remarkable in the negotiations for a very particular but entirely natural bitterness, since they had not been able to ally themselves with the stronger side and their defeat on his occasion had brought them nothing—on the contrary. The irredentists, spitting fire and flame, reproached the government for not having understood that all its efforts would have been better directed toward the Tyrol, and that an alliance with France was consequently indicated.

As the price of her good offices, England saw her latest acquisitions ratified, and the decisions made at several conventions granted her control over wide stretches of coastline, ensuring her future commerce.

IV

Has any more frightful spectacle ever been seen than the aftermath of that war?

What disorder there was in every State? Bankruptcy threatening, agricultural regions ravaged or abandoned for lack of workers; the most fertile plains reverted to the state of those heathlands where brambles choke the final seeds of fruitless vegetation; depopulated cities in the bosom of which troops of wretches in sordid rags, with pale and emaciated faces: such were the scenes offered to the gaze.

On the thresholds of hovels and palaces, one no longer encountered the cries of delight, but the interminable moans of tearful mothers, for the cadavers of their sons were littering the soil of the fatherland or some foreign territory.

Had barbarians passed that way? Had the Huns or the Mongols emerged from their distant lairs to gorge themselves once again upon Europe and pillage it? No, all those woes, all those disasters, were nothing but the result of a refined civilization, the consequences of a fratricidal conflict well worthy of a chastisement of celestial wrath.

In all the epochs of history, in every age of life, we are submitted to cruel ordeals: baneful days in which all energy totters, in which it seems that in the breath of adversity, the last glimmer of hope must infallibly be extinguished; but despair has not been disposed to triumph over human vitality any more than shadow can prevail over light.

In the aftermath of such shocks, it is rare not to see brave men surge forth, with firm and vigorous hands, who, if they are tormented within by the fires of boundless ambition, feel no less profoundly the woes of their fellow citizens and hasten by their sage counsel to reestablish justice on earth, to wipe away the tears of the poor and to strengthen the public order that has been shaken to its foundations.

This time, collapse seemed imminent; such a demoralizing experience had not enlightened anyone; far from being appeased, hatreds had been revived, more inveterate and deadlier than before. How could the only remedy whose effects would be certain—general disarmament—be applied? At that moment, it was necessary not to think of it, and to resolve to submit to the final consequences of human folly, to conserve armies more powerful than ever, to replace at all costs the materiel put out of service, which had become insufficient since the advent of the Lichtmann weapons.

Nothing better was found to do than to reduce to negligibility all budgets other than the military, and but for the efforts of commerce and industry, which were still struggling with the courage of desperation against countless difficulties, one might have believed, in fact, that Europe was reverting to barbarity.

There were no more public works; the roads were scarcely maintained; the staff of civil services was reduced by three quarters and ever more poorly remunerated. In consequence of the necessary reductions, the bearers of the best bonds were obtaining a derisory interest, and the Turkish debt appeared to be on the way to becoming a respectable investment. All these measures were, however, insufficient, as the needs of the economy soon brought about the introduction of fundamental reforms even in the organization of armies.

The truth, in its persistence, finally penetrated: the value of soldiers is a negligible factor by virtue of the increasing perfection of means of destruction, and only the number of men allied to the value of leaders is necessary. Therefore, the legislators renounced permanent armies. In peacetime, they maintained in a constant manner a considerable number of officers. Those officers only had troops under their orders for a period of six weeks per year. But the effective levy was enormous; in Germany and France it exceeded the figure of one and a half million. It needed more than three years for the entire army—more than five million combatants—to pass under the flag and receive training, and was now reduced to the necessary minimum judged indispensable to its employment on the battlefield.

The profession of arms, thus disengaged from the obsolete and vexatious prescriptions and obligations that cluttered the regulations, ceased to be unpopular. All adult citizens, often summoned and exercised, felt that they were really and constantly soldiers. That sentiment, having become generalized, beneficially replaced the former military education with a long sojourn in barracks. It was the armed nation in every sense of the term.

The officers, freed from the pettiest and least interesting preoccupations that had previously absorbed their activity and atrophied their faculties, were able to acquire and develop the veritable science of war. During the call-up of troops, they were able to apply to them the principles with the confidence and authority that knowledge confers.

That organization and the expedients of every kind permitted States to devote the necessary sums to their armaments. Orders flowed into Essen, where the Engineer rejected energetically the propositions of Prussia, which wanted to reserve the employment of the new weaponized engines to herself.

The factories soon became too small to satisfy all needs. A gigantic foundry rose up as if by enchantment at Ruhrort, on the banks of the Rhine, the motive force of which was utilized by ingenious artifice. No less than a hundred and fifty thousand workers were employed there, who had deserted similar factories that could no longer employ them.

It was then that Lichtmann had a luminous idea, which was to precipitate the realization of his projects. Knowing how difficult it was for Prussia to pay for its orders for cannons, armor plate and armored vehicles, the cost of which had risen to more than a billion, and also irritated by the pretentions of German artillerists, who wanted, as before the war, to control the manufacture of their materiel, he resolved to render himself completely independent. To that effect, he proposed that the Imperial Government exchange the territory of his factories and their surroundings for the complimentary delivery of the materiel under construction.

That offer roused the indignation of the politicians in Berlin. What! Re-create a free State in the middle of the Empire! But that would undermine the basis of the edifice so laboriously constructed half a century before, and set a deplorable example for Bavaria, Saxony and other provinces that still remembered their past independence. So a negative response was given to the Engineer—who was not disconcerted, and declared that, in the case of a definitive refusal, he would work exclusively for Russian and France, postponing the German orders until after the completion of those of her most powerful enemies.

That threat produced the effect that he expected. The sovereign's advisers, very perplexed, were not unaware that the execution of that plan would spell the certain doom of Prussia; on the other hand, to constrain the Engineer would have precipitated an immediate war for which they were not at all prepared. After concerted reflection, it was necessary to submit to the conditions of the stubborn canon manufacturer who suddenly seemed devoured by an inexplicable ambition.

From the mouth of the Ruhr, a tributary of the Rhine, to Wesel in the north and Dusseldorf in the south, the distances are almost equal, approximately twenty-five kilometers: a distance that was calculated to extend from the confluence to determine the dimensions of the new State along the river. From the two points thus obtained, the northern and southern frontiers extended eastwards following two lines of latitude until they encountered a meridian slightly to the west of Dortmund, which formed the eastern limit. The province ceded was thus a perfect square, following the example of territories in the New World. Prussia withdrew its troops and guaranteed the integrity of the territory to the Engineer. The latter baptized his possessions by the name of Canonenstadt.

The first act of the new sovereign was to expropriate, in the cause of public utility, all the immovable property in the country in order to have free control of the entire terrain. Then he formed a Governmental Council, adjoining to himself the five most intelligent engineers from his factories. He summoned them immediately in order to reveal his projects to them, and had no difficulty penetrating them with his ideas and communicating to them the unshakable conviction by which he was animated. Those improvised Statesmen then drew up by common accord the following declaration, destined to be published throughout the world and to serve as the constitution of Canonenstadt.

THE COOPERATIVE STATE OF CANONENSTADT

We, Litchmann, founder of Canonenstadt, assisted by the Council of Government, have decided the following:

Article 1. The Cooperative State of Canonenstadt has for its mission the manufacture of engines of war for the usage of other peoples.

Article 2. The citizens of the said State renouncing any other nationality, they have no preference for any foreign power.

Article 3. They are all equal. Length of service alone gives the right to the various positions in the hierarchy necessitated by the efficient division of labor within the factories. Only the director general and the five engineers forming the Council and the holders of the secrets of fabrication are appointed for life by a general assembly of citizens.

Article 4. The only labor authorized in the territory is that in the metallurgical factories, which are common property. The raw material for sustenance and other objects necessary to life that cannot be manufactured internally will be purchased from abroad by a committee of citizens who will distribute them at cost price to ad hoc *subsidiaries.*

Article 5. The working day is six hours. Every worker will receive per day, from the age of twenty years until his death, the sum of twenty marks in bills having no currency outside the State. Any acquisition from without is forbidden. Everyone will receive a house of a unique model. The land is the property of all. The profits of the State constitute a common fund put in reserve.

Article 6. The number of workers is fixed at three hundred thousand. The total population formed by them and their families will be fifteen hundred thousand. In the case of augmentation, lots will be drawn to determine the young people who will be obliged to leave the State. In case of diminution, foreign citizens will be admitted.

Article 7. Every year, a committee of workers will indicate the special work that is appropriate to each individual for twenty years in accordance with his strength and constitution. Education is free, obligatory and uniform. It is given to all children from six years of age until they become workers. Metallurgy is the principal subject of study.

Article 8. All crimes and misdemeanors are punished by banishment. Internal policing is confided to the inhabitants, who have an interest in not allowing the good fortune they enjoy to be compromised. The security of the frontiers will be ensured in due course by special methods.

Article 9. All workers present on the date of 1 January 1897 are citizens of the new state by right if they accept the conditions announced herein. Other inhabitants will be required to subscribe to them or to expatriate themselves.

Article 10. Until 1 March a committee formed by two engineer councilors and twenty of the oldest workers will receive requests for admission from foreign metallurgists. It will subsequently devote itself to the completion of the figures indicated in article 6.

Made at Canonenstadt 1 January 1897.

The President
LICHTMANN

A few days later, Paris was the theater of unexpected scenes. One morning, the entire working population of the suburbs, when the time to go to work brought them out of their homes, stopped in amazement at the sight of immense posters printed in large letters and pasted on all the walls, in front of which the agents of the police were shouting, gesticulating and arguing in the least peaceful fashion about the more-or-less seditious character of that appeal to the public.

Soon, the circulation of traffic was interrupted; coachmen were howling and swearing without being able to force a passage; gangs of street urchins were running around; women, intrigued, were trying to slip through the crowd in order to get a better view; and from the bosom of the multitude cries of astonishment and joy escaped, along with reflections and comments that, repeated from mouth to mouth, became a confused rumor of thousands of voices, waking up the laziest inhabitants of the capital in the depths of their alcoves.

Time went by and no one thought about his labor. The uniformed policemen agitated in vain, as all their attempts to dissipate the crowds having no result. Then they began to withdraw prudently to the nearest stations to await instructions from the Prefecture, who was already warned that a riot was imminent.

The precautions were superfluous, because once the initial moment of excitement had passed, everyone, having fully absorbed the terms of the proclamation that he had before his eyes, went on his way. The crowd dissipated of its own accord, and a few hours later, no one remained in front of the walls but a few late-rising employees and idlers who shrugged their shoulders on reading the document, whose implications they did not understand.

All the newspapers were filled with distorted accounts of these simple events and interminable polemics regarding Lichtmann's endeavor. In all the industrial centers the sensation was similarly lively; the solution to the social question was glimpsed at last: cooperation conceived on the largest scale.

In that fortunate State, therefore, the reforms demanded for such a long time by intelligent workers were going to be witnessed. The happiness of the people would be doubly assured by the suppression of frightful poverty and the reduction of odious labor. The latter, equally divided, would henceforth be a joy for all.

Previously, only the greed of the possessors of capital had delayed that result. The impulsion had been given, but nothing had yet been done, for only the ironworkers were to enjoy those just advantages. It required that great example to be followed, and that workers everywhere, having become the collaborators of the employer, should share equitably in the profits. Numerous conferences took place to hasten that rapprochement between the workers and the industrialists.

It was clearly demonstrated to the latter that their honor was at stake and that they ought not to remain behind the progress accomplished on the banks of the Rhine. Unfortunately, they did not want to be persuaded, declaring that the manufacture of cannons was presently the only industry flourishing, and that others would have difficulty following the indicated path. They promised nevertheless to study the question with the care that it merited.

V

At Canonenstadt, there was a rapid and enormous influx of requests for admission. From the four corners of the globe, stokers, founders, puddlers, forgers, welders. temperers, refiners, molders, shinglers, laminators, pourers, turners and fitters sent requests, and the committee was spoiled for choice. It was only by deploying the greatest activity that it was able to complete its work within the allotted time. The strictest equity presided over its operations, and its decisions, without appeal, could not be influenced by any pressure. By 1 March the population was constituted, and the new citizens began to arrive from all directions.

The new arrivals had to find immediate accommodation, which led to a few regrettable incidents. Force had to be employed to expel recalcitrant former inhabitants who wanted to continue to live in their native region without working, under the fallacious pretext that it was not their tradition. That exorbitant pretention naturally aroused a sharp indignation among the workers, who rapidly administered justice.

The territory purchased by the Engineer was then one of the richest regions in Germany. Industrial activity had developed there with astonishing vigor during the second half of the nineteenth century. In a few years, large towns had replaced simple villages, or had been built with an entirely American rapidity not far from points of extraction of the minerals and combustibles that constituted much of the subsoil of the Ruhr basin. The river in question was traveled by numerous vessels transporting annually, in addition to merchandise of every sort, more than one and a half million tons of coal. Ruhrort, at the mouth on the right bank of the Rhine, was the river port in which the most considerable commercial movement took place.

In the center of the province, Essen, which counted more than fifty thousand inhabitants, owed its prosperity primarily to the metallurgical factories founded by Krupp and subsequently directed by Lichtmann. All the neighboring towns—Mulheim, Duisburg, Steele, Altendorf, Haltingen, Styrum and Bochum—were merely immense agglomerations of factories producing iron and steel in the form of cannons, armor plating, rails, locomotives, etc.

Coal and metals were not the only sources of wealth in that fortunate region, however. To the south and not far from the recently traced frontier, enclaved within the new State, were the two sister towns Elberfeld and Barmen, occupying eight kilometers along the Wupper. More than fifty thousand inhabitants lived there who worked in the textile industry, spinning, weaving and dyeing, and also manufacturing musical instruments. In order to link all these centers of production together and to send their merchandise far and wide, the most elaborate railway network in Europe was spread out over the countryside. Finally, one will have a better idea of the manufacturing importance of that area of German soil when one knows that from Elberfeld and Barmen to Essen and Duisburg, the number of tall chimneys vomiting floods of black smoke was not surpassed by a single district of equal area in industrious England.

Well, all those towns and all those buildings already disposed in factories, prepared for work, and for which he had been obliged to pay very dearly, the Engineer, who had decided to break completely with the past, was resolved to demolish. He wanted an immense new city, which would combine all the improvements in viability, comfort, hygiene and elegance, and whose accumulation the present state of science and his genius would permit. Only metal would be employed in all the constructions that he was about to undertake.

He had drawn up the plan of the new State he envisaged a long time ago, and he had anticipated the slightest details, but its execution would require several years, and to begin with, the workers had to be accommodated in the existing houses. Those were demolished as the work advanced, and four years later, on the first day of the twentieth century, every trace of the former regime had vanished. Lichtmann's project was realized. Canonenstadt began to function routinely.

Among the thousand surprising conceptions hatched by the brains of engineers, which had taken on substance in the skillful hands of a host of smiths, the most remarkable of all were five colossal factories that appeared to be made for Cyclopes. One of them, the largest, was situated on the bank of the Rhine, on the site of the vanished Ruhrort.

The center of the State was marked by a vast roundabout with a two league perimeter, in the middle of which was a vast circular building. The administration offices, arranged in sectors, were gathered together around an immense hall, the seat of the government—or, rather the general management. Lichtmann and his colleagues were based there, and communicated from there with the aid of telephones and marvelously adapted microphones with all the section heads and secondary engineers in the factories. A multitude of wires communicated all the words pronounced at any point in the factories to sonorous funnels that ornamented the walls of the hall, while attentive phonographs recorded them, omitting nothing. The directors were therefore not unaware of anything that happened, and their will alone gave movement to the thousands of arms that contributed to the common endeavor.

The principal factory was a vast rectangle three kilometers long by one wide, divided into various bays by rows of columns that presented the appearance of giant cannons embedded in the ground. That forest of pillars sustained a light and elegant framework that launched audaciously from one to another, sometimes spanning a distance of three hundred feet with a single bound fifty meters above the ground.

From the outside, that hall, whose extremities extended to the horizon, had an imposing aspect, without the spectator experiencing the painful sensation of oppression often produced by great monuments. In fact, the two principal snags of analogous constructions of lesser dimensions had been avoided therein: a heavy and massive appearance of exaggerated solidity or a vague resemblance to a monumental cage.

A few bays were made to protrude from the façade, pleasantly disrupting the uniformity, breaking the principal lines here and there with their cleverly emphasized relief. Everything in the ensemble and the details satisfied both the eye and the taste of the artist, seduced by the agreeable superimposition of staged gables, the boldness of porticos, the severe elegance of cornices, and the correct design of bays of every size, well distributed without being lavish.

At intervals, superb bas-reliefs in cast steel, always representing some attribute of ancient or contemporary artillery, completed the decoration. The architect, who was none other than Lichtmann, had demonstrated superabundantly by means of that superb edifice that metal, like stone and wood, could be submissive to all the demands of the most conscientious artistry. He had just created the Metallic style, which would remain, by the same title as the Greek, Byzantine, Roman or Ogival styles, characteristic of its epoch.

As for the rotunda, it was veritably the soul of Canonenstadt, of which it directed and regulated the movements. Although its ensemble was less majestic than that of the factory, its admirable proportions and the beauty of its details made it a very remarkable monument. The immense cupola that surmounted it, and measured no less than six hundred feet in circumference, astonished the eye with its boldness and lightness. It was visible from all the extremities of the province by following with the gaze the broad avenues that converged on the rotunda.

There too, artillery bore all the expense of the decoration, but the artist had been able to vary his subject with so much imagination and artistry that one never wearied of discovering it in the thousand forms that he had given it. On seeing those compositions, which, for the most part, were masterpieces, one felt that one was truly in the empire of the cannon, which affirmed its supremacy everywhere. That central construction of Canonenstadt had been given the name Canonenpalast.

It was in the principal factory that the motive force and the apparatus of metal production were brought together. Foreign metallurgists permitted to visit it would doubtless have been very surprised not to find there any of the methods of fabrication in use in their own factories. Nowhere, over the entire the surface of the region, did one encounter the tall chimneys so abundantly distributed before the renovation of the country. At no point did one distinguish the slightest cloud of smoke above the buildings. No deleterious gases vitiated the atmosphere. Not a single particle of the fine dust that covers industrial cities like a black shroud rose up beneath the feet of the inhabitants. That was because the customary combustibles, wood and coal, were not employed to stoke the fires or reduce the minerals. The engineers had preferred to produce very economically, by means of the river, an enormous quantity of electricity, which furnished the motive force and heat they needed. Thus, the coal mines of the region, although very numerous and very rich, had been abandoned.

In the previous century, watercourses, considered as sources of work, had seen their importance diminish before the invasion of stream engines. The preference accorded to the latter was due to their constancy, not being subject to the accidents that so often vary the output of hydraulic machinery. To utilize streams and rivers, rapid falls were sought out, great inclinations of the bed giving a sufficient difference in level between two not-very-distant points. Everywhere that those conditions were not fulfilled, the current flowed unperturbed, satisfied to irrigate a rich valley without being submitted to any labor, expending the treasures of force that it contained in pure waste. Lichtmann extracted it from that mild quietude. As for the accidental or attending difficulties, his inventive genius provided the means to vanquish or avoid them.

From the southern extremity to the northern extremity of the section of the river that bathed his possessions, he constructed a diversion fifty meters wide and ten deep, which traversed the great factory along its axis. That canal was divided into two reaches whose difference in level was equal to that of the river at the two points of attachment, which is to say, nine meters. The waters of the superior reach, retained by metallic walls, fell onto an enormous wheel occupying the entire width of the smaller reservoir. Immense paddles glided smoothly over the cylindrical wall, which ensured that the two reaches did not lose a single drop of water with useful work. The machine, thus established, achieved an efficiency previously unknown, of over 98%.

With the average speed of the flow being 0.75 meters per second, 340,000 liters of water passed per second over the wheel, which furnished a disposable work of more than a million kilogram-meters. To obtain the same force, it would have required more than two hundred steam engines of a thousand horsepower each, collectively consuming eight thousand tons of coal every twenty-four hours, at an annual expense of thirty million francs.

A little more than a sixth of the water flow was diverted in that fashion. As the liquid mass is highly variable between periods of heavy rain and those of great dryness, when it falls to a third of its normal value, it was necessary to ensure a constant level in the millrace. This invariability was obtained by means of a superb dyke extended obliquely across the river, raising the average height of the water. The jetty was linked to a tapering arch similar to a monstrous funnel, in which the volume of water strictly necessary to the supply of the canal was engulfed, the excess being rejected downstream.

In periods of low water, the boats traveling along the river were enabled to cross the dyke easily by means of a new kind of lock. It consisted of a flotation reservoir into which boats penetrated, suddenly imprisoned by the closure of the gates. At that moment a colossal crane seized the reservoir full of water, raised it into the air, where it remained suspended by iron chains, and then, turning on its axis, lowered it carefully, to deposit it on the other side of the obstacle, where the boats were released.

It was not uncommon, in that mobile flotation tank, to see an entire flotilla of large-sized barges, which seemed astonished by that aerial transport, so contrary was it to their habits. On seeing the powerful machine lift its burden without apparent effort, the river-dwellers thought they were in the presence of one of the giants featured in certain local legends, lifting at the end of his long arms a plaything appropriate to his stature.

With this method, the delay caused to navigation was so minimal that the boatmen would have shown bad grace in complaining. They even discovered a new source of profits.

The tourists who explore the course of the Rhine belong to two categories. Some come in search of memories of the religious and martial heritage of the knights of the Middle Ages, and although they regret no longer finding in that magical land its grandiose and wild character, they still like to see filing before their eyes a display of old ruins and solitary burgs; they run after poetry and swoon in front of a tower. The others, on the magnificent steamboats as on the sidewalks of our great cities, in the midst of enchanted locations at which they scarcely glance, are attracted by the charms of the undines who spend the summer season traveling up and down the river; the comedy is the same; only the scenery has changed. Well, all those lovers of nature, attracted by the originality and novelty of the traversal of the dyke, now descended as far as Wesel; they could not dispense with going along the shore of Canonenstadt, and casting an interrogative eye over the mysterious

State, this strange city into which no one had the right to trespass.

In fact, an electrified fence protected the inhabitants against the curious and the importunate, and no foreigner had ever been authorized to pass over the threshold of the only gate in that barrier.

Not all the force produced by the river was employed in the great factory, which scarcely consumed a fifth of it to operate its pile drivers, laminators, cranes, mobile furnaces, etc. etc. Moreover, those machines were not, as one might believe, more powerful than those in rival establishments, for the metallic masses put to work were unremarkable with regard to dimensions, since the qualities of the metal permitted the thickness of the forged components to be reduced considerably. What absorbed the most work was the production of the heat necessary to the cupolas, blast furnaces, refining furnaces, furnaces for reduction or carburation, etc.

The extreme sections of the factory enclosed several series of large electricity generators of the Siemens system, modified by Lichtmann. The currents that they produced were employed in decomposing water in voluminous voltameters. The oxygen and hydrogen thus separated were received in numerous gasometers, which dispatched them to ovens where they were burned beneath flat sheets. In accordance with the quantities of gas consumed per hour and the dimensions of the ovens, all temperatures could easily be obtained, from the lowest to those necessary to melt the most refractory substances.

In the blast furnaces, the heat was created in the same fashion, but the pipes were injected with an excess of hydrogen to reduce the mineral. One thus extracted from them, not cast iron, but iron of great purity. Other furnaces similar to puddling ovens, but in which the operation was the inverse of the one normally effected, transformed that iron into hard or soft steel, at will, by means of the addition of small quantities of very pure combinants manufactured solely for that purpose. Considerable economies were thus realized, relative to ordinary metallurgical procedures. That is what permitted Canonenstadt to pay its workers so handsomely and to accumulate enormous wealth, as well.

One indispensable precaution was taken to avoid the freezing of the diversion canal in winter, an accident that would undoubtedly have occurred in that rigorous climate and would have paralyzed all movement in the factories. The machines that developed the necessary heat were aligned on both sides of the millrace, a short distance from its metallic walls. The water, warmed by that direct proximity and by steam coming from the combustion of the gases that were condensed there, maintained a temperature above ten degrees even in the worst cold spells.

The four factories situated at the angles of the province were constructed on the model of the first, but in less grandiose proportions. They received electric currents from it, transformed in their turn into work by machines analogous to those that produced them. It is well known, in fact, that machines of that sort are reversible and convert electricity into work or work into electricity at will.

The northwestern factory received blocks of raw metal in order to render them into the form of cannons or sheets of armor plate. The northeastern one was reserved for metallic constructions exclusively employed in Canonenstadt or sold externally, and material for the railways whose tracks were strewn seemingly infinitely over the entire surface area of the State. As for those of the south, one specialized in the fabrication of projectiles, the other in powder and nitroglycerine-based explosive agents used by armies.

Around the province, a broad roadway some fifteen feet wide formed a kind of exterior boulevard. It was linked to the central roundabout by hundreds of avenues that seemed to emerge from Canonenpalast like the spokes of a wheel from an enormous hub. All those arteries and other transversals were thronged by countless electrical vehicles. The rails of their tracks carried electric currents that it was sufficient to close by means of a simple commutator to activate the motor of the vehicle and determine the movement in one direction or the other.

Those vehicles were of very diverse models, from massive trucks designed to transport heavy loads to light coupés and stylish carriages employed by the feminine fraction of the population. The simple controls of the motors being familiar to everyone, including children, there was no need to equip them with specialist drivers, as everyone directed them at will and at the speed that suited his temperament or present occupation.

On the eastern frontier a strip of land two kilometers wide had been reserved as an experimental field. It was external to the fence, and it was there that the engineers met clients who desired to see the effect of the guns or examine the materiel before purchasing it. In the middle of the firing range, the single gateway opened through which the principal railway passed, connected to a station on the German railway network. Merchandise was transported there in order to be subsequently dispatched in all directions.

The space left free by the arteries of circulation had been converted into vast gardens in the midst of which were distributed the three hundred thousand houses required by the inhabitants. One could have compared Canonenstadt to an immense park in which no secondary enclosure indicated a private property or a reserved terrain. Everything there belonged to everyone, and nothing to any individual. The only exceptions to that principle were the houses granted for the exclusive use of the families who occupied them.

Iron and steel, sometimes aided by copper, lead, zinc and silver, were the only materials encountered in those constructions. The walls, formed of parallel metallic panels, enclosed a layer of air whose feeble conductivity protected the inhabitants with equal efficiency against the ardors of summer and the rigors of winter.

The furniture, variable according to the tastes and habits of the residents, emerged from the national factories, not excepting the carpets and wall hangings. It was possible to admire therein fabrics woven from steel, brass, aluminum or silver thread, sometimes more tenuous than silk, which the most capricious daughters of Eve would not have disdained, even in competition with the richest velvets and the most magnificent brocades; light items of furniture with polished, mat, damascened or moiré surfaces, whose elegance equaled that of the most exotic woods of Parisian industry; steel mirrors more brilliant than the best products of Saint-Gobain; and vases and trinkets of every sort, as beautiful in form and workmanship as the most highly-valued Sèvres and Saxe.

Only some of the fabrics of clothing and undergarments were not manufactured from metallic thread. It had been found, with reason, that their confection was the natural lot of women, and to that end they were furnished with raw materials from the outside.

Running through that city of disseminated houses, or that park decorated with three hundred thousand villas, the Ruhr—as placid now as it was laborious before, along with the Emscher, almost parallel to it, the Lippe that curved around the territory to the north and their numerous tributaries—no longer had any other mission but to transport the water necessary to domestic requirements to all the relevant points.

All of that was protected from curiosity-seekers and idlers by the aforementioned fence. It rested on a hollow metal foundation covered internally by an insulating layer on which the smaller part of the bars was fitted. At intervals, graceful columns containing enormous Ruhmkorff coils increased the solidity of the ensemble and charged the bars of the grille, which was, in consequence, nothing but a gigantic electric battery. Audacious individuals who approached the foundations, in spite of the prohibitions in all languages distributed in profusion along the frontiers, and placed a profane hand on one of the bars was immediately electrocuted.

That famous barrier, celebrated throughout the world, rapidly became the terror of the surrounding area after a few skeptics had tested its murderous properties at their own expense.

VI

In order to know Canonenstadt well it only remains to study its administration. It is very simple. The oldest workers, who number five thousand, are the deputy engineers or overseers. Some direct the workshops; others, undertaking long voyages, make the products of their homeland known abroad, striving to demonstrate their utility and advantages and then, as faithful emissaries, immediately reporting to the Council the success of their ventures. Those titles do not give them any right to an increase in salary. They merely receive houses of a special type, designated as no. 2, and special insignia on the uniform garments worn by all the inhabitants. The director and his five colleagues have the right to distinctions of the same nature. They are responsible for relations with other governments, approve measures as a last resort, and administer the reserve treasury, completing accounts that are distributed every year to the workers to keep them up to date with the situation of the public fortune. They are appointed for life and are only allowed to leave the State in grave circumstances, with the consent of a general assembly of the deputy engineers.

Thus, in the lower ranks of the hierarchy, there are indefatigable workers, full of solicitude for the common interest, attached to their duty as other men are to their passions, without any other desire than that of living well and practicing virtue. At their head are old men, even more venerable by virtue of their wisdom than their age, eager to render to their fellow citizens the greatest sum of service possible, glad to enjoy as a recompense, in the final moments of such a well-filled existence, the esteem of all, the peace of their conscience and the edifying spectacle, full of the charms of pleasure that absolute equality can give a people.

A utopia, a seductive dream, say the skeptics—but that dream, that utopia, has taken on form and acquired a powerful vitality in Canonenstadt. There are no more vain ambitions, no more quarrels, no more revolts; orders—or, rather, items of advice—are listened to with deference by the worker who receives them. Thus, in a family, sons obey their father. Everyone bows his head before a just reproach, thinking that his turn will come to lavish on his peers the fruits of his experience, and that all his actions ought to have for a motive and a goal the merit of such an honor.

The work in the factories, reduced to a few hours spent in the midst of amiable companions, becomes a pleasure, an attraction; it is an ear of wheat that one harvests, a flower that one picks, not a thorn on which one injures oneself. Other distractions soon succeed it, and intellectual relaxations temper the bitterness of bodily fatigue. A man, in fact, ought not to be left to his own devices; his sight embarrasses him, he cannot sustain it, ennui overtakes him. Sad and somber, he no longer thinks of anything but his misery and means of freeing himself from it. That is why he has an incessant need to amuse and distract himself.

The arts are not neglected, and the inhabitants, in that regard, can abandon themselves freely to their personal tastes and instinct.

"When one says that the arts render men effeminate, one is not speaking, at least, about those who apply themselves, since they are never in idleness, which, of all the vices, is the one that softens courage the most. It is, therefore, only a question of those who enjoy them."[10]

Certain in consequence of avoiding slackness, Lichtmann has no fear of encouraging the cultivation of the fine arts. His goal is to break the monotony of labor, to moderate character and maintain around him a frank cheerfulness, a sure indication of a soul satisfied with its lot. He hopes, in addition, that in a few generations, thanks to the uniformity of life, mutual contacts and identical occupations, that a general and median level of intellectual aspiration will eventually be established. At that moment, everything will be perfect, and he directs the education of the young in that direction.

But how slowly a great work is accomplished in this world! How many stones it needs to construct an edifice conceived by an ardent mind, how many materials he lacks and how many he is forced to reject!

So, our engineer sees with pleasure the population increase, an inevitable result among people who do not fear the division of an absent patrimony. He would rather, in fact, have to dispose of the excess of the maximum fixed by the constitution than have recourse every year to exterior elements, necessarily disparate, and the introduction of which would slow down the realization of his desires.

For the moment, the differences that exist between the character and aptitudes of individuals do not constitute a danger. No one has thought of availing himself of his talents, whatever they are, to obtain advantages over his fellow citizens, and if he tried, what advantages could he obtain? That consideration destroys any paltry

---

[10] Author's reference: "Montesquieu, *Lettres persanes*, lettre 106."

calculation, any sentiment of individual interest, and the value of productions is thereby increased. In consequence, only a few remarkable artists strive to give form to their chimeras, and the creation of any work of art—painting, sculpture, literature or music—is only appreciated as an agreeable pastime and not a means of charming one's fellow citizens.

Discord, however, would not have failed to slide slyly, like a snake in the grass, into this new terrestrial paradise and to cast trouble into feminine society, if a wise precaution had not prevented it from so doing. I will not say that an apple could have been, as before, the subject of the quarrel, for apple trees have fortunately been banished from the territory and coquetry is scarcely encouraged by the austere government that imposes on women as on men a uniformity of dress.

Lichtmann had thought deeply before promulgating that sumptuary law, because "plants, trees, and animals—everything that lives—naturally find themselves equipped with sufficient covering to defend themselves from the abuse of the weather, and so do we…it is easy to see that it is custom that has made impossible for us that which is not."[11]

A few years ago, was it not the dream of the virtuous chancellor to dress German women in chastity and the love of God? But even in the heavens, such an adornment has its deadly rivalries! What would come of it on earth?

Uniformity, in any case, does not exclude either style or elegance, and for the weaker sex, fashions are

---

[11] Author's reference: "Montaigne, *Essais (sur la coutume de se vêtir)*, 35." The essay in question is actually headed "Sur l'usage de se vêtir."

renewed at fixed intervals and carefully copied from those of Paris, minus those that might be ridiculous or contrary to hygiene—which simplifies them greatly.

The Romans established penal laws against those who refused the laws of marriage and wanted to enjoy a liberty contrary to their peers and to public utility. Following their example, celibacy is strictly forbidden in Canonenstadt; at twenty-one for young men and eighteen for young women, temperaments that might find equilibrium are carefully allied. But "if, of two people thus linked, there is one who is not appropriate to the design of nature, either by virtue of temperament or age, that one buries the other with them, rendering them equally useless."[12] Divorce is therefore permitted by law, but within reasonable limits designed to restrict overly pronounced tastes for change. Let us hasten to add that never have ladies so genteel, so dainty, so cheerful and so skilled in needlework yet completed human happiness. Ugly women are never encountered; shrews and harpies are unknown, and one never finds overly inquisitive ones—but is it not the same in every country in the world?

Thus, the family, the principal element of social strength, is constituted in Canonenstadt in an eminently solid fashion. The problem of property has been resolved to everyone's satisfaction. As for religion, that sublime consolation of the afflicted, the Engineer saw it less as a means of sanctification than a subject of ever-violent and often deadly disputes, and only envisaged it in that fashion. He did not settle upon any of those offered to humans to guide them on the short journey from cradle to tomb. Careful of material interests, however, he did not

---

[12] Author's reference: "Montesquieu, *Lettres persanes*."

think that he ought to neglect absolutely those of the spirit, for fear that, in being left to themselves, the people might be seduced by subversive theories. That is why, borrowing from all the systems thus far developed that which is truly useful, he created for the use of those under his administration a philosophy that, if not elevated, is at least practical, which is taught in the schools.

The fundamental principle of that doctrine might be summarized as: "Self-interest, properly understood, leads to the love of one's neighbor."

VII

19 February 1902

LATEST NEWS
Frightful symptoms in eastern Westphalia. Strange phenomena. Sinister noises. Population frightened. Thousands of victims.

Agence Havas.

That dispatch, spread throughout Europe as rapidly as electricity could transmit it, was initially published and commented on by the German newspapers, which recalled that for several years the soil of central Germany had been shaken by slight but very numerous quakes. Over twenty-five years, no less than two hundred and thirty-two of them had been clearly observed and recorded in the annals of science. Immediately, the public shivered in fear, scientists were struck by amazement, journalists swooned with joy and reporters buckled their suitcases.

Thousands of victims, said the dispatch: unfortunates in need of aid! That very evening, the committee of the French press convened in haste and adopted without dispute the project of the most original, the most grandiose, the most luxurious and the most magnificent feast that it had ever put on, to which the most charming fisherwomen in the entire world would be invited to inflame the most naïve of fishermen of foolish amour, with the praiseworthy aim of extorting fabulous alms from them.

The best-informed newspapers, however, did not give any details of the catastrophe. It was not until the

71

following evening that more precise information was obtained, which held the public breathless and intrigued the scientific world, but cooled the ardor of the party organizing committee somewhat. A cataclysm was imminent, but the victims were imaginary; there was no longer any reason to enjoy themselves!

In the Weser valley, not far from the small town of Peckelsheim, about ten thousand inhabitants—men, women and children—had precipitately quit their dwellings and fled in the greatest disorder, without thinking about protecting themselves from the intense cold that was assailing them at the time. Crazed by terror, those unfortunates had run through the surrounding region, devoid of resources, as if pursued by an invisible demon, intent on reviving the legend of the Wandering Jew in the century of positivism.

The crowd was still fleeing, spreading its fear by the stories told as it went. They had not seen anything, but for two long days they had heard frightening noises beneath their feet, occasionally interrupted by brief intervals of menacing silence, only to resume soon with an increasing intensity. "Man is a reed, the weakest in nature." A reed bends in the wind; this time, the people folded up in response to a sound wave.

It was not a distant storm, whose rumbles of thunder were arriving weakened and extended; the persistence and continuity of the phenomenon soon destroyed that illusion. There was no doubt about it; the mysterious sounds that were becoming more perceptible from one minute to the next were emerging from the bowels of the earth.

Then the memory of upheavals due to volcanic effervescence that had been renewed with a disquieting frequency in distant countries in recent years came to the minds of some. In a matter of seconds, a frightful panic took hold of them all. The bewildered peasants ran away, and a desert formed around the place from which the fatal rumbling seemed to be emerging. The fear spread to the citizens of Peckelsheim and several neighboring towns where nothing had been heard. No consideration could retain them, and not a single living being dared remain within a radius of five leagues, for even the animals, anxious and troubled, broke out of the enclosures in which they were imprisoned in order to follow their masters.

Then a long file of jostling men and women snaked along the roads, traversing villages that were depopulated as they approached, and, marching without respite and without aim, drew away with long strides from the accursed valley. Behind them, pell-mell, galloped horses, cattle, dogs, cats, rabbits and rats. The birds, fluttering fearfully, gathered in flocks to follow the general movement. It was a complete migration of a population that had left its common sense by the fireside.

When the rumor of the event reached Berlin, the members of the Royal Academy gathered to debate the issue and greeted it with suspicion. They refused to believe, as all the newspapers in the world were already announcing, in an upsurge of the terrestrial crust, perhaps the eruption of a new volcano, in the heart of Germany. The proximity of terrains of igneous origin in the Harz and the neighborhood of one of the earth's volcanic axes were not sufficient reasons to justify the possibility of such a catastrophe. All the geologists were, in fact, unanimous in declaring that the activity of the central fire was long extinct in that region and the nature and the disposition of the terrain did not permit the possibility that it might revive again.

On the other hand, according to the testimony of the witnesses of the phenomenon themselves, no movement had been felt; seismographs had not recorded the feeblest quake; the magnetic needle had not suffered any perturbation; and the telegraph had not brought news from any part of the globe of any earthquake or eruption whatsoever, and yet manifestations of internal force are rarely isolated.

After an earnest examination of all the hypotheses and a profound study of the symptoms, the learned assembly was convinced that the cause of the bizarre event, probably quite simple, had escaped the intellect of the inhabitants deprived by fear of the self-composure necessary to reflection. It decided that a committee of ten members, immediately sent to the location, would be charged with calming minds by divulging the origin of the ominous sound, which a scrupulous investigation, guided by the enlightenments of science, would not take long to explain.

The ten delegates included the most various, but the most characteristic, types of that special race of humans known as scientists. Are they even human? One cannot doubt it, for they possess, like the others, a head, a body, feet and hands. Are they beings superior to humans? That too cannot be doubted, for they all have a very clear idea of their immortality. Thus, at a single glance, in the middle of a host of travelers and employees, one would have been able to pick out those ten illustrious colleagues waiting impatiently for the special train that was to transport them to Peckelsheim and to glory.

As soon as they arrived, they observed that their instruments, with which they had furnished themselves at great cost, had not suffered from the journey, and that the unusual sounds had ceased. A trifle disappointed, they then traveled around the region in all directions, in search of some clue that would point them in the direction of the truth.

Their research was fruitless, however, and after having conscientiously devoted an entire day to it, they began to believe that the noises had only ever existed in the imagination of a few natives, whose fear had been communicated to all the others. For want of anything else, it was a phenomenon of suggestion worthy of analysis.

Reassured but downcast, they were getting ready to leave Peckelsheim and return to the Academy when, all of a sudden, a dull rumble became audible. One might have thought it the jolting of a thousand vehicles colliding with rocks, the sound of Vulcan's heavy hammer on the anvil, the sinister grating of fantastic chain dragged by gnomes, or the immense crepitation of the sea on a blazing beach.

Astonished, they stopped, they listened—and in those bodies already frozen by self-esteem, frissons attempted in vain to run through the flesh and chill the blood. They were as calm and impassive as the god Terminus, ready to examine such a rare phenomenon with an entirely fluid lucidity of mind.

Suddenly, the wind rose, initially caressing their curly wigs with a light breeze, but soon amplifying its fury; clouds heaped up and darkness covered the drama that was about to unfold with its mystery. The subterranean noises were still resounding.

Evidently, the honorable committee-members were in the presence of a terrestrial convulsion the nature of which escaped them. Might they be about to be swallowed up in some fracture of the ground, like victims claimed by infernal gods?

That idea was beginning to trouble their faculties of observation, but they lost them completely when the storm burst, when the howling wind, unleashed, opened up the cataracts of the sky, inundating the region with torrents of hail and sleet, pitilessly disemboweling the shelters under which the incomparable instruments of the Royal Academy were installed, and with a savagery that was even more unusual, scalping those venerable heads, leaving the bald pates of the wisest of men exposed to the wrath of the tempest.

Finally, the lightning died away in the clouds, the hurricane eased and the rain fell less densely. The scientific mission had lost its sound recording equipment, but its members were fortunately able to convince themselves that it still had twenty ears, and that, beneath its feet, the noise was sensibly decreasing.

"Saved!" exclaimed the cavernous voice of Herr Stern, an astronomer by profession and a poet in his spare time—and his large hand extended toward his colleagues, who, exhausted, streaming like gutters and bent down like old beech trees, only replied with a deplorable concert of coughs and sneezes.

Such a cacophony evidently demonstrated the necessity of suspending the series of observations, at least for that day. The Ten separated and, each obedient to the instincts of humanity, accommodated himself as best he could in the abandoned houses of a nearby village in order to spend the night.

That night, however, sleep did not weigh upon their eyelids; a nightmare pursued them in the shadows, for their duty was far from being accomplished. With attentive ears, they listened to the increasingly distant rumbles. A creaking weathervane, the rustle of dead leaves or the slightest breath of wind outside caused them to shiver and suspect an increase in intensity. Vain efforts and vain terrors—when daylight reappeared, the distant rumbling died away into a vague murmur.

It was high time; worn out by fatigue, exhausted by so much emotion, their brains enfeebled by continuous cerebral tension, they let themselves lapse into well-earned sleep.

Evening came, the moon emerged from a serene horizon and rose in her radiant beauty in the midst of a constellated firmament; not a single cloud patched that marvelous clarity with its shadow; the air was pure and the breeze was soft; an absolute calm reigned in the deserted plain.

A sonorous snoring, however, broke the silence. It was, in fact, the scientists who were snoring, and our ten Germans, after thirty-six hours without sleep, were not at fault in so doing. One of them eventually fell silent, opened his eyes, palpated himself, and then, shaking his limbs to rid them of the torpor that was numbing them, he recalled that, alas, his task had made no progress, since their entire task still remained. That awful thought drew them out of their lethargy one by one; soon, it obsessed them.

So, for several more days they explored the surroundings, demanding from the slightest movement of the terrain a plausible reason that would permit them not to return to their colleagues mute, exposed to their sarcasms. They were obliged to confess their impotence: the phenomenon had disappeared without yielding its secret.

On their return to Berlin they rendered an account of their mission, minutely detailing all the characteristics they had observed, without forgetting the horrible tempest of which they had been the victims. But it was proved to them that the storm in question, foreseen and announced by a dispatch from New York, had only raged over Germany after having raised up the waves of the Atlantic and ravaged France, and had no connection with the infernal racket that they had been charged with explaining. They drafted a report of their adventures, to form a sequel to that of the three Russians and three Englishmen by Jules Verne,[13] but did not draw any conclusion from it.

That document engendered memorable discussions in all the scholarly bodies in Germany and abroad, after which they all claimed to have removed the veils covering the mystery. As the explanations given were all different, violent polemics resulted, which impassioned the public, and it was feared momentarily that the question, scientific as it was, might become political by exciting national vanities to excess. In fact, the Germans reproached the French for an absence of method, and the latter did not hesitate to reply maliciously that the Germans had lacked ideas. Government stocks fell abruptly; the bellicose agitation immediately calmed down.

Only a few fanatics continued the contest, and no one had convinced his adversaries; the most complete obscurity did not cease to envelop the supernatural event.

In spite of that, the troubled district was repopulated. The timorous followed the bold, and all of them had soon returned to their dwellings. For a long time yet, however, in the tested region, peasants were seen paus-

---

[13] *Aventures de trois Russes et de trois Anglais dans l'Afrique australe* (1872; tr. as *The Adventures of Three Englishmen and Three Russians in Southern Africa* and as *Measuring a Meridian*)

ing in their labor, frightened by the rumbling wheels of a heavy cart on the nearby road. An English traveler who traversed the region last year published a collection of local legends in Bristol, including a poem in eight stanzas of eight lines of eight syllables, which recounted how the evil spirits populating the interior of the globe had broken their chains one day and attempted to irrupt onto the surface, threatening humans with total destruction, but fortunately, vanquished by the angels, they had been struck down and thrown back into their furnace.

These sublime lines are found therein, which the children of the region repeat with terror without comprehending them:

> The rumor approaches.
> The echo repeats it,
> It resembles the bell
> Of an accursed convent,
> Or the noise of a crowd
> Which turns and rolls
> And sometimes falls
> And sometimes grows.[14]

One morning, the engineer Lichtmann was in the central office of Canonenpalast, occupied in reading the newspapers of all lands that he received in great quantity. It was a servitude to which he subjected himself every day before examining the daily affairs of

---

[14] Author's reference: "V. Hugo, *Les Orientales; les Djinns*." *Les Orientales* was published in 1829; "Les Djinns" has more than eight stanzas and the lines of each vary in length, the first and last stanzas having very short lines while those in the middle expand considerably.

Canonenstadt. By a special favor, his genius saw through the chaos of obscure revelations, false news and erroneous assertions. So he was completely up to date with the progress of the world and hastened his wishes for the moment when he would be able to try to generalize his system with some chance of success.

He had just picked up the *National-Zeitung*, and his eyes were straying mechanically over the sheet unfolded before him, searching for articles worthy of interest, when he encountered the words IMMINENT PERIL printed in large letters at the head of an article in which the editor-in-chief, after having transcribed the dispatch from the Agence Havas of 19 February 1902, and commented on it in an emotional style, recounted, without having precise details, the fear and flight of an entire population, and reproached the government, which had been unable to anticipate the danger, for its incuriosity or malevolence.

Lichtmann had scarcely had time to scan the first lines when he leapt out of his seat, ran to the door and disappeared, to the great amazement of his colleagues, who were working in the same room. For them, in fact, what an unexpected spectacle it was to see a man who always seemed so calm so violently disturbed!

Having arrived outside, the engineer directed his rapid course—flying rather than running—toward the first electric vehicle that he spotted. He immediately launched the vehicle at top speed toward the northwest. Three kilometers from the palace, he stopped at the entrance to one of the old coalmines that had once served to supply the furnaces of Essen. Then he threw himself into an elevator stationed at the opening of a shaft, released the brake and allowed himself to fall, at the risk of breaking bones, into the depths of the mine.

He then found himself in an immense subterranean nave full of noise, where a few workers were agitating under the light of huge Voltaic disks suspended from the vault. Around that chamber, several circular holes, huge black stains in the illuminated walls, gave passage to numerous pipes of all dimensions, which, similar to water pipes, extended above the ground from one opening to another, or, by virtue of an abrupt change of direction rose up from a depth of five hundred feet toward the open sky along the walls of several vertical shafts. At the entrance to each hole, powerful machines whose wheels were spinning precipitately, seemingly devoted to an invisible labor.

A traveler transported into those regions would have found it very difficult to say what kind of operation was going on there. There could be no thought of an extraction of minerals or combustibles, for no carts were circulating and transporting materials extracted from the bowels of the earth, and no cart was carrying them up to the surface A lively imagination would be more likely to recognize forgers exercising their industry sheltered from indiscreet gazes, watching with anxious eyes the machines from which the illusory riches were emerging.

"Fritz!" a voice shouted.

The overseer thus addressed turned round, surprised, and bowed respectfully. A few orders were given to him. Immediately, a deathly silence fell in that sepulcher. The machines ceased to move; even the workers were immobilized at a word from the Engineer.

He did not say anything, however, and headed toward one of the holes. He stepped into a wagon in the form of a boat, which began to glide slowly along the rails that could be divined in the shadows, and plunged into the depths of an immense tunnel whose extremity could not be glimpsed.

The journey lasted almost three hours, although the speed was about two hundred and fifty meters a minute. Throughout that time, Lichtmann anxiously consulted the figures marked at intervals on the walls of the gallery, and a level placed close at hand in the axis of the wagon. Several times the tunnel had broadened out, and, in the large vaulted caverns, workers were contemplating with astonishment their inactive machines and the director, who passed by without stopping. The latter had taken a notebook from his pocket and sometimes made a rapid calculation, after which, with a gesture of disappointment, he resumed reading the numbers inscribed on the wall and the indications of his level.

Finally, he stopped abruptly in front of one of the numbers, drew closer to it in order to make sure that he was not mistaken, reflected profoundly, and began to trace several columns of figures in his notebook with a feverish hand. When he raised his head again, he uttered the words: "Too high," and then started the vehicle moving again, at a rapid speed that soon brought him to the end of the interminable tunnel. A black disk was discernible there, which seemed to close the tunnel, and where various sorts of iron conduit came to an end.

In response to his voice two men emerged, who climbed into the tram, and in less than half an hour, without making any calculations, he returned to his point of departure, where he ordered that the machines should not be started up again until he gave the instruction. He returned in haste to the Canonenpalast, where his anxious colleagues greeted him joyfully and bombarded him with questions about the cause of his abrupt disappearance and his prolonged absence.

VIII

Canonenstadt circumnavigates the western part of the long strip of ore-bearing and carboniferous terrain that extends westwards from Dusseldorf in the direction of Haarstrang. The engineer found the ferruginous ores there necessary to the production of steel, the principal element of his famous alloy.

It was completely lacking, however, in copper, lead, zinc and tin, of which he employed considerable quantities in the manufacture of numerous accessories of his cannons and all the objects in use in the province. Every year, therefore, he was obliged to buy those metals at a very high price, which depleted a significant fraction of his coffers.

Furthermore, as the annual consumption of steel, there even more than elsewhere, followed a rapidly increasing curve, it would not be long, with his own mines being exhausted, before he would be forced to import that material too, which, again, was the primary basis of his industry.

Already, in the past, the factory at Essen had started working with minerals imported from afar, especially the mines at Sayn, north of Coblentz, which had been acquired by Krupp—but Lichtmann had stopped exploiting them in order to avoid the inconveniences inseparable from having to send workers out of Canonenstadt. He thought, moreover, that in certain circumstances, however improbable but possible, the necessity of importing a major fraction of his materials from outside might put him at the mercy of his neighbors. So, as soon as the factories and the city were organized, he had had only had one thought: to shield himself from any inconvenient or troublesome eventuality; to ensure an independence that was not nominal, like the one he enjoyed already, but effective and final: a gigantic task, completely indispensable to Canonenstadt. Anyone else would have been deterred by the difficulties; he, confident in the inexhaustible resources of his imagination, was sure of a prompt and relatively easy victory. He smiled at fortune, and fortune heaped him with favors.

With an audacity approaching temerity, he talked about going to exploit the richest mines of the surrounding countries, unknown to their proprietors, and, in order to do that, to attack them in their deepest layers, while the others were operating in the opposite direction.

It was necessary, above all, to link his Estates to the regions that he intended to utilize by long subterranean tunnels, and that ambitious work represented more than doubling the length of all existing tunnels placed end to end, even including the Channel tunnel currently under construction.

For iron, he would go in a straight line directly under the valley on the Sayn, 110 kilometers from Canonenpalast, and to Iserlohn, a short distance from his eastern frontier. From there he would direct his tunnel toward the Harz, 230 kilometers away, where he would also find lead, copper and zinc. The same metals would be furnished by the territory of Sieregen. The Old Mountain, not far from Liège, would offer him zinc of superior quality. As for pyritic schists from which he would be able to extract aluminum, he would encounter them at various points alone the course of the various tunnels.

When those sources began to run out or to be impoverished, he would not hesitate to plunder from Bohemia and Saxony the rich seams of Erzgebirge, from

Cornithia those of Erzberg, and from Thuringia those of Suhl and Schmalkalden. If it were necessary, he would go under the Channel to steal their black-band ore from the English, or under the Baltic to appropriate the rich magnetic oxides of Sweden.

Before going to those extremes, he would require no less than seven hundred kilometers of tunnel to reach the first exploitable veins.

But the landowners, essentially conservative, would not gladly allow a hand to dip into their profits, nor the companies into their minerals, and the model State, like Caesar's wife, had to be above suspicion. In order to carry out the operation in secret, it was indispensable to avoid any compromising encounter with any extraction shaft or other already existent workings in the regions to be traversed. The tunnels, therefore, had to maintain an average depth of a thousand meters below the surface of the ground.

Having decided on that condition, Lichtmann had his engineers determine what the length and direction of the horizontal sections would be, as well as the inclination of the ramps of various conduits that, departing from a fifteen-hundred meter shaft already hollowed out not far from the Thur, would extend under Andreasberg in the Harz, beneath the valleys of the Sieg and the Sayn and into the entrails of the Old Mountain while maintaining the required depth.

He had checked all the calculations himself with the greatest care, and had immediately begun the work. After having studied the various models of drills, the most advanced rock drills, and the most recent perforators, which had served to pierce the Simplon and the submarine tunnel, he had become convinced that all that apparatus, even modified, would not be effective enough to carry out such a gigantic enterprise in a short time. Also, compounding his initial worries, though his tunnels would not have such large dimensions as those designed for the passage of trains, the means thus far employed to remove the extracted earth seemed to him to be slow and cumbersome.

That is why he had abandoned all the old procedures and invented a new machine: a sort of quartz-metal grindstone, with a slightly conical and dramatically striated frictional surface, wearing away the rock with which it was constantly in contact. The debris removal was now done by articulated brackets revolving with the apparatus and braced against the terrain, moving the waste out and around as the drill advanced. It was nothing other than the mechanically-realized action of the hindquarters of a horse making an effort to draw a heavy vehicle. The grindstone, equal in diameter to the hole to be bored, closed a cylinder within that contained, sealed and protected, the organs of the engine.

Toward the center of the rotating disk were vents that gave passage to an extremely violent current of air. That was furnished by enormous blowers and brought to the perforating apparatus by interminable conduits extended along the tunnel as it advanced. That wind contributed, along with centrifugal force, to drive the dust produced by the disaggregation of the rock toward the circumference.

The debris, then, drawn by the compressed air, was subsequently funneled into other conduits extending along the perimeter of the grindstone, which soon combined into a single trunk, to spout outside the tunnel the materials extracted from the depths of the excavation. That ingenious procedure eliminated the considerable manual labor and continual coming and going of receptacles ordinarily used for the removable of rubble. The waste material was used to fill in the old mines of Canonenstadt, with the result that the charming perspectives of the park were not interrupted by any of those useless and disgraceful hills of stones that are often heaped up around subterranean exploitations.

Each of those machines represented a great deal of work, which was of scant importance to Lichtmann, who appreciated rapidity of execution above all else. He had reason to be satisfied, for in the hardest granites and the most compact sandstones, as in the less consistent strata, the new perforator advanced about a thousand meters a day. It did not even allow itself to be stopped by the aqueous terrains that it sometimes encountered on its route. There, it was sufficient to increase the air pressure to clear the striations and the teeth of the grindstone completely of the mud that was clogging them, and permit them to bite without interruption into the surface of the rock. Only once every three or four days was it necessary to replace the rotating disk, when its blunted edges, having become less powerful, began to slow down the progress of the apparatus.

Where the terrains attacked were solid, the walls of the tunnel, perfectly regular and well-polished, did not require any ulterior buffering. Everywhere that the nature of the strata created a danger of partial collapses or the invasion of water, however, a second machine, following closely behind the first, unrolled a broad ribbon of metal in a spiral over the interior surface, amalgamated to prevent oxidation. A compressor immediately applied it to the rock, while a jet of oxyhydric gas, animated by the same helical movement, immediately welded its edges together. That task having been completed, the bottom rails were laid, beneath which, in the segment left free, ran the tubes and wires carrying the compressed air machines and electricity—which is to say, life, force and light.

The workers employed in the excavation had baptized the Engineer's new invention the Mole, by virtue of its analogy with those animals, which, shunning the light of the sun, hollow out unknown routes in their obscure domains in order to exploit riches without fear that anyone will dispute their possession.

At intervals, similar perforators enlarged the tunnel by hollowing out large excavations that would serve as relays or as stations during the main exploitation. The rails placed along the tunnels supported the wagons designed to transport workers from one extremity of the mine to the other. At every change of slope, at the origin of a horizontal section or a ramp, figures inscribed on the wall recorded the distance already covered and the inclination of each element, to facilitate the engineers' monitoring.

Every six hours, when a new shift of workers replaced the preceding one, the overseers directing them transmitted the information necessary to the continuation of the work. There was a map of the tunnel in the central channel, on which the exact location occupied by the machine was marked at the end of every shift.

Now, it happened one day that, because of an error in reading that plan, the location was indicated as being several miles in advance of the real position of the perforator. According to the plan, it should have been under a mountainous region and rising at a fairly steep slope in the flanks of the massif. That was what the apparatus did as soon as it was set in the new direction. The excavation proceeded thus for six days without anyone having any suspicion of the error that had been made, when everything in the mine suddenly stopped. Instantaneously, the blowers, the electric motors, and the rollers lining the walls were paralyzed. Even the men remained inert, thinking that an accident had befallen the great hydraulic machine or the electricity generators.

On reading the article in the *National-Zeitung*, Lichtmann had immediately realized that the town where the panic had occurred was directly above the Harz tunnel. Struck by the coincidence, he had glimpsed the truth and had raced to stop the machine while there was still time. When he arrived after that journey at the end of the long corridor in which he had verified the direction of all the sections, he had observed that the machine had risen to within less than 150 meters from the surface. If the newspaper had fallen into his hands a few hours later, the Mole would have emerged in the middle of the German countryside whose inhabitants it had frightened so much.

The idea that his secret had almost escaped, and the danger he had run, caused feverish frissons to run through all the Engineer's muscles. Having returned to Canonenpalast, without losing any time, he set about reviewing all the plans of the six tunnels with his colleagues; then he went to visit them to make sure that no other error had been committed. It was during that interruption of work that the Royal Academy's committee had pursued its investigation, without finding anything unexpected.

When Lichtmann was convinced that that routes followed everywhere else were in order, he set the perforators to work again. As for the eastern machine, the author of the accident, it was obliged to work in reverse—which is to say that the pipes replaced in front of the Mole the materials previously extracted, which it slowly compressed as it retreated, thus undoing the work of several days.

The Engineer had not wanted to leave the useless tunnel empty, for fear that the scientists might carry out soundings or that, by an unfortunate coincidence, a shaft dug in the future might encounter it. The Mole therefore placed seventy thousand cubic meters of rubble, corresponding to some seven kilometers of tunnel. After forty-eight hours of descent it was already four hundred meters below Peckelsheim, and the committee members, initially surprised by the abrupt reappearance of the sound, could no longer hear it.

The excavations continued after that without any further incident. Lichtmann, however, having become wary, often went to check on the workers.

Finally, after several months, all the tunnels were completed. The minerals sent by the Moles, which then served for their extraction, poured without interruption into the blast furnaces of the great factory. In all the exploited terrains, the perforators followed the metallic seams, thus tracing a new network of tunnels beneath that of the higher exploitation, without the miners or engineers of the latter suspecting the proximity of their redoubtable competitors.

The owners of those mines, who, until then, had supplied Canonenstadt with the metals it needed, saw that rich source of profits disappear. As the materiel sold by the Engineer always included a large quantity of those raw materials, they wondered with astonishment how he managed to produce them. They were obliged to resign themselves to not solving that enigma, and Lichtmann's reputation as a chemist was further enhanced.

IX

It had only been twenty years since Canonenstadt had been founded, and its flourishing industry had already conquered the esteem—and, better still, the clientele—of the entire world. Now, several models of cannon, each more perfected than the last, emerging from the factories at brief intervals, had obliged the great powers to renew their armaments simultaneously.

In that epoch, the Engineer furnished all the armies not only with artillery but also with portable weapons and all the vehicles of which they made use. His revolver-rifle, of small caliber but long range, had been endowed with an incredible lightness, thanks to the adoption of an elastic butt that reduced the recoil—and, in consequence, the fatigue of the shooter—to negligibility. The success of that firearm had been universal, and it was in the millions that the cases of them emerged from Lichtmann's factories.

It was to him, too, that mariners addressed themselves to procure armor plating and the various components integrated into the structure of warships or transport vessels, the quality and price of which could not be matched by any other contractor. In a few more years the oceans would no longer be traveled by a single ship that did not bear the mark of the celebrated manufacturer.

All the taxes that it was possible to raise served integrally to enrich Canonenstadt, and as the sum that was collected did not recirculate again, gold, which had become rare, saw its value increase rapidly. War had not broken out since 1896, but it was still in a latent state.

There was no lack of pretexts, and yet no one dared take the initiative, knowing that it would be gambling with high stakes, because the victors would certainly ensure that their adversaries could do them no further harm by annihilating them.

In 1896, there had still been fighting for a principle, for an idea; war was a duel between two peoples, courteous and polite champions who were regulating a question of honor, self-esteem or interest by means of arms. The victor profited from the victory, but did not abuse it beyond certain limits; the vanquished remained bruised, but not mortally wounded. In the twentieth century, the nations were ready to erase with a streak of blood even the name of the hereditary enemy. It was a hated of races that weighed upon Europe, like the vendettas of the ancient Corsican families.

All international conventions were torn up, the law trampled underfoot. The final phase of civilization was therefore approaching: the empire of force, to which the masses wanted to submit other masses, tamed as one tames beasts; and those crowds in revolt, raising their heads, were preparing a supreme struggle to survive or perish. The most seemingly insignificant event might be the cause of a catastrophe all the more terrible for being more belated.

Already, the purely scientific question raised by the subterranean noises heard at Peckelsheim had degenerated, by virtue of the rivalry of scholarly bodies and the consequential debates, into a political question of capital importance. Even individual disputes between foreigners took a form in which they were forcibly recognized as an exceedingly ominous symptom. Popular animosity was translated in ways that took on a character of savagery that became more emphatic every day. It was difficult to travel outside one's native land without being exposed to the obstinate malevolence of populations.

Russia continued to struggle impotently in the grip of nihilism, in spite of the incessant activity of the police, who, prompt to take alarm at any suspect appearance—an unfamiliar face, a word, or even a smile—discovered conspiracies everywhere and repressed them with terrible severity. Thus, three young Austrians sent by a company in Trieste to sell wheat in Odessa were denounced, arrested, tried, convicted and immediately sent to Siberia, victims of human injustice and the ingratitude of their fellow citizens, for the nourishment of whom they had courageously risked themselves.

German fury broke with no less rage over an attractive actress whose misfortunes were keenly felt in France. Poor Marie Loubka! All Paris had applauded the ravishing brunette whose strange beauty and romantic artistic temperament had so profoundly moved the blasé audience of the Comédie Française. *Hernani*[15] was her final triumph, and her numerous adorers still heard her golden voice in their dreams murmuring in their ear the words placed by the poet in the mouth of Doña Sol. A fatal impulse took her beyond the Rhine; she came from France, so she was booed in Darmstadt by the riotous population. Brawls bloodied the city. Prince Barichkine, who no longer left her side, departed with her for Dresden, and while they were promenading their amour beneath the blue sky of Saxony, they scarcely suspected that they were being condemned in Berlin. One day, they

---

[15] The play by Victor Hugo whose première in February 1830 was considered a key event in the fortunes of the French Romantic Movement.

disappeared, and the next, no one knew that the fortress of Königstein counted two inmates more.

The least of the dangers that one ran in traveling abroad was, therefore, that of being taken for a spy and treated as such. International commerce was no longer possible in the midst of such a tormented societies, and all the powers, in order to avoid an excessively imminent financial and social crisis, launched forth into distant enterprises whose ostensible aim was to provide sufficient outlets to their industries. In reality, the greater fear was that the military quality of their troops, and especially their leaders, might be diminished by such a long truce, and they also attempted to discover resources in conquests by pressuring the submissive peoples. All the expeditionary preparations were made in the greatest secrecy.

Immense spaces still unknown to white men, and reputedly rich, extended in the heart of Africa; it was in that direction that the sight of the French government extended, favored in that project by the Trans-Saharan railway, which had fortunately just been completed. Only then was the wisdom that had presided over the enterprise of that astonishing achievement, so long mocked, so ridiculous at first glance, finally realized. For several years no capitalist had wanted to risk funds on such a venture; now it was the link that attached the fatherland, across the desert, to a vast colonial empire whose wealth would amply compensate the shareholders for their expenses, a detour from previous exploitations.

The naval station of Senegal was reinforced; a few troops immediately disembarked and swelled the coastal garrisons and ensured the free navigation of the rivers. In the meantime, however, an entire column of infantry, cavalry and artillery was concentrated by the railway at

Kuniakoro. It was to follow the sole route blazed through the region, via Kemmu and Bangassi, to cross the Niger and then to divide into two corps, one of which would go up the Djoliba and the other the Ulaba, eventually to link up again near Sego, having obtained control of all the lands of the Mandingos and the Bambara.

The Mandingos, a brave, generous and intelligent people, had been submissive for a long time to French influence; they did not resist and became faithful allies. Only once, on the edge of a forest, did our valiant soldiers, struck at close range by an invisible enemy, believe that they were under considerable attack and deploy. The artillery took up position to rake the woods, but at the first salvo, all defense ceased, large hairy bodies fell to the ground, and the troops saluted with cries of joy the defeat of the chimpanzees, for it was them who had dared to interrupt the army.

All the way to Bangassi, everything went well, but the negroes of the Takrour, allies with the Fellatahs in a vast coalition against the whites, had massed on the right bank of the Djoliba. They had not, however, detected General Lamy Desrevues' advance scouts at the exit from the valley, where they were greeted by well-nourished musket fire, with the din of which the frightful cries uttered by the blacks mingled, and then the thunder of a battery unexpectedly unmasked. The battle lasted two days, and many cadavers littered the ground on either side, but the tigers and panthers willingly took charge of arresting the decomposition, and it is greatly regrettable that animals appropriate to ensuring the salubrity of the desert had to struggle against the antipathy of humans.

Colonel Panache secured the victory by his great flanking movement at Baumaku, and the rest of the army crossed the river, not without difficulty, at Manabugu. The enemy had retreated in great disorder but the troopers were so exhausted that the pursuit was renounced. They only resumed the forward march two days later, too late to catch up with the agile refugees.

A fortnight later, the advance guard arrived within view of Sego and signaled the presence of a vast quantity of tents scattered around the village, over which the blacks' flag was flying. All the fanatical and ferocious warriors had been summoned and had decided to defend up until the final extremity the capital of the Bambaras, then under the command of the fearsome Danfodiko, the sultan of the Fellatahs.

Astonishingly, numerous batteries were defending the approaches to the town, but fortunately, manned by negroes, they were more noisy than effective. The French, however, hesitated, because the enemy, a hundred times more numerous, would be bound to make inroads into their lines. Were they, then, about to lose the fruits of such a laborious campaign in a single day?

Suddenly, a cloud of dust rose up in the southeast, and a lively cannonade was heard. Danfodiko, momentarily surprised and disconcerted, rallied the savages in order to confront that unexpected attack, but soon, in full retreat, the latter piled up at the gates, crushing one another and trampling one another in order to take refuge in the town. That was what the multitude would have done if attention had not been suddenly attracted by rifle shots apparently coming from the terrace of the great mosque. At the same time, a white flag had been hoisted at the summit of the highest minaret, and a few unarmed horsemen advanced to meet the French column.

The amazement reached its peak when the negotiator was found to be a man with a pale face, of correct bearing and the purest language, who announced to the general that Danfodiko admitted defeat and was offering peace, but did not know to whom to surrender, for if it was the French that had started the battle, it was the English who had finished it. And, indeed, British uniforms, as if to confirm his assertions, were already appearing in the distance. He also added that a Portuguese expedition disembarked in Monrovia and, coming inland on the road to Musardu, had already arrived at Beleko, and that European susceptibilities, revived in the heart of Africa by the contact of the three powers, might well counterbalance the influence of their victories and favor a general uprising of indigenous nations if accord could not be rapidly established.

The person who was speaking was none other than Herr Schutz, Lichtmann's representative dealing with the indigenous of Takrour. In accordance with his advice, and in his presence, an armistice was signed the following day. General Lamy Desrevues, Lord Farsher and Admiral Don Diego d'Elvenar, summoned in haste, and Sultan Danfodiko drank the milk of a white camel from an ivory cup as a symbol of peace, and laid the basis for a political geography of that little-known region, to the great joy of collegians to come. The treaty was the occasion for great rejoicing, in the course of which the European soldiers, seduced by the natural grace of beautiful native women, took part in local dances and were drawn into an immense bamboula.

A week after the battle, everyone went their separate ways, contentedly, Danfodiko was consoled for his futile resistance by the glory that it had brought him, the victors were glad to have found adversaries worthy of them and to have been forced to conduct operations serious enough to hone their martial virtues. Their star, however, paled before a shinier one. Canonenstadt had just proved the extent of its moral authority by imposing its arbitration, its will and its laws on the foremost nations in the world. The latter, glad to have avoided a dangerous conflict, bowed down before the decisions of a modest engineer, and thus rendered homage to the merit of a man who, having emerged from the ranks of the workers, had raised himself by his genius to the sublime heights where, above conquerors, the rare benefactors of humanity soar.

X

Alone of all the great powers, Germany had not dispersed her forces. She took pleasure, by contrast, in concentrating them, and in admiring them; were not her military institutions her masterpiece? The able successor of a great man had been careful not to deflect his neighbors from their conquests in barbaric lands. A richer prey was offered to satisfy his covetousness in the heart of Europe, but, as a skilled diplomat, he seemed only to have eyes for events in Africa, boasting of his moderation, his scorn for riches, his love of peace—for "speech was given to man to conceal his thoughts."[16]

Things were at that point when, in the course of a discussion during a Parliamentary session, the Prime Minister thought the moment favorable and allowed the jealousy inspired in him by the prosperity of Canonenstadt to be divined.

A few days later, the Engineer, rightly troubled by the words that the Statesman had let slip, made his apprehensions known to his colleagues at the end of a meeting at which the financial accounts for the year 1922 had been finalized. It was on that occasion that he made the speech reproduced at the beginning of this story, in which he manifested both his satisfaction on the subject of the financial situation and serious anxiety about the state of minds outside.

---

[16] The quote as rendered was credited to Talleyrand, although it is probably apocryphal, and even if he did say it, he was only paraphrasing Voltaire.

As he had announced, he soon convened the governing council and the hundred most senior overseers, in order to propose to them measures appropriate to ensure the security of the territory, if it were menaced by external complications. His expression, even graver than usual, seemed to indicate the importance of the communications that he was about to make, and his audience listened with the greatest concentration when he began to speak.

"My dear collaborators, as a consequence of the successive improvements that have been made to them, our machines have arrived at a degree of perfection that it might be difficult to surpass in the future. That is why I have been obliged to seek a new field of study, which, less explored, might furnish our industry with new elements of progress. My initial investigations have already borne fruit, and I shall describe to you a new invention that will henceforth dethrone cannons by removing their principal role on the battlefield.

"The idea is not entirely new, and as early as 1883, as you know, a certain Nordenfelt manufactured machine guns capable of firing five hundred rounds a minute.[17] Those weapons could not compete against ours,

---

[17] Although variants of the Gatling gun, patented in 1861, had been used in the American Civil War and the Franco-Prussian War, they had been largely replaced at the time the present story was written by Nordenfelt Guns, patented in 1873. The author is obviously not aware that the Nordenfelts would soon be overtaken by the much more efficient Maxim Gun, whose prototype was first demonstrated in October 1884, and which became the ancestor of the machine guns employed in the Great War of 1914-18. From the author's temporal standpoint, the alternative history, in which machine guns fall into disuse

because the projectiles they fired were too small, the range too short and the terrain covered too limited. Those machines, fallen into forgetfulness, are about to reemerge with improvements that will earn them the confidence of artillerymen and place them in the front rank of firearms.

According to my calculations, my machine gun, formed from a sheaf of a hundred divergent barrels, will project to a range of twenty kilometers more than ten thousand projectiles a minute. Each of those shells, weighing five hundred grams, will burst into twenty-five shards, producing two hundred and fifty thousand fragments, which will scythe in the fashion of our present cannons a surface area two thousand meters wide and as many deep.

"You will be convinced of the efficacy of that spray in forthcoming trials, in which you will observe that over the four million square meters exposed to the fire, there will be not one that is not furrowed by at least ten shards. It is certain that under that rain, no living being will be able to survive, and in a matter of minutes, that destructive action can be extended over a considerable zone of terrain, embracing entire districts. More than ever, it will be unnecessary to see the enemy to suppress him radically. It will only be a matter, in fact, of directing the spray in any direction in which one merely suspects the presence of adverse troops.

"Although, in these conditions, I think that a conflict ought not to last more than three or four minutes, a serious difficulty resides in the large number of projectiles to be transported. I estimate that two hundred thou-

---

until Lichtmann invents his super-powered version, was not implausible.

sand machine gun shots—which, collectively, represents twenty minutes of combat—will be quite sufficient for a campaign. Wars will become, in fact, very short, for there is no danger that beaten armies will reform after a defeat. In spite of that, one arrives at the enormous figure of a hundred thousand kilograms to carry per machine gun, plus the weight of the powder charges.

"I have, I believe, solved the problem in a very satisfactory manner, which I shall indicate to you in due course. Let me tell you right away, however, that I was on the point of offering these devices to the European artilleries when, the states of minds among our neighbors having troubled me, I thought it would be as well to keep them for the service of the army that I desire, with your assent, to form as soon as possible.

"Be assured that I am profoundly saddened to have to go to this extremity. I had hoped that the services rendered to the world every day by Canonenstadt would shield us from evil intentions, but before such ingratitude on the part of humankind, hesitation on our part would be imprudent and culpable. It is our duty to ensure our defense and to be prompt in putting ourselves in a position to annihilate the illegitimate hopes that our apparent weakness might encourage. Our fence, adequate to protect us from the curious, cannot protect us against a serious attack, for the destruction of the underlay by cannon fire would eliminate all its defensive value."

The Assembly was greatly disturbed by these revelations, but full of confidence in the sagacity of its President; it remained calm, and none of the clamors were heard that are the usual prerogative of those sorts of meetings in moments of crisis. All the audience members, visibly embarrassed, reflected profoundly and communicated their ideas to one another in low voices before giving their opinions.

Finally, the oldest of the overseers stood up and made the following observations:

"It is with the certainty of being the interpreter of all that I express to our dear President the admiration and gratitude inspired in us by his enlightened prudence and his solicitude for the general wellbeing. We would certainly have preferred to remain in our modest role as useful workers, and the glory of marching in the forefront of progress would have been sufficient for us, but since it is necessary, we are ready to attempt to acquire another. Is it not to be feared, however, that our small number will not permit us to organize an army strong enough to rival that of other States, and, above all, to withstand the enormous destructive force that present artillery will not fail to deliver?"

When the orator fell silent, the attitude of the overseers showed very clearly that they shared all the anxieties that had just been manifest. They were too well judged to astonish Lichtmann, whose response was not long in coming.

"I anticipated that objection," he said, "so I have thought of a unimpeachable refutation. Be reassured, therefore: our army will only consist of five hundred men, including the officers, and with that effective force we shall form several units, which will be able to operate in multiple directions."

At these words all the members of the conference looked at one another in bewilderment, wondering whether the director's brain, overtaxed by so much work, was not slightly unhinged. The latter divined their thoughts, contented himself with smiling, and continued:

"At present, the battlefront of an army cannot surpass, or even attain, thirty kilometers, because of the difficulty that a single commanding general would have in knowing what is happening over such an extent and transmitting his orders in good time. With fifteen machine-gunners I can cover the entire extent of that terrain, and the troops occupying it can be annihilated in a matter of minutes.

"One of our armed units will therefore consist of fifteen machines, and one man will be sufficient to operate each of them. Each one occupies, in fact, the front of a kind of cylindrical carriage moved by an electrical accumulator contained in its flanks. That accumulator contains sufficient stored fluid to furnish a twenty-four hour march.

"When the motor is activated, six legs articulated in the same fashion as those of an animal, the movements of which are controlled by pistons and crankshafts that are both simple and sturdy. The apparatus, thus provided with veritable limbs, will be able to travel over any kind of terrain, climb or descend the steepest slopes, and if necessary scaling escarpments and crossing rivers in a matter of seconds. Ordinarily, it moves like a galloping horse with a speed that can attain forty kilometers an hour.

"It carries twenty thousand projectiles and weighs no more than eighteen thousand kilograms. The charges are delivered automatically from the reservoir that contains them in the funnel of the machine gun. Movement and fire are produced at will by means of a commutator placed under the operator's hand. The latter is enclosed in a kind of cabin on top of the whole system.

"The machine is somewhat reminiscent of a locomotive without a funnel, mounted on legs. The man, comfortably seated in an armchair fitted with springs, scarcely perceives the jolts due to the strides of the apparatus, and in very little time he can acquire the experience necessary for the efficient employment of his weapon.

"To complete the supply of projectiles, six tenders of the same form will follow the machine guns, just as ammunition trucks follow their cannon. They have the same weight and contain thirty thousand rounds each. At the required moment, the driver of a tender links his apparatus to that of the gunner, which absorbs the contents mechanically.

"Finally, other similar vehicles, each carrying forty-seven charged accumulators, will permit the replacement of those in other machines when they have exhausted the disposable force that they contain. The latter vehicles will number fifteen for an army of fifteen machine guns and ninety ammunition tenders. It will then dispose of its contents sixteen times in twenty-four hours of marching—which is to say, more than fifteen thousand kilometers per electromotor.

"In a fortnight, therefore, we shall be able to travel the length and breadth of Europe in every direction, fighting several battles. An army thus constituted will be commanded by a single general, supported by a general staff of four officers and five further officers each commanding a group of three machine-gunners and their auxiliary vehicles. All of them will be mounted in electrogallopers similar to the preceding ones, but lighter and capable of traveling at sixty kilometers an hour. They will have five thousand rounds for their personal defense, and they will be sheltered from all danger by their speed alone.

"The total personnel of an army unit will therefore be ten officers and 155 machine operators, making a total of 165. Now, take note of the simplification of tactics resulting from that organization. In less than half an hour, our troops can be deployed before an enemy, out of its range, and in the same time the general's orders can extend from one wing to the other, whereas, in order to effect similar maneuvers, our adversaries would require several hours, if not an entire day.

"We shall also be able to utilize our speed in another far more advantageous fashion; it will always permit us to surprise the enemy corps on the march and destroy them before they are able to see us and respond. Infantry and cavalry are impotent against the armor plating of our machines, if, by chance, they succeed in getting close to them. As for artillery, assuming that it has time to take up a position, it will disappear as soon as its first cannon shot reveals its position to us. In order to discover the enemy easily, an optical apparatus of great power will constantly display to each machine-gunner, enclosed in his cabin, the horizon that extends before him. In that fashion, nothing can escape his investigations, and as soon as the enemy appears, he can crush it with his fire.

"In order to camp, the army can gather in open spaces that it can easily choose, thanks to its mobility. The men will then be free to emerge from their lodgings, after having reconnoitered the surroundings, in order to avoid being surprised by any partisans against whom they might be momentarily disarmed. When security is not absolute, they will remain inside their machines, where food supplies for a month will be stored. That reclusion will not prevent them from communication with one another by means of whistles employed for the transmission of orders during combat.

"The only operation that we cannot undertake is an attack on a fortress against which our projectiles would be insufficient. We could make it impossible for the defenders to maintain a single man on the ramparts, but that would not lead to any decisive result. Imminently, I hope to be in a position to fill that lacuna and destroy enemy emplacements by another method, without leaving Canonenstadt."

Although long accustomed to the admirable conceptions of the Engineer, his audience could not contain their enthusiasm when he had finished explaining the principles of his new invention, which would revolutionize the military world. Alexander, Hannibal, Caesar and Napoléon paled by comparison with Lichtmann. Their genius and their most savant schemes would have been rendered moot by the simple tactics and comprehensive strategy that he had just revealed. In his modesty, however, he was amply rewarded by the grateful acclamations that his collaborators lavished upon him.

When calm was re-established, he thanked them in an emotional tone, telling them that their patriotism and the solidity of their social convictions inspired confidence in him. Carried away by the general ardor, he ended up by proclaiming: "Rather destroy humanity entirely than fall back under the laws of a government imbued with the most monstrous prejudices, which leaves the laboring classes, the only ones worthy of interest, in such complete poverty."

The very next day, the construction of the electromobile machine-guns and other auxiliary vehicles was begun. The work progressed rapidly, to the exclusion of any other, and was completed in a week, after which that superb materiel of war was arranged in front of the great factory in perfect order.

The old artillerists—those legendary maniacs for whom order, regularity and symmetry came well ahead of the science of combat, and whose esthetics did not rise to any more beautiful conception than that of straight lines formed by six guns followed by their ammunition trucks—would have died of jealousy. But the era of the firing-line was past, and that simple alignment only attracted their gaze because of the spectacle of the new materiel.

In the factory where artifices of every nature and explosive substances were manufactured, fever had gripped the machines and the workers. The latter, without worrying about the danger, handled villainous substances of various colors, more capricious than spoiled children and more terrible in their noisy games, with great dexterity, for an imprudent hand never touched them twice—irrefutable proof that the smallest bodies often contain more energy than the largest. All that work concluded, without accident, in the production of enormous quantities of ammonium picrate, pyroxyl and dynamite, but even the engineers charged with that specialty did not know what purpose was to be served by that overwhelming mass of explosive materials, for which the existing storage facilities were inadequate.

XI

The politics of Herr von Minskopf, the German Chancellor, was found at fault this time. He had counted too much on the gorillas and the negroes. The gorillas had fled and the negroes, who were still reliant in politics on their natural knowledge and guided by one of Lichtmann's emissaries, had just let him down outrageously by virtue of the treaty of Sego. He had been too hasty, in order to appease the Reichstag cabal, in opening his heart to his enemies. He had won the vote that he was pursuing, but had aroused all the diplomats against him.

Since speeches menacing to Canonenstadt had been pronounced in Germany, the attention of the public, initially captured by the exploits of Danfodiko, and in France by the arrival at the zoological gardens of a consignment of orangutan prisoners,[18] had been diverted

---

[18] There are no orangutans in Africa, but the Comte de Buffon, author of the standard Natural History still in use in France in the 1880s had confused the great ape species on the basis of unreliable second-hand reports, conflating Asian orangutans with one of the two African species he based loosely on accounts of chimpanzees and gorillas. His contemporary, Linnaeus, did not make the same mistake, but was seduced by apocryphal tales of orangutan intelligence into wondering whether they ought to be classified in the genus *Homo* as near-humans. So-called orangutans, bearing very little resemblance to the actual species, are extensively featured in a military role in Alfred Robida's satirical account of the adventures of Saturnin Farandoul, which the author of the present text might well have read.

back to the problematic existence of that province and its mysterious appearances, to which people had gradually become accustomed. The press commented on the awkward situation that might be produced, and uneasy governments were much preoccupied with the projects being elaborated in Berlin. They watched with jealous eyes for any action that might prejudice the arsenal from which their armaments emerged, and whose independence was for them a question of capital importance.

While all gazes were thus turned toward him, Lichtmann, confident in his electromachine guns, was thinking about the future without anxiety, when an unexpected event demonstrated to him the necessity of taking the greatest precautions to keep the secret of his preparations.

One morning, he was informed that one of the bars in the fence on the northern side had been partly cut through during the night. The noise made by the operators had attracted a few workers, and the malefactors had fled, leaving behind one of their tools, broken by the unexpected resistance of the obstacle.

That item of evidence, having been brought to Canonenpalast, was scrupulously examined in a secret session by the members of the government, who, after passing it from hand to hand, declared that they recognized these cutters with their insulating handles, with one side having given way under the violent effort to which it had been submitted.

The President suspended the deliberations in order to go to the place where the attempted break-in had occurred; he noticed there that the bar that was attacked, along with its neighbors, were linked to the underlay by a metallic chain; the assailants had thus been protected from a fortuitous closure of the contact.

After making these observations, he returned to the hall of deliberations, to which the council was summoned to give its advice on the measures to be taken in order to prevent a recurrence of such an attempt—which, had it succeeded, might have had disastrous consequences. With the means employed they could certainly only have made a narrow opening, sufficient to permit the passage of a single individual, perhaps followed by a number of others, but vulgar thieves would not have been audacious enough to try to cross the boundary without being assured of a considerable profit. Now, no easily carried object of value was in the vicinity, and they certainly had no knowledge of the treasury reserve or the location it occupied under Canonenpalast.

Precautions had, in any case, been taken in the latter regard, of a kind unknown to the Banque de France, but much in use in the eighteenth century in the tombs of rajahs. An inscription in flamboyant Gothic letters first invited the sacrilegious profaner to leave any hope of return at the door. Frightful apparatus, whose surveillance of the vicinity was absolute, garnished the walls of the shaft leading to the mysterious cellars. Those vigilant guardians would have seized in passing and crushed with their arms of steel the imprudent or criminal individual who had gone into the corridor without possessing the secret that rendered them inactive. That secret was only known to the six directors.

Even supposing a clever thief had succeeded in getting to the bottom of the tunnel, he would have brought back nothing but his disappointment. Instead of a vast lighted room in the midst of which stacks of gold coins and ingots of small dimension were glittering, their gleams fascinating the privileged mortal admitted into that miser's Eden, there was nothing but a dark cellar under the gloomy vault of which the perspective would appear of compact masses of yellow metal cast in thick iron chests.

Each of those precious parallelepipeds weighed 322,580 kilograms and was worth exactly a billion. There were three rows of ten, and a fourth had been commenced that only numbered three as yet: enormous blocks aligned in that sepulchral temple of fortune like menhirs in the plains of Armorica devoted to the worship of the druids; stones as brilliant as they were useless, extracted from the depths of the globe and buried there again. Products of a diabolical reaction of dust, mud, sweat and blood, those gods of the world had retreated underground again, leaving human folly to its agonizing struggle, without recourse against the will of one man: the man of light; the prophet of progress; Lichtmann.

To all the questions asked of them, the engineers were unanimous in replying that they were in the presence of an attempt at espionage. It therefore became very evident that their neighbors were thinking of attacking them. Was not the first thing to do, in such a case, in fact, to take account of the configuration of the place and its means of defense? Military men as prudent as Germany's would not fail to take that step.

The council was still in session when a balloon was detected above Canonenstadt. It was the third in a week. The frequency of those aerostatic trials was striking. Might it not be another mode of investigation employed by the enemy?

The session was quickly suspended again and the six councilors, in Indian file, with the President in the lead, climbed a veritable astronomer's stairway as rapidly as gravity would permit, onto the esplanade that surmounted the palace. The balloon descended with majestic slowness, and a light breeze blowing from the north soon pushed it toward Canonenpalast, but so gently that it seemed to be floating rather than navigating through the air.

It was barely 300 meters from the ground, and our six sages, reaching the goal of their ascension, were able to install themselves in excellent armchairs facing no less excellent telescopes with which to observe, while getting their breath back, the evolutions of the giant balloon and the slightest movements of its passengers. The latter were devoting themselves to a scrupulous study of the topography of the area, searching it with their gaze in every direction, parading the focus of their instruments along the avenues.

Suddenly, they perceived that they were being attentively watched themselves from the height of the cupola, and, throwing ballast overboard, disappeared into the air.

The President's hand bell was obliged to remind the engineers that the governors ought to be preoccupied with the interest of their country rather than the study of heavenly phenomena, and that the interrupted session had not been officially concluded.

They did not take long to close the discussion, because no one was any longer in any doubt; although slightly modified, probably by design, the balloon was the model adopted by the German military aerostatic corps.

Fortunately, thanks to those two discoveries, all immediate danger was set aside. The aeronauts had not been able to take specific note of the electromachine-guns, whose external form did not indicate their usage. The goal of the aerial reconnaissance, undoubtedly, was only the research of precise information in order to move confidently in Canonenstadt if the fence were successfully breached. However, it had become urgent to hide the veritable means of resistance, and as imminent maneuvers had been scheduled in order to habituate the workers to the operation of the machines, it was decided to carry them out in secret.

For that purpose, construction was immediately begun of an immense hall three thousand meters long by two thousand wide, which was built facing the principal factory. The building had only one door, carefully guarded; the army would be based therein and workers would only be allowed to enter after being recognized by several of their fellow citizens. With those precautions they could be sure that no stranger astray in the maze of the province would be able to witness the trials incognito.

In spite of the preliminary reconnaissance operations that Herr von Minskopf had instituted, it must not be thought that he had the intention of hurrying things and resorting to violence unless it was absolutely necessary. He hoped to save appearances by first engaging in artful negotiations and to arrive at his goal by persuasion, convinced that a little diplomacy would not hurt and would give him a fine role to play. With what joy he would resume the ensuing politics that had been the glory of one of his predecessors, and whose traditions would be lost if they were left in neglect for too long. A few fine arguments, supported by the display of a single army corps, would suffice, in his opinion, to bring about the submission of that State, whose population certainly would not dare to match itself against the imperial troops, so disciplined and in possession of all the secrets of war. The series of annexations that seemed closed had merely been interrupted; his clever schemes were about to add a new item.

Infatuated with his ideas, he declared, in a Parliamentary session that the revision of the treaty concluded with the Engineer in 1896 had been recognized as necessary.

"Without wishing to put the existence of Canonenstadt at risk," he said, "the Government finds that the existence of that State is a serious obstacle to our rapid concentration in the west, because several railways have been abolished and cannot be easily replaced. The War Office is continually made aware of the inconvenience of the situation, which it is necessary to remedy as soon as possible. In addition, it is probable that a ambitious enemy, less scrupulous than us, would not respect the neutrality of that province, the protectorate of which would become a heavy responsibility. It is therefore just to request, and, if necessary, to demand: firstly, that a German railway traverses Canonenstadt and that the bridges previously existing on the Rhine are reestablished in order to link the provinces of the left bank with the rest of the Empire; and, secondly, that an indemnity of twenty million thalers be paid by the Engineer in exchange for the guarantee of the integrity of his territory."

That declaration, skillfully brought forth in the course of a stormy discussion of the budget, appeared to the members of the parliament to bear the stamp of the greatest justice, and enabled them to glimpse a remedy, or at least a palliative, for the financial difficulties. It was, therefore, warmly welcomed, all the more so as the worthy patriots had never ceased to consider the metallurgist's province as a challenge thrown down to the complete unification of the great nation.

A few days later, a special envoy, General Baron von Kenntnissheim, was charged with taking these proposals to Lichtmann. The latter received him coldly. He suspected the objective of the embassy and, in spite of his habitual phlegm, had difficulty containing his indignation.

Visibly embarrassed by his interlocutor's expression, the General sought to disguise beneath flattering words the painful mission that he had to fulfill.

The Engineer interrupted him. "Let's leave my discoveries and ideas aside, please, General. You're not charged, I know, with bringing me a purchase order from your Government, and I've finished delivering the materiel requested of me. Get to the point and admit that you've come here today to reclaim the land that you sold to me."

"Germany, sir, is powerful enough to have nothing to gain by the acquisition of a parcel of land like the one you occupy."

"I know Germany, and I know that Germans are avid and that any treasure seems good to them. Gratitude is not one of their virtues."

"Perhaps, but the road that leads to glory and power is the only good one."

"Do you believe that you are following it by attacking me?"

"But we have never had any such thought!"

"Well, why have you come here if not to bring me an ultimatum and to declare that you are ready to annex Canonenstadt as you have annexed so many other provinces? What have you to reply to me? Have I not divined your master's intentions?"

The General, exasperated by seeing the politics of Herr von Minskopf, so just and so measured, thus unmasked and denigrated, could no longer contain himself and decided to expose the conditions that the latter deigned to put on the existence of Canonenstadt.

Lichtmann, however, had already drawn himself up to his full height; his eyes were flashing, his lips were pursed with disdain and his contracted features betrayed the violence of the internal battle he was fighting in order not to let his anger burst forth.

"Never!" he cried. "I will never consent to let my State be traversed by a German railway line, and above all by German agents. The fundamental principles on which the existence of the State is based formally oppose the introduction of foreigners and their passage, no matter how rapid. Holstein, too, was only asked to be traversed by a railway line. The day after I allowed the smallest parcel of my rights to be alienated, Canonenstadt would suffer the same fate as that Duchy."

"Germany would undoubtedly be proud, sir, to count among the estates that compose her a manufacturing city like yours, but I repeat to you that she does not want to absorb it; once again, she is only thinking of defending herself against her enemies and protecting you."

"You speak of a protectorate. General, I'm willing to renounce it. It's true that the treaty of 1896 still binds the Empire in that matter, and circumstances have not changed since that time, but even if they had, the convention, having not anticipated anything in that regard, can only be modified by the common accord of both contracting patties."

"The Emperor demands it, sir."

"And I oppose it, with all my strength."

"On what strength do you think you can rely to...?"

"On what strength? Oh, that's true, General, I don't have millions of men to oppose to you; I'm only an engineer; I only direct worthy workers and don't command a single soldier. Is it on that basis that you found your pretentions to constrain me to an engagement that my honor and my conscience reprove? I refuse to subscribe to it, and urge you not to have recourse to violence. I advise you not to do anything."

"Violence is, indeed, repugnant to us, and in your interests as well as ours, I would like to try to demonstrate to you your impotence to stand up to us, and to avoid a crisis that you seem eager to incite."

"Is it me, then, who is summoning it?"

"Yes, by your obstinacy."

"Let's leave it there, General; all your arguments cannot persuade me. You have in your favor the number of your bayonets, and the cannons that I have furnished you. I am strong in my inviolability, recognized by all the powers; to scorn it would attract the anger of all of Europe upon you."

"Europe is busy enough elsewhere. You refuse, then?"

"I refuse absolutely, and in the event that you try to carry out your threats, I shall appeal to all the civilized nations."

"I have nothing more to do, then, but withdraw. I am sorry that the steps I have taken have not been successful, and I hope that your ideas, modified by reflection, will lead you in a few days to adhere to the proposals of the Emperor, who holds you in the highest esteem."

The plenipotentiary had failed completely in his mission. Was that his fault? He returned to Berlin, convinced that it was not due to his lack of skill, but to the stubbornness of the Engineer that it was necessary to attribute the unfortunate result. So, why so much diplomacy when one had in one's hands such a beautiful army, commanded by generals of incontestable merit? If he were Prime Minister, he would not waste time in futile negotiations and would have quickly swept that Lilliputian republic away. Nevertheless, he had to make a report of his trip to the embassy to the chancellor and ask for further instructions.

For his part, the Engineer thought that there was no more time to lose, and occupied himself with organizing and exercising his personnel in a number of maneuvers, detailed and collective.

The firing trials had been carried out before uniting the machine guns, properly speaking, with the electromotors, and the engineer's calculations had been completely verified by the results obtained, with regard to rapidity, dispersion and the number of fragments. Who would the combatants be? Although they ought not to be running any great danger, equality nevertheless demanded that their designation be made by drawing lots. Everyone sensed the gravity of the situation and submitted in advance, were he to be selected or rejected, to the obligations that would be incumbent upon him.

The ceremony took place in the factory, with the greatest simplicity and without the noisy manifestations that accompany it in certain populations. That calm in strength would have been a precious subject of dissertation for philosophers if there had been any there. Four hundred and seventy soldiers were thus chosen from among the workers. The same procedure designated deputy engineers to fulfill the role of officers. As for generals, Lichtmann reserved the choice to be made among his colleagues until the moment came. In the meantime he assumed the direction of the maneuvers himself, which lasted four days.

During the first two, the soldiers were taught to operate their machines at all speeds in the great hall, identified as a gigantic racetrack ten kilometers around. Soon, all the machines were executing the most varied evolutions, at the signal of an officer, with a remarkable coordination. It was a grandiose spectacle, that of the electromachine-guns, with their shiny plump bellies and flanks, from which robust limbs extended and retracted rhythmically, endowing them with a graceful and rapid movement. The future generals watched those superb giants with pride, as well as those new warriors, whose composure was assured and whose discipline could not be compromised by the attending action of dangers and privations. In a matter of hours, the instruction of a driver was complete, so accustomed were they to adapting to the most various and complicated machinery.

That done, the engineer explained to his officers the ideas already developed in the session, now famous, in which he had first spoken about the army. He told them, among other things, that the interval of two kilometers was a maximum, and that there would often be an advantage in diminishing it in order to augment the density of the fire and the effect produced. As it was reduced, by half, to a third or a quarter, the number of fragments sweeping every meter of terrain would be doubled, tripled or quadrupled, which would abridge the battle proportionately.

He decided then that each set of three machines would constitute a corps analogous to those of other armies. One of them could be detached if necessary and act in an independent fashion on the flanks or behind the enemy, who would be impotent to oppose such movements.

Having put these principles in place, he employed the last two days in exercises of deployment and concentration, on a small scale, because of the relative absence of failed maneuvers. The instruction of the officers and the soldiers could then be considered as perfect, and Lichtmann charged the five oldest with drafting, in accordance with his indications, a new treatise on military artistry appropriate to the new army. That work, which ought to be reduced to a brochure of 25 demi-octavo pages at the most, would nevertheless provide the solution to all problems relative to tactics, strategy, the direction of fire, encampment, information services, etc.—all the subdivisions, once so complicated but now so simple, of the art of war.

With that book, which would be distributed to all the schools, all the inhabitants would soon become consummate generals, which would ensure Canonenstadt a new and crushing superiority over all other peoples.

XII

When the ambassador returned to Berlin bringing Lichtmann's response, the Prime Minister flew into a violent temper. What? That pygmy dared to scorn the protectorate of the great Empire! He had the audacity to call its good faith into question! That was too much. The man must certainly be mad to stand up without hesitation to the most powerful nation in the world. Such arrogance merited an exemplary repression, and if he believed that he had rendered himself indispensable as a manufacturers of cannons, he would soon be shown that they could do without him, by utilizing the experience of a few of his engineers. They would be paid for that as dearly as was necessary. Cannot everything be bought, and during their master's exile, would his most skillful auxiliaries not be only too happy to choose between poverty and the honors that would be lavished upon them?

During that explosion, the unfortunate delegate, his head bowed, cursed the mission that he had previously received with so much joy, which had evidently earned him a complete disgrace.

Fortunately, the minister soon calmed down, and after having reflected, reassured his subaltern with a further mark of confidence.

"Go back to Lichtmann, Baron von Kenntnissheim; if he is obstinate in refusing the conditions already posed, well, an army corps will go to establish itself in Canonenstadt until they accept it, and will levy a contribution of a hundred thalers per month of delay in the signature of the new treaty."

That abuse of force aroused general indignation when the demands became known abroad. All sympathies, especially among the invasive host of socialists, anarchists, nihilists and other reformers, all contained with difficulty since the beginning of the century, were with the little people, whose courage was admired. But no one was under any illusion as to the outcome of the conflict, for it was impossible that the Germany army would not rapidly confront such a feeble population.

The governments opposed to the empire of the North, frightened by the turn that events had taken, were very perplexed; the weakness of Canonenstadt did not permit them to come opportunely to its aid; furthermore, as the invaders would be able rapidly to put their hands on the enormous reserves accumulated in the inventors stores, the moment was ill-chosen to declare war. No national question had ever excited minds so keenly.

In order to give more weight to the words of her plenipotentiary, and show that they were no vain threat, Germany immediately mobilized two army corps. But the Engineer gave proof of an admirable steadfastness; he did not want to hear anything, rejected the advice of the diplomat who attempted to demonstrate his imprudence to him, and would not withdraw any of his previous conclusions.

"I would rather see the State that I have founded disappear than expose it by precipitating the loss of its autonomy, or by divulging the secrets that are its sole reason for being."

Both surprised and furious at such stubbornness, Herr von Minskopf broke off the negotiations that were turning to his shame. Nothing more remained but to act vigorously.

On his orders, the corps concentrated at Ham marched to the frontier, and General von Brandt, its commander-in-chief, informed Lichtmann that if he had not surrendered by seven a.m. on the sixth of September, he would proceed with the annihilation of the fence by cannon fire. Afterwards, his troops would enter the intractable territory and take possession of it. While awaiting the expiry of the deadline, he established his army in a good position parallel to the fence, on the eastern side, about ten kilometers away.

On the morning of the day indicated, forty batteries, having once emerged from the factories of Canonenstadt, were now directed against those who had forged them. That circumstance made no small contribution to entertaining a mild gaiety among the officers of the operational corps. Behind the artillery line, the infantry amassed in several columns and were ready to advance as soon as a sufficient passage had been contrived.

The besieged, for their part, had not remained inactive. Three army corps appeared at night through the door of the enclosed drill field and placed themselves along the fence, facing the enemy army. That movement, effected in less than a quarter of an hour, did not attract the attention of the enemy scouts. They had been careful to carry out at the same time, on the open experimental field, a great displacement of the materiel that was already to be found there in considerable quantity. It was brought closer to the door, as if to shelter it from the assailants' first attempts, with the result that the movement of the machine guns, mingled with the general confusion, did not awaken the suspicion of the nearest posts.

At dawn, everything was ready in von Brandt's army. The battle line was marvelously traced, the discipline of the troops irreproachable. Enthusiasm reigned among the soldiers. The officers, with smiles on their lips, gave their final instructions and made sure that no detail had been neglected. Everyone, at his post, watched out for the general's signal to act in accordance with the orders distributed the previous day.

At six fifty-five, a black oriflamme suddenly appeared at the summit of Canonenpalast. The enemy general staff had just perceived it and was wondering what it signified when a noise similar to that of a multitude of enormous rattles struck the hundred thousand German ears, while an exceedingly dense hail of steel descended upon the army.

By seven o'clock, that rain had ceased; a deathly silence reigned over the battlefield. Around the cannons, not a single man remained standing. The regiments in the rear were no longer anything but heaps of shredded cadavers. The commanding general, who had come to the front rank in order to observe and make his final dispositions, had fallen, horribly mutilated, in the midst of this officers, who were scythed down at the same time. Only a few battalions that had not yet arrived in the line or had been placed in reserve, filled with fear by the horrible crackling sound they heard, had escaped the general destruction by fleeing.

The next day, it was learned in Berlin that 47,295 men had been killed. Stupor took possession of everyone at that news. Who could have anticipated such a result?

They thought they had only to carry out a marching maneuver to attain the objective without firing a shot, and they had been annihilated without even suspecting the storm. A bleak consternation succeeded the initial astonishment, and then depression and a profound grief.

The sovereign was beside himself; in his delirium, he first blamed for his fate poor von Brandt, who had rendered his soul, and then von Minskopf, all the diplomats and the army, which had not been up to its task. Even the most faithful courtiers displayed their terror by their attitude and their fear of further disasters if they persisted in the fatal enterprise.

The majority of the ministers, astounded, saw only one means of countering Lichtmann's ruses and avoiding greater misfortunes, which was to offer peace—a honorable peace, for the Engineer would surely be content with a complete renunciation of the conditions they had tried to impose on him. That was what they thought, but they dared not say so. To make peace was to declare themselves defeated; and to add to the humiliation of the defeat the even more poignant humiliation of being constrained to yield after having taken up arms to dictate the law.

At odds with those feeble hearts, the Prime Minister, with a firmness and a grandeur of soul that rendered him well worthy of his noble position, revived their flagging courage. He remarked, with justice, that for a nation with three million combatants at its disposal, the destruction of fifty thousand soldiers was not an event that ought to discourage spirits. After all, they were only men, and the fatherland must remain great, proud and glorious. One ought not to think about the dead except to avenge them, nor of the setback suffered except to retaliate.

It was, he said, simply a matter of assembling a council formed of the most experienced generals, who would plot the course to be followed to defeat the infernal Engineer without exposing themselves to excessively cruel losses.

That idea appeared very reasonable, and was immediately adopted. Twenty warriors known for their science and wisdom were summoned by telegraph. They hastened to the capital. They were immediately convened, and got a handle on the problem.

That conclave included the men of the era most versed in the art of war. The majority had been studying it all their lives, and had brought scrupulous improvement to it. The presidency fell to Feld-Marschall von Helheim, whose advice was always heeded because of his great age and his profound experience, gloriously acquired. For him, all vain discourse was a delay in vengeance, a peril for national honor; he was therefore in haste to open the debate.

To their extreme embarrassment, however, the enemy had proved that it was as impossible to attack from the front as from the flank; its mode of defense utterly ruined modern tactics. In any event, they were heading for the sacrifice of a part of the nation, and even soldiers recoiled before that bloody perspective. Their brief words, as staccato as commands, whistled through the air in the midst of noisy interpellations, and sharp negations interrupted overly vehement orators. Peace had fled that warrior assembly. Three hours went by, and the debate was still going on; irritation was reaching its paroxysm.

Then von Helheim took the floor.

"What has happened ought to have been anticipated—which is to say, that the Engineer would place along his frontier an enormous quantity of the cannons at his disposal. The unfortunate and lamented General von Brandt did not think of that, and moreover, he committed a great imprudence informing his adversary of the time at which he would open fire. That is a courtesy to be relegated among the ancient prejudices of war, and it astonishes me to find it in this epoch in one of my colleagues. In any case, it has permitted the enemy to anticipate us by peppering our position before we had time to respond to him.

"That Lichtmann is unassailable on his own ground, I believe; but everyone knows that the province of Canonenstadt obtains from outside what it necessary to its functioning, and that it is impossible for it to produce internally what is necessary to the primary necessities of life. In addition, it lacks means of transport and an army organized to wage war externally. In order to obtain its submission, therefore, the surest means is to establish, out of range of its cannons, a strict and sufficiently prolonged blockade.

"I estimate that, in order to enjoy complete security, the line of investment should be drawn fifty kilometers from the besieged city. It will thus have a development of six hundred kilometers—an exaggerated development, you might say, but take note that we can maintain an average of two men per meter. The surveillance will be exercised principally on the routes of communication ending at Canonenstadt, and attention will be focused on the roads practical for convoys, for any re-provisioning operated by individuals crossing the lines is negligible. That will reduce the inconvenience of an overly extensive perimeter; but we will soon arrive at the figure of twelve hundred thousand men.

"As that is a significant fraction of the army, it is to be feared that other powers might take advantage of it to trouble us. In that anticipation, let us place the least experienced men in the composition of the blockade, reserving our best troops, and invite our allies also to mobilize their troops, in order to be prepared for any eventuality. They will be amply compensated for that effort and their sacrifices by the considerable sums that the rebels have amassed over the years, and which we can demand from them. To shelter us henceforth from difficulties of the same sort we shall attach the enemy province to the empire from which it should never have been separated and, by appropriating its manufacturing methods, we will become the arbiters of the world."

The truth and good sense of these words seemed striking to the council. Nothing more remained to say. The President had explained the situation with the greatest clarity and indicated the path to follow in a simple and precise manner that left no room for the slightest objection. Prudence and the vigor of execution, the two principal qualities of any plan of operation, were both satisfied by the means proposed. Success was certain.

The man who had conceived the general scheme with so much clarity was better equipped than anyone else to organize its details. So, before breaking up, the council expressed the desire to see General von Helheim appointed as commander-in-chief. The sovereign thought that he ought to accede to that desire.

When the resolutions taken became known in official spheres, those who had thought the day before about making peace no longer understood how they had entertained that idea for a moment. They rejected it strongly for fear of being accused of a culpable lack of confidence in the destiny of the fatherland. They now felt that the initial check, instead of being an unfortunate occurrence, was, on the contrary, an honest pretext for taking complete possession of the neighboring State. There would be good days once again for the annexationists.

That same evening, instructions were sent to the ambassadors in all allied nations. A long circular explained the situation to them, at least in part, along with the numerous advantages that might be obtained from it, and invited them to make the generous offer to their friends to share in those advantages. All that was so evident, and a revenge for 1896 so clear indicated, that the interested ministers allowed themselves to be convinced, and sent their concurrence without delay.

Two days later, half of Europe put its entire valid population on a war footing. Let us add that the other half did likewise, as a simple measure of precaution.

The following is a summary of the instructions dictated by Generalissimo von Helheim. It can be seen that, penetrated by the grandeur of the objective and the desire to avoid any contrary misfortune, he had not hesitated to adopt the most energetic means and had resolutely rejected half-measures.

The investment corps would be formed by three armies, each of four hundred thousand men. They would be concentrated at Hanover, Cassel and Mayence, and would be ready to march on 25 September, to blockade Canonenstadt after eight stages of marching. The points of concentration, chosen far enough away from the frontier, did not permit any small isolated corps to be exposed to the Engineer's enterprises, if by chance he wanted to hinder the investment by organizing bands of partisans in haste.

The army of Mayence would operate on the left bank of the Rhine, maintaining its wings on the river in order to link up with the armies of the East, at Emmerich to the north, at Cologne to the south. Between those two points it would follow the Dutch frontier as far as Aix-la-Chapelle, to extend from there to Deutz, where it would link up with the Cassel army. The latter would have its center at Siegen and direct its line of surveillance toward Soest, where it would link up with the left wing of the third army, which would lend a hand to the first, passing via Munster.

From the fifteenth onward, all the garrisons and men conscripted to military service would evacuate the interior of the circle thus traced, taking away or destroying the food supplies contained there. The population, forced to move out, would be encamped behind the troops, at a sufficient distance to avoid disorder and would be nourished at the expense of the State for as long as the siege lasted.

Thus, there was a zone of twenty thousand square kilometers that the Feld-Marschall transformed into a desert. More than three million inhabitants, expelled from their homes for an indeterminate time abandoned their towns and villages to the wrath of the enemy. Cities of a hundred thousand souls, such as Dusseldorf and Crefeld, remained devoid of their inhabitants, methodically removed by soldiers, reminiscent of admirably conserved modern Pompeiis exhumed the day before, where a deathly silence replaced the immense and confused noise formed by the thousand sounds of civilization. The stronghold of Wesel, which touched Canonenstadt to the northwest, saw its garrison leave after three days employed in transporting its military equipment, destined for the army, to the Dutch frontier.

On the river, where navigation was abruptly interrupted below Cologne, thousands of cargo vessels, still laden with iron, coal and textiles, hastily moored in the docks and along the banks, seemed to be waiting for their absent sailors. Some, detached by the current, followed the watercourse, sometimes colliding with the banks and remaining becalmed there briefly before being gripped again by the flow, until some new obstacle stopped them and, dislocated by those violent and repeated impacts, the water invaded them to drag their cargoes to the river bottom. The phenomenal crane of Canonenstadt, resting there from its quotidian labor, only emerged from is immobility occasionally in order to transfer the barges arrested in their chaotic course by the dam, against which they accumulated.

As the troops withdrew from the condemned zone, the railway personnel accompanied them, taking the locomotives and all the traction materiel that had not been used for the general migration. The rails were taken up and removed over long stretches in order to prohibit the use of the lines to the besieged. The bridges were cut, the tunnels blocked, while careful searches ensured than no livestock remained in stables and that no nourishing substance had been forgotten in the food stores.

Lichtmann had easily perceived the projects elaborated by the high council; they had not been hidden from anyone. Why would they have made a mystery of them? Was success not certain and the denouement fatal? Was the Engineer's impotence not evident? So the newspapers displayed the plan of operations to the eyes of their readers, analyzed it expertly and complacently discussed the consequences of the victory. They returned to the theme repeatedly, obsessing their subscribers; but the superficial embroideries of light pens did not disguise the serious basis of less officious communications. By the time they stopped arriving at Canonenstadt, the President was amply informed; it would have been sufficient for him to know the assembly points of the blockading army.

The void created around him did not alarm him. He still had provisions of food in the State's docks for a fortnight. By rationing them moderately, he calculated that there was more than he needed to reach the end of the crisis without too many privations.

Nothing had changed in the appearances of the province, and the factories were as active as usual. The workers scarcely thought about becoming anxious on seeing their director, even calmer than usual, passing through the factories and giving advice with his habitual benevolence. Their wives were obliged by that assurance not to manifest too much anxiety at the idea of their isolation or too much repugnance for the new cuisine to which the rigors of a siege might be about to submit their delicate stomachs. Love can surmount many ordeals; it operated miracles in the city; the women were admirable in their heroism and their example gave the world the lesson that, in a besieged city, one should only consider as useless mouths those of people who lack courage.

It was only on 23 September that Lichtmann gathered his officers, and after having designated three of his governmental colleagues to command the armies, he revealed the dispositions that he intended to make during the campaign, on the result of which everyone's fate depended.

It was necessary both to begin and end the war with a lightning strike, to annihilate the enemy before the exhaustion of existing provisions, and for that, a perfect understanding was indispensable.

These were the resolutions that were definitively settled: to each of the assailant armies an army of electromachine-guns would be opposed. The movement would take place on the night of the twenty-fifth and all three would move simultaneously to within thirty kilometers of the respective adversaries. The average distance to travel, slightly over two hundred kilometers, would be crossed in five hours. They would then wait for daybreak, and in the morning, when the unsuspecting enemy troops were in the middle of their second stage, the officers, having reconnoitered the routes, would direct their machines at the head of each column and commence fire a few minutes before reaching them.

Then, marching at top speed from the advance guard to the rearguard over the battalions destroyed, they would only stop after the complete annihilation of the adverse troops. The later would have neither the time to reconnoiter nor the leisure to deploy a single item of artillery.

Lichtmann announced that he would follow one of the armies of the east personally and would give further orders after the combat. Only the corps on the left bank would return to Canonenstadt after the victory.

XIII

A short distance to the south of Cassel, the Fulda, whose upper reaches placidly hollow out their bed through the rocks of the Hess plateau, sees its valley suddenly broaden out at the approach to the city, which a landgrave enriched by the traffic of his subjects has embellished superbly. The river then runs through a circular depression in the center of which it curves, and then leaves to the left the town with its numerous palaces to mingle its waters with those of its sister, the Werra. All around, the horizon is limited by a ring of mountains covered with forests.

To the west, the gaze is attracted by the steep slopes of the Habichtswald, dominated by the magnificent castle of Wilhelmshöhe, a blithe imitation of Versailles. It was in that ancient royal residence that General von Helheim had established himself, with his general staff, to preside over the concentration of the army of the center and expedite his orders to his lieutenants who were in command at Mayence and Hanover.

Before his eyes, in the immense camp that surrounded the town, four hundred thousand soldiers were amassed, who were to collaborate in the enslavement of Canonenstadt. At every moment, trains arriving from the most distant provinces of the empire were vomiting forth battalions, squadrons and cannons, which, in turn, disembarked hastily and extended along the roads. But the disorder was only apparent and the confusion temporary. Order was soon re-established, and the moving masses were rapidly directed to their stations by impassive officers of the general staff, who, darting a glance over their maps covered in strokes of multicolored pencils, indicated to the leaders the routes to follow and the places of destination.

On 24 September the incessant movement of locomotives had slowed considerably. All the components of the complicated machine known as an army had been united, and the ensemble was ready to function efficiently. The general was satisfied; all his strategic anticipations had been verified; not a minute had been lost and the news from the other assembly points announced that there, too, all the rules of logistics had been strictly applied.

The next morning, at four o'clock, a general rumor was heard from Munden to Zwehren in that agglomeration of living beings. They were all agitating simultaneously, urgently, colliding with one another, like ants disturbed in their labor by a pitiless hand leveling their dwelling. Bugles and trumpets sounded, and to their strident notes, repeated by the echoes of the Habichtswald, the cries and joyful songs of the soldiers responded, along with the whinnying of horses and the barking of dogs, disagreeably troubled in their sleep by that unusual dissonance of chords.

Local inhabitants gripped by enthusiasm had accompanied their temporary guests to the assembly point, and more than one blonde Hessian maid, skillfully hidden behind her white curtains, followed with eyes that were still humid the victor of her enchanted dreams, who drew away pensively and, lost in the noisy crowd, tried to find his way but only found the adorable memory of an amorous night. The population, ever avid for great military spectacles, was up and about; the army was about to march away.

It was one of those mornings of which the end of September sometimes reserves the surprise, in which the lukewarm atmosphere is already no longer heated by the ardors of summer without having yet suffered the assaults of the bitter north wind. A gentle breeze was agitating the foliage gently, with the branches shivering at that caress and fine droplets falling from their tips and dripping onto the mosses of the woods. The sun was still hiding its fiery globe below the horizon; the light was pale and rosy, as if filtered by the immense stained-glass windows of a cathedral; an azure sky could be divined behind the milky transparency of a vaporous gauze; the hills were lost in the mist, and the contours of objects floated indecisively in that haze. Awakened birds were chirping as they fluttered in the bushes; wild flowers closed from dusk to dawn were opening their corollas and giving off a subtle perfume by which the air was embalmed. The day promised to be delightful!

The mist dissipated slowly. Suddenly, the first rays of sunlight began to gild the summits of the hills; the tufted tresses of the tall trees stood out more clearly. The sun emerged then above a fleecy train and teased from the admiration of the harmony the freshest tones, combined with the warmest tints of autumn. The castle of Wilhelmshöhe and, further away, at the top of the mountain, the Castle of the Giant, with its colossal bronze statue of Hercules, were scarcely discernible, still drowned in the white clouds that were rising from the valley.

Already the advance guards were moving off, following parallel routes. Busy couriers were flying in all directions, linking the great general staff with the commandants of the columns. Von Helheim, on horseback in the middle of a group of staff officers, was watching the departure personally, and his physiognomy reflected the interior joy he felt on seeing those long serpents of somber color undulating over the flanks of the hills and ducking their heads under the woods that crowned the occidental crests. He complimented his old companion-in-arms, Feld-Marschall von Wachelndstein, who, placed at the head of the eleventh corps, presented his troops to him. Both of them bowed to salute the passage of the standards, covered in decorations that were going forth to conquer a factory and a treasure.

Behind those two old relics, thus far respected by bullets, an imposing escort of colossi in bright uniforms attracted one's gaze; they were the white hussars, who had been charged with forming a guard of honor, and their youth, their exuberant strength, their gigantic stature and splendid costumes caused the virile old age and noble simplicity of the great dignitaries of the Empire to stand out even more clearly. They were there, revolvers in hand, impassive spectators of the file, which only lacked the trumpets of Joshua to bring down the redoubtable fence defending the entrance to the promised land. They did not seem to notice the admiration they excited to the highest degree among the youths, the children and their nurses and the idlers of all ages who ran in their wake to the gates of Cassel. They were handsome, and knew it, but discipline blinded their pride.

A cloud of dust rises up; the ground trembles.

What is that noise? The batteries of the horse artillery pass at a trot, enveloped by a dense whirlwind. Then come the heavy vehicles of the eleventh brigade; through the dusty waves that these stir up, black beings move. They are the cannoneers, faithfully following their guns. Gray-black trousers and dark blue tunics ornamented with red piping, with boiled leather caps surmounted by a ball of yellow metal—such is the somber equipment with which a sage government opposed to pomp had provided for them. Needless to say, beneath those austere exteriors beat hearts forever cheerful, forever devoted. The artillerymen's tread is heavy, but their voices are light when it is a matter of intoning their favorite song:

Wie ziehen wir so frölich
Mit Sang und Klang hinaus!
Beschirmet ist ja immer
Des Artilleristen Haus.
Es schreckt uns nicht
Des Feides Übermacht,
Wir führen ja den Donner
Der heissen Schlacht.[19]

Observe also with what verve they all repeat it!

A graver note succeeds that refrain; it is the tread of innumerable infantrymen who, with rifles on their shoulders and pipes in their mouths, are counting melancholically the miles of the route, so slow to unfurl. Here and there, soldiers crushed by the weight of their burden, fatigued or wounded by the march, pause on the edge of the road; sometimes, too, an officer reprimands the laggards or exhorts them to recover their courage, and, preaching by example, hastens their pace to make them

---

[19] Author's reference: "Hackländer, *Humoristiche Schriften.*" The reference is to Friedrich Wilhelm Hackländer (1816-1877), whose first success as a writer was an account of his military service, which prompted him to offer voluminously detailed accounts of all his other experiences. The work cited, actually entitled *Humoristiche Erzählungen*, was published in 1847.

re-enter the rank. Then the unfortunates in question, at least to appease their thirst, raise the waterbottles to their lips that they were careful to fill on departure: sources too soon run dry; they have quickly exhausted their contents.

Here are the battalions that come from Giessen, Gotha, Hildburghausen and as far away as Weimar to join the eleventh corps; then the Bavarians, the regiments of the Emperor Fredrick of Prussia, the King of Saxe, and Prince Leopold, extracted from their magical garrison at Nuremburg or the musical solemnities of Bayreuth. After them, others still! They have to hasten their paces toward the Occident; the Orient is vomiting incessantly. Along the flanks of the columns prance proudly mounted officers of the general staff, always on the move, always glad to make their importance as leaders of various units felt in sharp reproaches regarding the advancement or retardation, and the alignment of their troops.

As for the cavalrymen, distributed alongside those interminable queues, proud of their brilliant uniforms and indisputable superiority, they scarcely dart a pitying or disdainful glance at the unfortunates condemned to carrying themselves. There is no other success than for those graceful horsemen and wielders of the saber; they appear, and the people quivering at the sight of them welcome them with flattering murmurs, for which they repay in smiles.

The blue and yellow hussars, the squadrons of the third and the eleventh Uhlans, are the heroes of the last war. It was they who, at the battle of Hochspeyer, launched themselves so resolutely at the enemy batteries, carving out with thrusts of the saber and the lance a reputation for bravery of which the regiments are justly proud. For a quarter of a century, they have lived tranquilly on their laurels, profiting from the exploits of their elders—that is what malevolent tongues say; others affirm that they are not degenerate; the truth is that they do not yet have the habit of pillage, but they aspire to acquire it.

Finally, at the rear come the reserves, escorted by a few battalions, the convoys of food supplies, munitions, baggage, ambulances: vehicles of every form and nature, in all weights and all dimensions, designed to satisfy the numerous needs of a society on the march.

Ten hours after the advance guards had departed, when the latter would have arrived at the end of their first stage a long time ago, the convoys would not yet have moved off. All of that was happening, flowing and rolling, with a regular slowness giving the impression of an endless chain. One almost expected to see the first groups reappear after the last, to recommence incessantly a circular transition, in the same way that the adroit actors hide behind the scenery of a phenomenal theater to show themselves again to the eyes of the deluded spectators. And that was not yet all; long rows of immobile and unharnessed vehicles were silhouetted in the plain; their horses, attached to long parallel ropes, were stamping their hooves, irritated by remaining idle beside the others. But they were not to depart until the next day, or even later; they were the reserve provisions, whose over-proximity would have encumbered the army and compromised the liberty of its movements.

For two hours, the general in command had been contemplating the file. At the sight of that human flood, tamed by a severe discipline, he savored the delightful emotion that any man feels who, having reached the summit of grandeur and clad in an absolute authority over his fellows, can dispose of their fate at his whim and decide their salvation or destruction with a gesture. A heavy responsibility had weighed upon him for several days; instead of being overwhelmed by it, he seemed this morning to be less burdened with cares. Lighter and freer than usual—a rare thing for a military man, he had acquired the conviction that everything was perfect.

The war itself could not be serious; the most complicated of operations consisted of bringing together in a short period of time so many disparate elements. That task accomplished and the marching orders expedited, all the way to the investment of Canonenstadt, it only remained to let the well-designed mechanism go in the direction that had been so skillfully imparted to it. So, before following the army, he wanted to prove his satisfaction by thanking his auxiliaries for the intelligence and zeal they had deployed. On returning to Wilhelmshöhe, the general staff found a splendid lunch offered by the general—in order, he said, while smiling, to compensate them for the privations they were going to have to suffer.

As redoubtable as von Helheim was on the battlefield, one discovered him at the table to be a cheerful companion. Descended from his pedestal, in the midst of hearty drinkers, he matched the most intrepid, and in a century when physical strength is losing its luster, in which a man is soon no more than a ruin among the ruins that he heaps up around him, his companions were pleased to consider him as a rival of Bassompierre.[20] Thanks to him, the wines of France and the wines of the Rhine flowed in gilded waves into crystal cups, and under their generous influence, the most cordial gaiety

---

[20] The courtier François de Bassompierre (1579-1646) was made famous by his posthumously-published *Mémoires.*

never ceased to reign during the meal. The entire clan of young officers, buckled into their elegant uniforms as if in corsets, noisily manifested themselves in bellicose outbursts in which they loudly regretted not having to deal with a more serious enemy, which would furnish opportunities for the troops to show their valor, and also more chances of advancement.

Fortunately, that was merely a game postponed, and after the occupation of Canonenstadt, advantage could be taken of the general mobilization of the army and the prodigious resources of which they would then dispose to invade the whole of Europe. Frivolous minds, stuffed with illusions, ardent in pursuit of an ungraspable phantom of gory, too ignorant of the vicissitudes of life to stop at positive advantages when unexpected ones surged forth—these are lieutenants!

The superior officers, generals and old colonels with energetic but fatigued faces, drank without getting so heated. The collections that ornamented their chests absolved them from showing their love of glory in such an expansive manner. They contented themselves with smiling benevolently at the speeches of their young rivals. Deep down, they thought them very naïve, and dreamed about the incalculable millions that were attributed to the Engineer, compared with which the ransoms once demanded of vanquished enemies were derisory sums. Those riches were going to permit their gracious sovereign to award them good pensions or endow them with magnificent estates by way of national recompense. It was time for repose finally to succeed fatigues, and a life of ordeals and sacrifices fully deserved to be thus crowned. For the moment, they calculated internally the figure to which their gratification might rise.

It was with an indescribable enthusiasm that all of them, young and old, those with admitted desires and those with secret ambitions, welcomed the toast to the Emperor that his representative the feld-marschall proposed. Three cups were emptied in his honor, and immediately afterwards, the General gave the signal to depart.

The horses were awaiting their riders, some of whom, weighed down by age or overly copious libations, had to be respectfully hoisted into their saddles by soldiers accustomed to that service.

As a man who knew that corporeal fatigues are harmful to the clarity of mental conceptions, von Helheim took to the road in a vehicle, accompanied by the officer who had his confidence. In a few hours, he was in Gudenberg, at the center of the army, where the various corps, camped at short distances from one another, were distributed in a line perpendicular to the course of the Eder. That river had the general direction to be followed during the first days. Then leaving its valley, they would traverse the Westerwald to reach Siegen, where the split would take place to the right toward Soest and to the left toward Cologne, to establish the line of investment.

The day had been trying for the troops. The soldiers, informed men aware that it would be the same every day and that the dangers to be run were negligible, spent the night in absolute quietude, dreaming of the marvels of Canonenstadt, which had been the topic of all conversations for some time. Those belonging to the corps raised in the vicinity of the enemy province, in particular, obtained a good deal of success among their comrades from distant regions by recounting the legends that had arisen in their region around the singular State that was so careful of its isolation. Those precautions evidently had the objective of protecting the treasures possessed by the inhabitants, and no one doubted that the expedition would make him rich.

In the advance locations, where the service was severely assured by discipline and respect for regulations, the sentinels spread out around the guard posts, feeling a complete security, having neglected the surveillance of the surroundings somewhat in order to dream about the agreeable surprises that awaited them.

XIV

On the twenty-fifth, at ten o'clock in the evening, Lichtmann's armies had emerged from Canonenstadt. The army of the left bank, having closed the hermetic portholes that permitted air to penetrate into the drivers' cabins, and had plunged into the Rhine, from which it emerged to set foot in enemy territory, after a duration of forty-seven seconds. Then it headed toward Mayence in a single column. The other two marched on their adversaries in the same order.

The night was fine but dark; only the stars were shining in the sky and the new moon did not reflect its rays upon the polished components of the machine guns, whose imposing mass stood out more blackly in the obscurity. Their legs, animated by a rapid movement, were scarcely discernible, and the well-greased articulations did not grate audibly. The silence was only troubled by the rhythmic impact of their feet on the hard ground of the roads.

In the desert zone, they initially encountered only rare malefactors who were looting houses as their leisure. Disturbed in their occupations, frightened by the noise of the convoy, they fled at its approach without looking behind them. Soon they entered into the inhabited region and were obliged to traverse numerous villages aligned along the road, sizeable burgs and sometimes towns in which the noise took on a more forbidding intensity.

The inhabitants, awoken with a start, approached the windows curiously to seek the cause of the nocturnal racket; frightened, they recoiled, thinking that they were still dreaming, unable to understand how the road, suddenly transformed into a railway track, could be giving passage to the fantastic train that they had glimpsed. But the tumult gradually diminished and faded away in the distance. The vision disappeared, and nothing remained but the astonishment of having been the victim of an illusion and the vague anxiety that one experiences in the wake of an unexplained event. Those poor folk, abruptly snatched from their beds by the strange phenomenon, tried in vain to recall sleep, and awaited with anguish the first light of day, which might perhaps restore calm to their chimerically haunted minds.

The following day, three simultaneous battles took place, one in Hameln on the Weser, the second in Fritzlar on the Eder and the third at Kreuznach, not far from Mayence. On those three points, the mortal hail furnished by the machine guns began to fall without any indication of danger being signaled to the armies on the march.

As they did not believe that there would be any contact with the enemy, the cavalry that was scouting for the columns had not pushed its investigations very far forward of the front, and had been unable to discover the adversary. Only at Kreuznach, one squadron launched in advance had suddenly found itself face to face with the bizarre convoy. Sensing peril, it had immediately retraced its steps, full tilt, in the direction of the advance guards—but it was too late; the machine guns, without pausing to destroy the little troop, had accelerated their pace and in a matter of seconds had obtained a considerable advance on it. Soon, the unfortunate scouts heard the sinister tremors that announced the commencement of the combat.

Surprised by that sudden attack, entire regiments fell as one man, toppled by the whirlwind of iron that did not spare anyone, crushing skulls, perforating chests and shredding limbs before the unfortunate mutilated individuals were able to know what terrible enemy was sacrificing them thus to its frightful wrath. Cadavers covered the ground in a thick and uninterrupted layer.

Not all those bodies, however, were lying inert, clinging with the energy of desperation to a last chance of salvation. Some were wriggling in the dust and mud, and although exhausted, were trying to make themselves a rampart of the bodies of their comrades in order to shelter themselves from the projectiles that were still raining down. A precaution often futile, alas!

The clinking of weapons, the rolling of runaway carriages, the whinnying of frightened horses, and the whistling of the grapeshot were only a fraction of the daunting concert of the battlefields: the accompaniment of a funeral dirge, a horrible song that was impossible to forget once it had been heard. To the suffocated pleas, those cries of pain of the wounded, the gasps of the dying were met with blasphemies and maledictions by all those for whom duty is a vain word and who were expiating in that supreme moment the error of a life too egotistical to finish in grandeur. With that heart-rending expression of an immense distress, a few voices resigned to the sacrifice were mingled.

Armies have been seen to battle against an adversary ten times superior in number, to struggle against the unchained elements, to brave cold, hunger and disease, to succumb after frustrating combats to so many ordeals and fatigues, and still retain until the moment of death a noble countenance. The hope of bringing victory sooner or later to their flags or saving their possessions and the sincere conviction of being useful to the fatherland and defending a just cause sustain them in adversity. The imperial troops were confronting a very different struggle; number, courage and even weapons were devoid of effect—so despair burst forth everywhere, and the expiring victims uttered a last cry for treason.

No, treason was not the cause of the disaster. The plan of campaign was marvelously conceived, the details well ordered; the officers and soldiers had obeyed their orders. All of them were at their posts.

The veritable author of the catastrophe was neither von Helheim nor any of the military leaders; it was the diplomat whose politics, by its insatiable greed, had ignited that bloody quarrel. After having suffered one disastrous defeat, he had wanted to efface the memory of it and had prepared another more irreparable. He had fallen into the trap of his own schemes and had dragged the entire nation into a slaughter such as it had never seen throughout the centuries,

What had the cavalry been doing, however? Why had they not warned the generals about the danger that threatened them? They had every right to ask that question.

The enemy took responsibility for the reply. Those who were still breathing, in a last glance veiled by death, saw them pass like a flash of lightning. They saw through thick smoke monsters with blackened flanks striding through the mass of cadavers, cutting a violent passage through it, throwing to the right and left thousands of arms and legs separated from their trunks. A fiery spray preceded them, and they were spewing grapeshot. In their path, a red rain soaked the dust; rivulets of blood ran in the ditches alongside the road, filling them to the brim, and those waves carried human debris.

In seven minutes, near Mayence and Fritzlar, the machines had swept away all the troops that they had found before them. The battle of Hameln was longer because the enemy army had been obliged to restrict its front in order to pass through the gorge in the mountainous ridges that extended to the south of Hanover. It had only formed three columns, and the first machine guns engaged had been slowed in their march by the vehicles and corpses accumulated in certain narrow passages. They ran out of ammunition and the fire was interrupted until the arrival of the replacements left in the rear. There, the carnage lasted twenty-three minutes, which permitted a considerable number of enemies to escape. Moreover, on the three battlefields, by virtue of an excusable sentiment of humanity, the soldiers of Canonenstadt had stopped when the rearmost regiments, mad with terror on seeing those preceding them fall, had dispersed in all directions, incapable of offering the slightest resistance to their elusive adversary.

In spite of that, according to official documents, the total losses of the three armies were 727,325 killed and 151,753 wounded. On the side of the victors only one machine, hindered by bodies and stopped by a mass of overturned cannons, had suffered some damage to its internal organs. On inspection, it was found to be out of service. In order to prevent the enemy from having the opportunity to study it and enlighten themselves as to the causes of their ruination, the mechanism was dismantled on the spot and its pieces, loaded onto the other electromotors, were dispersed in all the watercourses that were encountered nearby.

While the three battles were in progress in which so many human lives were scythed down with lightning rapidity, another drama no less moving was unfolding at the confluence of the Rhine and the Moselle. Coblentz, one of the most important fortresses in the Empire, collapsed in a horrible earthquake.

Suddenly, the hills on the right bank of the river, from Niederberg to Horcheim, covered with their redoubtable fortifications, appeared to tremble on their fractured foundations. In vain the bunkers of Ehrenbreitstein, hollowed out in the rock, had defied the most massive artillery; in vain the strongholds with which the plateau of Pfaffendorf had covered the course of the Rhine and forbade its navigation to any fleet attempting to descend the river: those defenses, elevated at enormous cost to oppose the enterprises of an external enemy, ceded to the irresistible effort of a superhuman power, ready to crumble and to be engulfed in the waters that rose up in liquid mountains.

On the opposite bank, the great Fort Alexander, which watches over the city from the height of the massif of Chartreuse, was seized by a sudden vertigo. In the old city, the ancient Cathedral of Saint Castor felt itself shiver and seemed only to be hanging onto its foundations with difficulty. After a few seconds of hesitation, without any other sound being heard but a dull rumbling, hills, edifices and walls all collapsed into an immense heap of rubble.

The trembling ground, ripped by long fissures and hollowed out by gaping holes, emitted thick clouds of black dust, with torrents of white smoke. The sky was obscured by them, and in broad daylight, darkness instantly covered that scene of desolation. The houses and walls, collapsing noisily, crushed the unfortunates they sheltered as they fell. Stones, bricks, boulders and inhabitants were hurled around pell-mell by the sudden explosion.

The Rhine and the Moselle, both suddenly stopped in their courses, rose up in proud waves, which, suddenly liberated, covered everything that they encountered, smashing angrily into and sweeping away the promontory at whose tip Coblentz had existed.

In less than a minute, the physiognomy of the country had become unrecognizable; instead of those correct monuments, those gigantic bunkers, that cheerful countryside whose crops blossomed under human hands and human will, one saw bizarre heaps of brutally disparate elements and was astonished to find them in contact with one another: a frightful chaos of heavy rocks, dislocated edifices and fragmented ramparts stacked on top of one another. One might have thought them pieces of an enormous game of patience thrown in disorder by capricious Titans, under which lay, undiscoverable, the cadavers of the fifty thousand human beings engulfed by the catastrophe.

The Rhine paused in its course momentarily, encroaching on its banks and scaling the hills that narrowed its valley upstream. Soon, however, it resumed its original direction, deflected here and there by mounds of debris that its swollen waters undermined furiously in order to flatten the obstacles opposed to their progress.

Finally, the Moselle, whose mouth was obstructed, now covered with a broad liquid expanse the whole of the plain extending below the confluence, all the way to the hill of Weissenthurm, where the obelisk stands erected to the memory of Hoche by his soldiers.[21]

---

[21] Lazare Hoche (1768-1797) was the French general in the Revolutionary Wars who was in command of the armies of the Moselle and the Rhine.

It was for that upheaval that the greater part of the dynamite manufactured had served some time before in Canonenstadt. By thus destroying one of the largest fortified locations in Europe, the Engineer had wanted to impress the imaginations of his enemies even more, if that were possible, than by the mere destruction of their armies. As soon as war had been certain, halting the works of mineral extraction under the valley of the Sieg, he had sent his Moles not in search of further metal-bearing terrains but to construct tunnels under Coblentz and Mayence.

The distance to travel to reach the first of those fortresses was only fifteen kilometers, and it had been possible to begin a vast network of conduits immediately under the condemned city, ending in shafts that extended upwards toward the surface. Those shafts gave access to enormous blast-holes, and those centers of collapse had been loaded with more than two hundred thousand kilograms of explosive material. In addition, a forceful cramming had promised an effective strength that the mass of dynamite, great as it seemed, would otherwise have been impotent to produce. The distribution of the charges had been calculated in a manner to dislocate the terrain of the city and the surroundings without provoking violent explosions that would have dammed the river with falling debris and deprived Canonenstadt temporarily of its motive force.

In the direction of Mayence the excavation was not completed. As for Cologne, which could be attained rapidly, Lichtmann had refrained from razing it because of the resources that had been accumulated there for the blockading army, and which would serve him for initial resupply after the victory.

XV

In the evening after the three battles the Engineer concentrated his two eastern armies in the middle of a plain not far from Munster in order to confer with the generals.

He was, it is necessary to admit, rather perplexed, and more than ever aware of the weak aspects of his military organization. He could not, like Napoléon, take advantage of the victory to march on the enemy capital and dictate the peace there. Omnipotent in open country, it would be imprudent to penetrate into an overexcited large city and to set foot outside the machines in order to undertake negotiations. Even less could he send a single officer to assign a place where negotiations would take place, for he feared that the exasperated population would destroy an apparatus left by itself and would not respect the envoy.

Another important reason to be added to the preceding ones in preventing him from taking that course was that he wanted to maintain ignorance for as long as possible regarding the external disposition of his machines, which must have appeared to be fabulous monsters to those who had glimpsed them during the conflict and had succeeded in escaping.

Foreseeing all these difficulties, he had instructed that the Harz tunnel be continued in the direction of Berlin, and would have preferred to act on that city rather than Coblentz, but the branch to be excavated was no less than thirty miles long; time had not permitted him to complete it and the extremity was still more than a hundred kilometers from the banks of the Spree. Driving the machines very aggressively, it would have required another two months to attain the objective.

He therefore resolved to return to Canonenstadt and to wait there for the proposals of the German cabinet. He contented himself with telegraphing, from the office of a small locality in the confines of the desert zone, to grant "out of pure kindness," a suspension of arms, and said that he was entirely willing, although victorious, to receive a plenipotentiary to sign a peace treaty.

Fifty hours after their departure, the machine guns went back through the fence. The absence of the army of the west had only lasted one day. None of the factories had suspended its production.

News of the disaster reached the imperial court on the evening of the combat; immediately divulged, it was announced in the middle of a theatrical performance, and before such a calamity the entire audience got up, the curtain was lowered and the crowd dispersed silently. Soon, the fugitives arrived in the city and their stories added details to the event that shook all minds. Of a hundred and seventeen generals, only eleven had survived, and seven of those eleven had already gone mad. Two ministers, including the one who had counseled the fateful war, met the same fate. Profoundly wounded in his vanity, Herr von Minskopf had been unable to resist the black treason of fortune, the unexpected blow that had ruined his dearest hopes.

Strange destiny! The man whose insatiable desires had troubled the peace of Europe, who had single-handedly disentangled all the conspiracies, discovered all the secrets and thwarted all the designs of his adversaries for thirty years, fallen today not only from all grandeur but even from human dignity, having become the target of hatred and public fury, was to end wretchedly in a lunatic asylum—a life worthy of a far finer end!

The general in command, who, as we have seen was following his troops a day behind, had only arrived on the battlefield to contemplate the sad spectacle of his army strewn on the ground. Mute with horror, he had been unable to recover the power of speech, and could only translate his impressions by means of gestures and fearful gazes.

People expected to see the avalanche of iron described with terror by those it had spared falling on the capital at any moment. The population believed that its end was near. It was even worse when news of the catastrophe at Coblentz arrived from Neuwied. The inhabitants, at the peak of terror, wondered if the ground was going to open up beneath their feet. Many dared not even go back to their homes; a host of them quit the city, and in official spheres, the question arose of whether the seat of government ought not to be transported elsewhere. Fortunately Lichtmann's telegram arrived to reassure minds, and it was decided to rely on his generosity.

Other complications cropped up, however.

The results of the forty-eight hour campaign were not known precisely in Europe until three days later, and only via the German newspapers. A large number of reporters had received authorization to follow the armies, but they had shared in the misfortunes and end of a part of the accredited military missions accompanying the generals. The survivors had needed to recover their spirits before being in a state to send dispatches.

When the situation was finally clarified, the neighboring powers hastened to exploit it. They had all raised their voices in Lichtmann's favor; that was, to be sure, all that they had done for him, for they had abandoned him to his own resources and had watched the disproportionate duel placidly, but as Prussia, in summoning all its contingents to the flag, had forced them to complete their own readiness for war, they demanded by way of indemnity some increase in territory of the return of provinces previously taken from them. They protested, it is true, their love of peace, but they desired it on their terms, with demands that only rendered war more likely—for how could all those desires be granted, which only agreed on one point: to parse out the spoils of the weakest.

The treaties of 1896 had to be revised; the balance of power was no longer the same between the people since the successes obtained by Lichtmann had, so to speak, annihilated the army that weighed the most in the destinies of the continent, and the equilibrium was destroyed. But if general peace were at the price of a sage redrafting of the map of Europe, that was a long way from imposing excessive and humiliating conditions without reason on a nation of the first rank, from which it would evidently be impatient to escape. The conduct that was adopted in her regard might, therefore, either lead to a lasting arrangement, if the negotiations were sufficiently moderate to save the honor and susceptibilities of Prussia, or a desperate, perpetually re-igniting war.

Meanwhile, as if the future were not somber enough, everyone allowed themselves to be carried away at the whim of their passions, and after having expanded many times in bitter reproaches regarding the dire politics of the great man who had just disappeared from the world stage, took aim at the same goal and became intoxicated by the hope of imposing their supremacy on the Occident.

Russia demanded the province of Posen, which, as a Slavic region wrenched from Poland, belonged to her alone.

Austria refused to compromise herself any longer with such a feeble ally and even appeared disposed to turn against her. Silesia tempted her strongly and Russia was ready to let her take it, on one condition: the cession of a few Slavic territories within the confines of Transylvania. The Hapsburg heir could already see himself reconstituting to his advantage the Holy Germanic Empire, and, in order to arrive at his ends, not only favored the views of his gigantic neighbor but also sounded out the courts of Bavaria and Saxe, secretly promising them his collaboration if they wanted to recover their independence.

France demanded the Rhine as a frontier, and promised in the course of negotiations to offer an alliance with the Engineer, who would have become her neighbor.

In the midst of those great nations ready to support their hypothetical rights with weapons in hand, only Denmark, still loyal and faithful to her allies, did not raise her voice to reclaim her duchies. Italy decided, if the spoliation were accomplished, to demand a part of the Tyrol as the price of her silence.

On the Russian and French frontiers, the troops were already mobilized and assembled in compact masses. What could be done to resist such pretentions and avoid such pressing danger? The only possible resource was to implore the assistance of Canonenstadt. The finest diplomat was sent there with a mission to accept all conditions and sign a treaty of alliance at any price.

Lichtmann received the German emissary in the pavilion of the exterior railway station, where he had the habit of offering the broadest hospitality to his clients, and where the conversations had earlier taken place with the first ambassador charged with dictating the law to him. After having listened to the envoy's grievances and envisioned the proportions that the war threatened to assume, his expression darkened, to the great alarm of his interlocutor.

"In the course of my career," he said, after a few moments of silence, "I've encountered many errors and many abuses; I've seen despotism sacrifice to its own interests the grandeur of the country over which it had extended its iron scepter; I've seen triumphant liberty degenerate into excessive license and cause misfortunes among the nations as great as those occasioned by tyranny. I've seen princes and peoples not recoiling from any crime in order to satisfy their hatreds; I've seen horrible and above all illegitimate wars, treaties founded on brute force and, by virtue of that alone, devoid of stability or duration; and after sixty years of a life spent observing these turpitudes, it was reserved for me to find today the human species more vicious, more incorrigible than I had yet imagined."

As he pronounced those last words, he was pacing back and forth, his eyes ardent, seemingly searching for a solution that escaped him. Then, turning to the visibly distressed diplomat, he said: "Yesterday you hoped to exploit my weakness; I've beaten and crushed you. Now, here come the others who want to exploit your ruin. Has the lesson I've inflicted on you not engendered salutary reflections in them? Well, wait and see.

"Enter into discussions with your enemies; I know from experience that your government excels marvelously in negotiation. Negotiate with them, then; if necessary, make them glimpse complete satisfaction, temporize, and in a month, come to see me again.

"I only demand that tomorrow, you re-establish the means of communication destroyed in the desert zone, and that our relations become once again what they were before recent events. The abandoned region will be repopulated, with the exception of a strip two miles wide along the frontier of Canonenstadt."

That response was not calculated to reassure the delegate, who had hoped to return to Berlin with more positive assurances. In truth, the Engineer's demands were trivial, but that refusal to mingle at least provisionally in European affairs was very disquieting. Might he desire to see his enemies crushed again, or, driven by a personal interest, might he want a war that would procure him new orders for cannons? However, it would doubtless be risking exposure to his anger not to follow his advice to the letter. Besides which, it was good and the only practicable course in such difficult circumstances.

In consequence, the foreign powers, France and their allies, were promised a prompt and entirely peaceful solution. But before establishing the delimitation of the provinces to be ceded, it was necessary to weigh maturely the rights of everyone to the possession of the lands in litigation and, before anything else, to regulate the form of the negotiations that were about to be opened. The German diplomats therefore insinuated that it would be as well to fix a few important points in advance. Ought they to talk to each power separately, or should an international congress be charged with discussing the conditions of a general peace? On what territory should the plenipotentiaries meet?

Time was thus wasted—or, rather, gained—in steps taken regarding these various alternatives. It was only after a fortnight that an accord was reached, and it was agreed that the congress would be held at Sandwich, a small town in the county of Kent in England, where the representatives of the powers would not have to fear any act of nature influencing the debate. Preliminary conferences established the bases on which the negotiations would be founded.

Lichtmann had returned to Canonenstadt somewhat agitated after leaving the ambassador.

He was striding back and forth on his own in the council room. The metallic floor resonated beneath his feet; he paid no heed to it.

He was thinking.

Telephonic mouths were repeating in the distance the sound of that presidential pacing between four walls replete with ears. The unbearable buzzing of flies, abundant at that time of year, mingled disrespectfully with the monotonous cadence of that coming and going. The sun darted a few oblique beams into the abode of the government, like glances curious to complicate the scene, and with reason, for the sun illuminated the world and Lichtmann was his prophet, and that prophet was reflecting before launching one final warning into the world and giving it one final lesson. He had believed that his military successes would open the eyes of the most obstinate and that the world was ripe for the realization of his projects.

The goal was still remote, and he experienced a keen disillusionment in consequence. He thought at first of declaring war on the French and others in order to destroy a considerable number of them, as he had of the

Germans. Certainly they merited a terrible chastisement as much. But that means, which consisted of suppressing a considerable fraction of humanity in order to ensure the happiness of the remainder, seemed to him to be a trifle radical. Furthermore, he was opposed by the existence of numerous fortresses in France and elsewhere, and admitted that if the entire world joined forces against him, by adopting a certain tactic that he could anticipate, the operations might be a long drawn out and success, and although certain, dearly purchased.

Then he decided to employ a method that he had had in mind since the end of the campaign, and which had been the cause of the only condition he had imposed on the German plenipotentiary.

An immense terrestrial globe displayed its roundness in the center of the hall. He headed straight toward it and considered it attentively. His expression had resumed its serenity; the angel Azrael understood in the heights of Heaven that he would soon have to watch over two more great tombs.

The Engineer scanned the continent with his gaze, his eyes settling alternatively on Canonenstadt, France and Russia, and he made a few notes. Then he sat down, and devoted himself for two full hours to calculations that he interrupted in order to draw geometrical figures. Soon, large sheets of paper were filled with them; his pen never wearied of soiling the virginal whiteness with black hieroglyphs before which the faithful adepts of the Polytechnique cult would not have failed to prostrate themselves fervently, but of which the profane reader might perhaps be glad not to find the insipid enumeration here. Let it suffice to say that Lichtmann understood it.

He yielded to mathematical inspiration as the poet recites the verses that the muse dictates to him amorously. When he had finished, his head fell into his hands and he contemplated his work. He found that it was good.

He then wrote a few figures in his notebook and had his colleagues summoned. They did not take long to respond to his appeal. Furnished with a theodolite, they went out to climb into a vehicle that took them at full electricity toward the gate of the State.

To the south of Dortmund and toward the center of the firing range, a mountainous ridge detached from the Haardstrang tapers away beside the Ruhr, which it deflects. It was on that crest, which looms over the surrounding plain by four hundred feet, that the engineers stopped. After having the engineers who had accompanied them establish a solid base, they installed the theodolite and determined two lines with the aid of the instrument, one of which cut the meridian at an angle of $47°26'40''$ toward the northeast, and the other directed southeastwards, making an angle with the line that joins the poles of $126°44$. With those two directions having been carefully labeled, they gave the order to carry out several soundings in the neighboring terrain. Then they returned to Canonenstadt and went to the access shaft to the subterranean realm.

They hastened into it and took the Harz tunnel. Having arrived under Dortmund, which was doubtless standing above that minor cavern, they prescribed the commencement of a new tunnel going up to the surface, and spent some time discussing its dimensions and form.

From that day on, an extraordinary activity seemed to occupy all the workers, although they did not know exactly what kind of work they were doing. Accustomed to the admirable inventions of their leaders, however, they abandoned themselves with no less ardor to the execution of the sometimes bizarre instructions they received. The daily period of work was increased, exceptionally, to eight hours, and in the great factory, all the furnaces, the temperature of which was raised to the extreme, melted with a kind of rage masses of metal to which they were not accustomed. Streams of molten metal soon flowed from their flanks, the dazzling floods of which combined into a seething river to traverse the entire province. One might have thought it a torrent into which the lava of a fully active volcano was flowing. That metallic flood went to plunge into a subterranean conduit open in the middle of the polygon.

The raw metal was soon in short supply, and, with the extraction machines not being able to furnish sufficient metal, entire buildings were demolished, including bays of the factory itself, and their debris, as well as the materiel already completed, was thrown into the insatiable crucibles, emerging in liquid form to supply the streams and fill the invisible gulf that absorbed molten excretion with an avidity that never relented.

That went on for a fortnight. In the meantime, Lichtmann, almost constantly underground, only appeared on the surface to cast a rapid glance over the progress of the exterior works. Then it was the turn of the gunpowder works to be seized by a frenetic ardor.

The grindstones were not inactive for a moment. Night and day they crushed and pulverized relentlessly the black mixture of sulfur, saltpeter and carbon. The pancakes were cut up into particles of phenomenal dimensions, and the latter immediately disappeared into the mouth of the shaft, drawn into the tubes by a violent current of air produced by the blowers.

XVI

It was the beginning of November.

It was raining in Paris. The air was cold, and the sky was speckled with large black patches whose capricious contours, by an insensible gradation of tints, faded to an ermine tint at the edges. Here and there, fleecy masses lost in space ran away before the west wind, taking on the bizarre forms as they fled in which a dreamer or an artist sometimes believes that he has found his chimera.

The gaze that plunged between the rare interstices of these vagabond clouds was lost in the immensity, whose azure splashed as if it were a whim by an impressionist hand, and then disappeared behind a spectrum of dirty tones, which was not at all reassuring for the rest of the day. Since eleven o'clock, the downpour had not ceased to batter the asphalt and lash faces. The Place de la Concorde, seen from the summit of the obelisk, presented the aspect of an agitated forest of umbrellas, and yet their owners, immobilized by the crowd, were scarcely thinking of sheltering under their narrow cover. The umbrellas were streaming, the garments were streaming and the square was a lake further swollen by the two fountains dedicated to river and maritime navigation, which, in spite of the design to receive in their basins the 6,716 cubic meters of water so gracefully launched into the air every day, have the bad habit of watering the passers-by as much as the sea nymphs.

The popular flood extended far into the Champs-Élysées, the Rue Royale, the Tuileries and the Rue de Rivoli. The quay and the bridge neighboring the Legislative body would not have been able to receive a single extra occupant, for there was not an inch of pavement that was not being utilized. The whole world was waiting impatiently for the end of the Parliamentary session.

Cries of every sort were heard; noisy clamors and lively discussions animated a few groups, which seemed to be on the brink of passing from unparliamentary words to more disturbing manifestations.

A dull rumble stifled those individual quarrels, however. Opinion was scarcely divided, and woe be to anyone who opposed its torrent. They were not curiosity-seekers, braving the inclemency of the season, which had been stationed for several hours before the twelve Corinthian columns of the portico of the Palais Bourbon. They paid scarcely any attention to the colossal statues of Sully, Colbert, l'Hôpital and d'Aguesseau, who were considering them from the height of their plaster seats with an impassive serenity. They had seen many others! These were no longer rioters come to break down the doors and impose their will on the representatives of the people. They were patriots, and from all mouths, one word was escaping more frequently and more expressively than any other: war!

Inside, the session was stormy.

The benches decorated with multicolored garments, overflowing with alert pretty faces placed as sentinels to encourage their favorite orators, and who were not listening in silence to the long reproaches addressed to the Government for allowing itself to be played by foreign diplomacy in the negotiations that had been going on for a month. The electrified feminine audience shivered with pleasure on seeing Monsieur Descombats race to the podium.

Monsieur Descombats: "Messieurs, a week ago, the minister brought here firm, clear and patriotic declarations, to which the Chambre and the country responded with their applause. Did those declarations have no other end than to make us forget the derisory slowness of the negotiations?" (Excited rumors heard on several benches.) "I will withdraw 'derisory' if you insist. The causes of that exterior conduct are carefully hidden from us; but the unrest that the various branches of the public fortune are experiencing and the injury inflicted on public dignity force us today to demand a categorical explanation from the Government..." (Exclamations, various movements, bravos to the left.)

The Minister of Foreign Affairs: "I have only one thing to reply to the honorable orator. The negotiations we are conducting with Germany are not yet concluded."

A voice: "They ought to be."

"Don't interrupt..."

The Minister: "We are expecting, in order to communicate it to you, the response to the ultimatum that we have sent to the cabinet in Berlin. Our desire was to conserve for Europe the benefits of peace, and in spite of our legitimate impatience, we could not desert the congress. We have sought by all means honorably to resolve a difficulty that we did not create..."

Several voices: "That's true.... Yes, very good."

The Minister: "Our very moderate demands have, however, been welcomed in such a fashion that the outcome of the affair does not seem to be in doubt."

General Crattair: "It never has been. These procrastinations have been disastrous. The enemy has taken advantage of the time that you have benevolently granted him. He has reorganized, and although we are still certain of victory, it will cost us a hundred times more than it would have cost us a fortnight ago."

At that moment an usher hands a sealed note to the Minister of Foreign Affairs, which he opens with a feverish hand. He goes pale and passes it to his colleagues.

Five hundred voices shake the ceiling: "The dispatch! Read the dispatch!"

The hemicycle is invaded; there are conversations, cries, insults; there is jostling; no one heard the frenetic agitation of the President's hand-bell. The latter then covers his head, and that simple demonstration restores calm to the Assembly.

The President of the Council gets to his feet and, after a brief explanation of the situation, reads the dispatch rejecting the terms of the ultimatum. A great excitement takes possession of the entire audience.

A voice: "It's a challenge."

Monsieur de la Salpêtrière: "One does not take impertinence so far."

The Minister finally concludes with a request for supplementary funds.

The President of the Chambre: "I shall consult the Chambre regarding an emergency vote." (Exclamations, bravos.)

Monsieur Beaujeu: "I demand to speak..." (The agitation is redoubled; Monsieur Beaujeu sits down.)

The President: "Would those who are in favor of an emergency vote please rise."

The entire Chambre rises, with the exception of a handful of members.

Fifty voices shout in chorus: "Stand up, then, stand up!" (Loud protests.)

Monsieur Quartier: "If there is one minute, one second, in which history gazes at us, Messieurs, it is this minute, this second, do you not think?"

"Yes, yes, closure!" (The noise drowns out the voice of the orator.)

Monsieur Quartier: "Will you please listen to me? You did not want to listen in 1896 either…and you were punished for that…"

A voice: "In 1896 you didn't want anything."

Monsieur Quartier: "I was right…"

Several voices: ""Closure!"

Monsieur Quartier: "The war for which you are voting will plunge thousands of families into mourning…"

"Enough! Closure!"

Monsieur Quartier: "Since you do not want to hear me, I protest in the face of the world and posterity against an unjust war. History will judge. I'm stepping down."

"Yes, get down! Bravo! Closure!"

The war was decided by an immense majority, and notification was hastily sent to the commanding generals, who had already joined their armies at the frontier.

When the result of the count spread through the crowd, there was nothing but delirious joy, exclamations of triumph and explosions of enthusiasm; from those hundred thousand dilated chests a powerful cry erupted: "*Vive la France!*"

All the faces were cheerful; people were extending their hands to one another, congratulating one another as if on a domestic good fortune, so deeply was that passionate love of the fatherland anchored in their souls, fickle but generous. Everyone raised his voice to make himself heard to his neighbor, who, occupied in developing his own ideas on the manner in which the operations ought to be conducted, was not paying attention to anyone else.

Why, though, was that human flood undulating? Why that long shiver, from the Madeleine to the Quai d'Orsay? The people looked up, and fell silent.

On the pedestal of the statue of Strasbourg, hoisted up by a thousand arms, a man was standing, a pygmy beside the giant, but a pygmy whose stentorian voice, in spite of the wind and rain, was able to dominate the noise and cover with its resounding tones the immense audience that had been given to him. How proud and masculine he was, draped in his flag! Sometimes, his patriotic song rose up, loud and majestic; sometimes, its fiery tone made the audience shiver; and everyone was breathless under the charm of that inspired music.

And he was still singing when, suddenly, an arm rose into the air, immediately imitated by a thousand others, pointing into the sky, at a black dot between two clouds.

Was it a precursory sign of the end of the world? No trumpets were sounding at the four corners of the world.

It was more like a balloon, floating over Belleville at an enormous height. It grew in size rapidly; already its dimensions equaled those of the full moon; its disk had a perfect roundness, but there was no trace of a nacelle.

Amazement was succeeded by curiosity.

The unknown body then had an apparent diameter of more than a meter; it was evidently heading for the Place de la Concorde.

Instinctively, all heads ducked. Was it not an asteroid launched out of its orbit that was about to crash on our planet?

Curiosity was succeeded by fear.

The multitude was gripped by panic; the flight began, terrible and pitiless, the strong crushing the weak in order to forge a passage. Driven by irresistible currents, hundreds of individuals were precipitated into the Seine; compact clusters of unfortunates clung onto one another desperately, almost damming the river in the vicinity of the bridge. Their arms were knotted in convulsive grips; then their muscles relaxed and the swollen waters covered their prey.

Up above, the terrified crowd had renounced its movement. It waited with bleak despair for the arrival of the exploding meteor. Now, as vast as the cupola of the Invalides, it seemed to be touching the houses.

Then a noise burst forth unheard by human ears: the violent impact of two colliding worlds, with the grinding of horrible frictions of stone, sinister gratings, a universal collapse. No one could see anything any longer. The errant star had not fallen on the square, but the frightened people had nevertheless been knocked down in the mud. Suddenly, a mighty explosion shook the ground, breaking all eardrums, and a hail of stone fell upon the crowd, killing or wounding the bellicose individuals of a few moments earlier...

The immense vessel of the Opéra had just been punctured by a bomb twenty meters in diameter, weighing five hundred kilograms, which, crashing through the vault, crushing the orchestra, hollowed out a monstrous crater beneath the monument, in the depths of which it exploded, reducing to dust houses, mansions, edifices and palaces from the Madeleine to the Bourse and the Gare de l'Ouest to the Palais Royal.

At the location of the most beautiful and richest quarter of Paris, a gaping gulf was fuming like the mouth of a volcano, and everything around it was nothing but ruins and rubble.

At the other extremity of Europe, Russia, irritated, like France, by the obstacles raised by diplomacy to a prompt conclusion to affairs in the Occident, was impatient to appeal to the judgment of God.

The Tsar had announced that on the twenty-fifth of October (the fifth of November in the Gregorian calendar) he would pass in review the troops ready to leave for the frontier. All measures had been taken to display the magnificence of the court to the wonderstruck eyes of the Orthodox, without that solemnity being troubled by one of the abominable assassination attempts all too frequent in that country.

On the left bank of the Neva, between the palace of the Senate and the palace of the Admiralty, coiffed with its superb tower of gilded bronze, extends a vast square whose quays are licked by the river in passing, and at which the principal avenues terminate. It is almost in the center of the capital. There, on an enormous block of granite fished out of the marshes of Finland, is the equestrian statue of Peter the Great. The bronze Tsar mounts that rock at the gallop, and indicates with an imperious gesture the fortress that his caprice caused to surged forth in the middle of the bog.

It was at the feet of that great man, who created the grandeur of Russia, that the Emperor wanted to affirm, in the face of his people, the glamour of a power that had not fallen.

The population of Saint Petersburg, composed in the majority of emigrants from all parts of the Empire, is very mixed, but that day, at a very early hour, the city, invaded by a legion of foreigners, presented even more than usual a bizarre aspect and an extraordinary animation. At the announcement of the war, the various populations living between Finland and Kamchatka, Lapland and Turkestan, had decided to send deputations to bring the homage of their devotion to the Tsar, to proclaim their submission and their inviolable attachment to this sacred person. Their rich and strange costumes and their immense astrakhan bonnets gave their vivid physiognomy a cachet at which the svelte Poles, clad in boldly-cut garments in bright colors, could not help smiling in admiration.

A gray-clad Lithuanian, devoid of fringes and braid, was gazing in a melancholy fashion at the preparations for the sumptuous review while an adorably pert young woman suspended from his arm pointed out to him, with a hint of irony, the embroideries of red and blue thread that ornamented the apron of a gracious young Russian, whose brown eyes had doubtless caused offence to her own beautiful blue eyes.

Everywhere, muzjiks with broad faces and sturdy shoulders displayed their long, thick beards as if to mock the founder of the monarchy, for, in spite of whom, they still wore them.

The Russian nobles worship strength, and it pleased them to see their prince, the representative of God on earth, appeared to them surrounded by the imposing aura of the sovereign presence.

A battalion of Karelian giants had difficulty containing the vast crowd, which, perpetually shoved by new arrivals, was beginning to obstruct the vicinity of the square. The troops, under the orders of General Field-Marshal Prince Khonckhierdforsstouttchine, were gathered on the superb Tsaritzynsko-Louga, which serves as a drill-field, or were arranged along the great avenues, bordering the sidewalks with an impenetrable hedge. Forty-five thousand men were under arms.

At a quarter to noon, cannon shots announced that the Tsar was leaving the Winter Palace, and soon, with all the guns of the Citadel of St. Peter and St. Paul, responding to that signal, bounded on their carriages and saluted the prince seventy-one times. Then the bells rang; orchestras, fanfares and drums drowned out the acclamations of the crowd with their loud sonorities. The windows and the skylights were crowded with curious enthusiasts jealously conserving their places.

The cortege finally appeared, preceded by a platoon of military police, several sotnias of Cossacks and a squadron of Uhlans. Then came the representatives of the high nobility led by the Marshal Prince Gogol Widtfverrowdviy, who, as the possessor of the entire territory of Kamel, is the sole proprietor of the taverns of the region; the Grand Marshals of the Court, and the members of the Council of the Empire. The Emperor was at the head of a brilliant general staff of ministers, aides-de-camp, major-generals and lieutenant-generals sparkling with decorations. Distinguishable in his wake were the Prince of Sweden and the Khan Berekuzbeck, who commands twenty thousand kibitkas[22] of Turkmen from Merv.

Finally, behind the Grand Dukes on horseback, the Empress and the Grand Duchesses advanced in carriag-

---

[22] Author's note: "Tents."

es, escorted by pages and two squadrons of mounted guards.

Two magnificent stages, decorated with the national colors, decked with trophies and banners, had been set up to receive the imperial family and the great dignitaries of the capital.

The Empress, followed by her ladies in waiting, came to sit down on a gilded silver throne encrusted with precious stones. The bright red velvet curtains, the pillars ornamented with the emblems and arms of submissive provinces and all the splendid dresses worn with supreme elegance by seductive and coquettish women dazzled the eyes, and the heady perfume wafting from that box intoxicated more than one page.

The Emperor, costumed as a general, went to place himself with his back to the Neva facing the statue of Peter the Great; there he handed the diamond-studded plaque of the Order of Saint Alexander Nevsky to the Grand Duke Wladimir Gropoulowiewitch, and the file-past began.

First came the cadets of the Alexandrof, led by Tsarkoïé-Zélo; then the infantry of the guard, the regiments of Preobrajensky and Semenowsky, the nucleus of the Russian army, formed more than two centuries before by the battalion of entertainers with whom the Tsarevitch Peter, still a child, played soldiers.

The monarch gazed with pleasure at the superb troops who were passing before him, while the crowd, maintained by an active and numerous police force, admired the deployment of uniforms, sabers and bayonets.

Acclamations were unleashed when the regiment of hussars of which the Emperor is the chief halted before His Majesty and then set off again at the charge. But the greatest success was won by the Cossacks, grim in their tawny beards, mounted on their small horses of the steppes, so difficult to contain in spite of the rude hands of their riders.

After having filed past the Tsar, the troops continued their march along the Nevsky Prospekt, the boulevard frequented by the high life of the capital. In spite of its breadth, the grandiose avenue could not contain all of the population that had tried to gather there. The less fortunate, pushed back into the lateral streets, were only enjoying the spectacle in imagination, while the privileged hung in dense clusters from the windows of houses and numerous palaces, or on the ledges of the churches that embellished the great Petersburgian artery.

Suddenly, gazes were diverted to the west, in the direction of Petershof, where an unfamiliar phenomenon had appeared; a dark patch was displayed against the faded blue of the sky; it was extending rapidly. A body was falling.

The tumult caused by that strange apparition was soon so great that the procession stopped and, in spite of discipline, the officers and soldiers also turned round to look at the black disk. The anxious multitude, their eyes staring, sensed that something extraordinary was about to happen.

There was no more doubt about it now: the frightful patch, now enormous, was heading for the city; as if moved by the same spring, those thousands of people fell to their knees, invoking God and the Tsar before that infernal wonder.

Impassive, mute and grave, the Emperor turned round and blessed his people.

Abruptly, the ball disappeared, but dull rumbles were immediately heard, as if a furious tempest had been unleashed over the bay, and an enormous wall of water fell upon the city, covering it entirely, while the islands of Wasilewsky and Goutouyewsky were invaded by the waves, and the sea came to bathe at the base of the Winter Palace and the grandiose massif of the Admiralty.

That first assault was succeeded by a second, more violent, preceded by a frightful commotion that made the building tremble, while in the harbor, the heavy iron-clads, the merchant vessels and the pleasure boats, hurled into the air, fell back to plunge into the profound furrows that laid bare in places the sandy bed of the gulf.

Kronstadt, the impenetrable fortress, groaned under the torment and thought about collapsing under the stress. It saw with fear the flood invading its bunkers through gun-ports through which monstrous cannon extended their barrels outside, ready to vomit death.

That black dot, that patch, that disk, which the Tsar's prayer had buried in the sea, was a bomb similar to the one that had caused such great ravages in Paris the day before—but the city of Peter the Great got away with a fright and a cold bath in salt water.

XVII

The two catastrophes in Paris and Saint Petersburg, which had cost the lives of three hundred thousand individuals, were due to Lichtmann's latest invention. At the place to which he had gone a month earlier with a theodolite, in order to mark the direction of the two capitals, two somber tunnels opened with polished walls, a hundred meters long, which penetrated underground at an angle of forty-five degrees. They were simply two monumental mortars constructed in secret. In spitting out their projectiles they had also cleared from their orifices the fragments of earth deliberately left to hide them. It was to cast the two bombs in place and construct the sixty-foot-thick walls of those gun-barrels that the floods of molten metal had served by virtue of flowing underground for a fortnight.

The projectile destined for Paris, launched by 25,635 kilograms of powder with an initial velocity of 3,236 meters per second, had arrived at its goal crossing the 460 kilometers that separated the point of departure from the point of descent in three minutes fifty-six seconds.

As for the one launched at Saint Petersburg, its aim had been slightly less accurate because of the enormous range, the 1,704,300 meters that it was necessary to attain. But the two mortars were there, ready to fire again in case of need, and Lichtmann had just calculated that by adding 527 livres of powder to the charge of 42,300 kilograms employed the first time, the second projectile sent to Russia would arrive precisely on the precious dome of St. Isaac in seven minutes forty-three seconds.

A second proof would have been unnecessary, though. On the banks of the Seine, as on the shore of the Baltic, martial enthusiasm had noticeably cooled. An immense discouragement and a bleak sadness had succeeded the joy of the preceding days. It was necessary to incline humbly before the man who disposed of such means of action and launched shells the size of houses.

From all the courts of Europe, emissaries were sent to Canonenstadt to implore the clemency of the Engineer and discover why he had so cruelly chastised his best clients—for the capitals that were still intact, not at all reassured, had no desire to suffer the fate of those unfortunate cities, and there was no humiliation that they would not have accepted in order to avoid it. The fatal patch described by the newspapers was present in the minds of their inhabitants, and they only raised their eyes toward the sky tremulously for fear of seeing the terrible threat hanging there.

Lichtmann, informed of the imminent arrival of the plenipotentiaries, felt that he had become this time, without contest, the arbiter of the world. The psychological moment had come to stop war forever and to give the people of the future the leisure necessary to direct their activity into the path he had traced out in founding Canonenstadt. Thus, he refused to receive the European delegates, collectively or separately. It was not to a few but to all the delegates of humankind that he wanted to dictate his will. He sent for ambassadors from the States that had not sent any, even from the most ignored peoples. That took a rather long time, during which a remarkable collection of diplomats could be observed in Dusseldorf, which would have delighted the most savant philologists and the most conscientious ethnographers.

That assembly of intelligent primates—or, at least, reputed as such—had doubled the population of the city where they awaited impatiently for the Engineer to condescend to hear them. In a matter of days, following their respective affinities, solid links of amity began to be established by those individuals of such diverse races, covered by such different garments. Those agreeable relationships were to have fortunate effects in the future and prepared the universal alliance the mere mention of which had once made sensible people smile, and the realization of which was now certain for all clear-sighted people.

It was, therefore, a spectacle full of promise that was visible in all the public places in Dusseldorf, where Kaffirs and Eskimos, Turks and New Zealanders were continually in conversation.

Finally, the assembly was complete. The day arrived when all human specimens were represented there. Then, for the first time, Lichtmann opened the gate to his Estates and brought the delegates together in the great hall of Canonenstadt, to which they were ferried by electric trams constructed for the occasion.

Taking his place on an elevated seat that had been prepared for him, not as a matter of vulgar triumph but only in order that everyone could hear his voice, the Engineer pronounced the following words, which were ineradicably engraved in the memories of the listeners who were hanging on his words.

"My brothers, a new era is about to begin. It will be the era of peace.

"Purge your hearts of the egotistical sentiments and paltry interests that have inspired your thoughts and actions thus far. Relegate them into the past, in order that they might fall into forgetfulness.

"Let us love one another.

"I have acquired the right to speak as a master; let those who have attempted to contest it learn that in two months, with my machines of war, I can go around the world destroying everything in my passage, as the latest battles have demonstrated. Know also that New York and San Francisco, as well as Edo and Peking, are not safe from my bombs, and that I can destroy those cities at a stroke by means of projectiles more powerful than those that have tested Paris and Saint Petersburg.

"Let my will be accomplished on earth. I want, from this day forward, over the entire surface of the globe, armies to be dissolved and fortresses razed, and their cannons sent to Canonenstadt in order to be transformed there into gigantic columns, which will in the future bear sole witness to the fratricidal struggles too long maintained by humans.

"In recompense for the benefits that it is imposing on humanity, the Cooperative State of Canonenstadt will reserve a monopoly on the manufacture of steel, leaving you free to exploit as you please all the other branches of industry and commerce.

"In order to ensure the world the maintenance of peace, I shall also reserve for myself and my successors the right to entertain engines of war, to improve them further, in order to re-establish concord, if it is threatened, while radically suppressing the combatants of the contending parties. *Et nunc reges intelligite erudimini qui judicatis terram.*[23]

---

[23] The quotation, slightly misprinted in the original text, is from the Latin version of the Bible, from *Psalms* 2:10. The equivalent text in the King James version is: "Be wise now therefore, O ye kings, be instructed, ye judges of the earth."

"I have spoken."

The plenipotentiaries found no response to this strange speech—which, in any case, did not admit any. That solution, which they scarcely expected, plunged them into a profound astonishment. They had believed that they were only addressing a skillful cannon merchant intoxicated by success, happy to treat on an equal basis the most powerful States of the world. Far from that, Lichtmann appeared to them now as the superior genius that he was, the regulator of the future destiny of our planet.

Several governments considered the results of their missions to be derisory and many of the illustrious diplomats, previously honored, fell into disgrace. Everywhere there were criticisms and hesitations.

The memory of recent events, however, plus the fear of chastisement and the pressure of public opinion, eventually convinced the most recalcitrant to yield. The Engineer's speech, published everywhere, translated into all languages dead and living, posted in barracks and in palaces, necropolises and modern cities by unknown and ungraspable agents, had aroused the enthusiasm of peoples, finally glimpsing a conclusion to their miseries.

From that moment on, the world has lived in the most perfect tranquility. Finances were gradually reestablished, and budgets were reduced to a quarter of what they had been in 1925. The day was seen coming when all constitutions would be modeled on that of Canonenstadt, where the celebrated formula "the right of every man to live by labor" was effaced in favor the more obligatory law of societies to come: "the duty of man is to live by labor."

The wellbeing and happiness of all is the price of a strict observation of that principle, as old as the world, but thus far misunderstood or applied unintelligently.

There are no more heroes, no more great captains to whom statues are erected, but populations console themselves for that by raising those of Lichtmann. There are already 21,753 of them in Europe, and the smallest localities want to offer him theirs. In other parts of the world, statistics are still mute in that regard.

In spite of that, the great man has not been overwhelmed by pride, and often seems plunged into a black depression.

That is because, even in Canonenstadt, the land of the elect, he believes that he can distinguish among his dear workers the nascent seeds of egotism.

"Perhaps," he sometimes says to his intimates, "when I am no longer here, they and their descendants will want to exercise power before their turn has come. If they succeed in taking possession of the apparatus of war, might they not make use of it to oppress their fellow citizens?"

At that idea, the old man's eyes fill with tears. He trembles every time the army undertakes training exercises with its engines. He has diminished the danger by reducing those exercises to the strict minimum, and changing the soldiers frequently, but his dearest wish is to suppress that apparatus completely—an impossibility, for in several States, a few conspirators retained solely by fear would immediately take advantage of his impotence.

As for us, we who do not want to see the future in such dark tones are convinced at the sage Engineer, carried away by his love of humanity, is exaggerating the inconveniences of the inequality of characters and individual aspirations.

We believe that, as wisdom and equity reign henceforth as sovereigns of the world, no one will ever have the culpable thought of sowing trouble among the reconciled peoples again.

So let it be!

"So let it be!" I repeated, loudly, on completing the reading of that bizarre lucubration, and I returned the manuscript to my friend Dr. K***, the director of the lunatic asylum of X***.

"Well," he said to me, "what do you think of the poor fellow?"

"But is there any reason to complain, if he imagines that we're there? His madness doesn't seem to me to be too dangerous—why is he here? Do you hope to cure him?"

"Alas, no. All the remedies that have been tried have failed."

"In that case, why keep him—could he not be set free without inconvenience?"

"I don't believe so. Know, to begin with, that it was him who caused the explosion in 1882 in the Rue Dufour, which fortunately had no fatal consequences. His madness having been observed, he was locked up here, and although he's ordinarily quite calm, he sometimes has terrible crises. He carries stones in his pockets constantly, which he claims to be dynamite cartridges; he often says that our poor earth is mined, and that before long it will explode in a multitude of fragments small enough for their inhabitants to live on them in peace. At other times, he isn't sure about that, and would prefer that no living being survived."

"It's certainly a curious case. Have you encountered others like it?"

"No others so well characterized, but I have no doubt that in a few years, unfortunates afflicted by explosion madness will become numerous."

On that hardly reassuring note, I took my leave of my savant friend, and since that day, the memory of the poor madman has pursued me, and sometimes inspires me with dread as to my own mental equilibrium.

NAVAL BATTLES OF THE FUTURE
by Maurice Loir

A midshipman in the Mediterranean naval squadron who took part in the naval operations of the war against the Triple Alliance recorded his impressions, emotions and hopes hour by hour in a pocket notebook in the course of the great events that no one has forgotten. Although the journal has a personal and intimate character, it is quite complete. We thought that the public might read these rapid notes, written without pretention and in a tone of sincerity that renders them very touching, with interest. Modern warships, so powerful and so complex, can be seen there in action; the difficulties inherent in the guidance of squadrons is revealed, and finally, the noble courage deployed by our mariners for the defense and glory of the fatherland is once again observable.

Anchored at Toulon aboard the Formidable, *22 April 190**

It's eight o'clock. I've just come down to the quarterdeck, harassed by fatigue, having done nothing but run around giving urgent orders during my watch on deck. The orders were performed quickly and well executed, thank God. What ardor and zest the men show! If I've sometimes had occasion to find them a little slow to obey the blasts of the bosun's whistle, I couldn't make any such reproach today. Those worthy men know that the moment is solemn, decisive. The eternal jokers on board, who are always ready to laugh at anything, have shut up since yesterday. It was in the greatest silence—a religious silence—that the movements were carried out.

From the bosun to the least of the matelots, they were all serious. By their silent attitude—meditative, one might say—one divines that they're deeply conscious of the enormous duty that's incumbent upon them. The war that threatens us, the declaration of which we're expecting at any minute, doesn't seem to be causing them overmuch apprehension. There's been talk of a possible war for so long, and it's been repeated so long that it might break out suddenly, that all minds are ready to receive the redoubtable news without surprise.

In the midshipmen's quarters, I've found my colleagues debating with an extraordinary animation the merits of an offensive, which is unanimously regarded as a certain guarantee of victory. May God hear them!

8.30

The admiral has just come back aboard. He's been advised by the ministry that the response to the French ultimatum won't be known before tomorrow morning. We're, then, going to spend another nervous night. For everyone here, in the week since the Franco-Italian conflict burst forth, has been in a state of incredible overexcitement. We're in haste to be sure of our fate. Uncertainty is the worst of evils. "What will tomorrow bring?" as the poet says. For us, it's peace or war. And the anguish caused by that frightful alternative is calculated to give us a fever.

The newspapers are admirably calm. I confess that I hadn't thought them capable of such sagacity. They're not indulging either in ridiculous provocations or vain bluster. They're awaiting events with a great deal of calm and dignity, almost with confidence.

All things considered, I share their confidence. I believe that our army is the equal of those of Germany, Italy and Austria, and as for our fleet, in spite of all the attacks that have been lavished upon it, I believe it to be capable of playing with honor the redoubtable role that will devolve to it. We have lacunae or weak spots in our naval organization, but so do our enemies in theirs. Only they haven't had, like us, the stupidity to proclaim the imperfections they must have perceived to the whole world. I can't believe, and don't want to believe, that our squadrons are inferior to their mission.

Just now, on deck, during the short respite the prayers said at the evening roll call gave us, I looked toward the harbor. It was superb in the soft dusk of a beautiful summer day. In the direction of Marseilles, the sun, already having disappeared behind the mountains of Provence, was still illuminating the horizon and seemed to be setting it ablaze. In the other direction, the hills of the Îles d'Hyères were drowned in the somber vapors of a distant mist. Around me, the squadrons were formed up in perfect order: eighteen battleships, twenty-two cruisers, forty-five torpedo boats, waiting motionlessly at anchor for destiny to be determined. And I told myself that all those ships, imposing in number, to which so many engineers and mariners had devoted the best of their science, couldn't be worse that the ships put in line by our enemies.

The frontline forces in the Mediterranean have been arranged into three squadrons: the active squadron, nine battleships, nine cruisers and nine ocean-going torpedo boats; the reserve squadron, six battleships, six cruisers and six ocean-going torpedo boats; and the independent squadron, three battleships, five cruisers and five ocean-going torpedo boats. All those vessels are in addition to those whose mission is to defend the coasts, which form the second line.

The vice-admiral commanding the active squadron has received an admiral's commission; he can organize all the movements he judges appropriate of all the naval forces in the Mediterranean. But as soon as one naval force or one gathering of ships is out of range of his signals, whoever is the senior officer will be entirely responsible for operations.

We're ready. The activity deployed in Toulon is marvelous, and I know, from letters sent from Cherbourg and Brest, that there's also prodigious activity out there. The day before yesterday twelve torpedo boats left for Algeria and Tunisia, where they've gone to reinforce the mobile defense, with the battleships *Vauban, Bayard* and *Duguesclin,* and the cruisers *Lapérouse* and *Du Petit-Thouars.* Yesterday, six torpedo boats, the cruiser *Rolland* and the armored gunboat *Mitraille* left for Corsica. The torpedo boats and coastguard vessels *Océan, Achéron* and *Fusée,* bound for *Villefranche* and other points of the Provence coast, have been at their posts since this morning. As for the squadrons, they're as ready as they can be. All the crews are complete, and all the orders have been given to the commandants in a series of conferences held in the admiral's quarters twice a day. There's no more to do than set a match to the fires of the boilers; three hours later, the harbor will be empty, and we'll be at sea.

By contrast, it's said in the Paris newspapers that the Italian navy is in complete disarray. That's doubtless exaggerated, but there might be a basis of truth in the information. We're not surprised that their mobilization has been slow; they've always be short of matelots, so they must have enormous difficulty manning their entire fleet, while we can muster all our reserves from the Nord and the Midi without effort.

As for the French crews and officers, everyone knows that they're the equal of the Germans and Italians. For abnegation and courage, none of us cedes anything to our adversaries. We're resolved to any sacrifice. This war is the supreme struggle, in which the existence and honor of France is at stake.

10 o'clock

I was right to anticipate a sleepless night. No one has any thought of repose. We're too anxious. There's nothing but comings and goings everywhere, as in broad daylight, aboard the worthy *Formidable*. Since I can't sleep, I'll copy in this journal the list of Italian and Austrian ships with the designation of their squadron and their station. It's a document that the general staff has just communicated.

Italy has for combat vessels eighteen battleships, twelve cruisers, seven torpedo boats and eight torpedo corvettes.

One squadron has its base of operations in Spezzia. It consists of the *Italia*, the *Sardegna*, the *Sicilia*, ships of the line; the *Elba*, the *Dogali* and the *Umbria*, cruisers; the *Partenope*, the *Urania* and the *Catalafini*, torpedo cruisers; the *Montebello*, the *Monzabano* and the *Tripoli*, torpedo corvettes; making twelve ships plus six ocean-going torpedo boats.

A second squadron has its base of operations at Maddalena. It consists of the *Lepanto*, the *Re Umberto*, the *Ruggiero de Lauria*, ships of the line; the *Piemonte*, the *Etruria* and the *Lombardia*, cruisers; the *Minerva*, the *Iribe*, the *Aretusa*, torpedo cruisers; the *Goito*, the

Folgore and the *Saetta*, torpedo corvettes; making twelve ships plus six ocean-going torpedo boats.

A reserve squadron concentrated at Spezzia consists of the *Francesco Morosini*, the *Andrea Doria*, the *Duilio*, the *Dandolo*, ships of the line; the *Bausan*, the *Vesuvio*, the *Marco Polo*, the *Stromboli* and the *Fieramiosca*, cruisers; the *Terpischore*, torpedo cruiser; the *Confienza* and the *Euridice*, torpedo corvettes, which makes another twelve ships, plus eight ocean-going torpedo boats.

The seven old battleships *Maria Pia*, *Castelfidardo*, *San Martino*, *Ancona*, *Affondatore*, *Principe Amedeo* and *Palestro*, with the old cruisers, torpedo scouts and ocean-going torpedo boats form seven divisions, each of which is charged with defending Genoa, Livorno, Civita Vecchia, Naples, Palermo, Catania and the Otranto canal. The last named also disposes of the battleship *Roma* and the cruiser *Etna*. Spezzia, Maddalena, Tarente and Venice don't have a special squadron for their defense.

Austria has constituted a mobile squadron composed of the battleships *Rudolf* and *Stephanie*, the cruisers *Franz Josef* and *Elisabeth*, the torpedo cruisers *Leopard* and *Panthere*, the torpedo corvettes *Meteor* and *Satellite*, plus four ocean-going torpedo boats. The author Austrian vessels are affected to the defense of the Adriatic coasts.

Our first concern, on waking up, has been to ask for news. There is none. The telegraph that links our *Formidable* directly to the telegraph office in Toulon, by means of a submarine cable, hasn't stopped functioning all night, but all the dispatches coming from Paris— which is to say, the most important—have been transmitted in cipher and the profane can't know what they contain.

23 April, 6 o'clock

The admiral has sent a signal to the squadron asking for the state of its various preparations. Five minutes later everyone replied: *Materiel embarked, personnel complete*, except for the *Amiral Baudin*, which will be ready within the hour, and the *Tage*, the *Dragonne* and the *Audacieux*, which won't be finished with repairs to the engines that they have to make until eight o'clock. Thus, in two hours the entire fleet will be ready to put to sea.

A midshipman on the admiral's staff, who had been sent to the maritime Prefecture with an urgent message has come back on board. He's been questioned. He doesn't know any more than we do, but he tells us that the animation in the city is extraordinary. He's crossed the path of companies of marine infantry in campaign gear, going to the railway station, and detachments of land or marine artillery taking the road o the forts overlooking Toulon. He brought us a few copies of the *Petit Marseillais*, which were snatched from hand to hand in the hope of finding something there to aliment our natural curiosity—but in vain. News from Paris is scarce, almost nothing. The government has evidently given orders for the newspapers to say as little as possible.

8 o'clock

It's forty-eight hours since the officers were ordered aboard. Now that all the dispositions for getting under way and combat have been made, there's no inconvenience in letting us communicate with the shore. The admiral has been asked to grant us that favor for an hour or two. He's consented to it. The officers will have their liberty today at half past noon, after lunch, with orders to return on board at two-thirty. Even so, they have to remain attentive to any cannon shot that might recall them on board in the interval, if it's urgent.

We can see two big transport ships of the Indo-China service, the *Mytho* and the *Shamrock*, leaving port, which are coming to carry out engine trials in the bay, at a fixed point. They've been fitted out as hospital ships, with numerous medical personnel, and will receive casualties after combat. By virtue of the new conventions, the need for which was keenly felt, those ships will be regarded as neutral. They're painted white, with their battery lines green, in order to be more recognizable, and they'll also fly the white flag with the red cross of the Geneva Convention immediately above their national flag. They'll bring help to the wounded and shipwreck victims of the belligerents without distinction of nationality. They'll follow the squadrons at a distance; they'll be assigned routes and rendezvous points in order that they won't be encumbering impediments before the battle.

Behind the *Mytho* and the *Shamrock*, three large steamers of the Maritime Mail emerge from the harbor, the *Saghalien*, the *Australien* and the *Armand Béhic*, transformed into auxiliary cruisers. They've been fitted with 14cm cannons and cannon revolvers; their crews are complemented by fusiliers, artillerymen and signalers. They're ready to pursue our enemies' commercial vessels.

9.50

The die is cast! The signal to "light the fires" has just been given from the mainmast of the *Formidable*. War has been declared!

The admiral has just received the following dispatch, which he has communicated to the squadron: *France's ultimatum having been rejected by Italy, as well as the offer of mediation by the king of Portugal, the government has ordered its ambassadors in Rome, Berlin and Vienna to leave their residences without delay. The Minister of War has received orders to mobilize the army immediately. Conform to the instructions sent in yesterday's dispatches nos. 714 and 715, and the secret program sent the day before yesterday by special courier. In addressing this final telegram to you, the government sends you its best wishes for success. It expects that the national army of the Mediterranean will legitimate the high hopes that the country has placed in it.*

The admiral followed this dispatch with a declaration along the following lines: *War, which had appeared threatening for forty-eight hours, has been officially declared. The admiral will have the honor of leading the Mediterranean squadrons, united under their commander-in-chief, against the enemy. He is convinced that everyone will do his duty and that every ship will remain faithful to the navy's proud motto: Honor and Fatherland. Vive la France!*

Thick clouds of black smoke are escaping from the funnels of the ships. The harbor is obscured, for there is not the slightest breath of air. The weather is superb. It takes two and a half hours to build up pressure. We shall, therefore, be under way at about noon. For where? We don't know. The admiral has authorized communication with the shore for two hours. The launch is ready. Those who have a father, mother or family in Toulon are going to say their last farewells. I'm staying aboard to write; the orderly will leave in an hour with the last batch of mail.

I've written to my mother, Aunt Marie, Madeleine and Henri. I've told them that I love them, that I'll be thinking about them, that I'll be brave, but that they're not to worry... Now, I have tears in my eyes as I write this journal, for it is as if I were never to write to them again. I resent those tears, as if they were evidence of a lack of courage—but no; when I interrogate myself, I feel as firm and resolute as can be. I'm weeping because my heart is overflowing with tenderness and gratitude for those who surrounded by childhood, protected my youth and have given me the strength to be a man in these days of proof that are commencing. Everything that I've written to them I found in a letter that a comrade showed me yesterday.

It's from Jules Sandeau, a ship's lieutenant in 1870, written on the eve of a battle. I'll transcribe it in this journal because it's more personal than my own letters and translates better than I can the sentiments that everyone here, I believe, experiences at such a solemn moment.

In a few hours we'll be at grips with the enemy; we'll be fighting on almost equal terms. I'm quite calm and sure of myself. I have your dear thoughts in my heart; they will protect me, I'm sure. If I'm killed, however, my poor dears. Tell yourselves that your child died accomplishing the foremost of his duties, defending the honor of his country.

I've just received your letters of 25 August. You love our dear France; you don't resent her for having taken your son.

At this hour, the most solemn and grave of my life, my entire soul is with you.

Last night, perhaps the last opportunity I shall have to think, I remembered my childhood and youth, which you surrounded with so much love. All those times were good; destiny had made my life very sweet; I would be ungrateful to think otherwise. But all that makes me emotional, and I don't want to be emotional.

I have confidence in our crews, we ought not to be, and cannot be, defeated. For myself, I shall never see our flag lowered.

I am at your knees, my father and beloved mother. It's there that from the bottom of my heart that I pray to God to give us the strength to avenge our dear father-land here.

I should have lived better, but on looking deep inside myself, I feel that I've always been honest; I don't find any bad deeds or wicked thoughts, and I can hold my head high at the hour that is sounding.

Adieu; I love you with all the force of my heart; may God give us victory.

J. Sandeau.

The vice-admirals and commandants have been summoned to a conference by the admiral to receive final orders. They've all arrived with more serious expressions than usual. Their conversations on deck before going in to see the big chief were very reserved. They were chatting in low voices. While I was looking at them, reminding myself what a heavy and redoubtable responsibility weighs upon those among them who'll have to take a *Marceau* or a *Courbet* into fire tomorrow, or even this evening, the commandant of the *Formidable* called me over. He's told me that throughout the duration of the war I'll be on his personal staff; I'll follow him everywhere, remaining at his side in order to transmit his orders and take account of their execution. I sensed myself going pale on learning that I'm to occupy that position of confidence and honor.

The commandant saw that, because he took me by the shoulder in a familiar manner and asked me: "Is that clear?" I replied with a "Yes, Commandant," that nearly stuck in my throat. I was so proud of being chosen that I couldn't say anything more.

The approaching departure is animating the bay in a curious fashion. Launches and dinghies are going back and forth in all directions. The boats transporting the Toulonnais to La Seyne are black with people. As they pass through the lines of the squadron, the passengers wave their handkerchiefs. The merchants with their small boats loaded with provisions are accosting the ships for the last time.

11 o'clock

The white and blue flag signaling the general rally has been unfurled from our mainmast. The cannon signaling the rally has been fired. The commandants have emerged from the admiral's conference and returned to their ships, pensive and serious. The launches will be back soon; we can see them rowing toward us vigorously.

The officers and midshipmen coming back from shore have told us about the demonstration that was produced when they left the quay. Half the population had come to see the launches. When the whistles blew to command the first strokes of the oars, long cheers were launched by the Toulonnais, mingled with repeated cries of "*Vive la marine!*" and "*Vive la France!*" The officers waved their caps and the matelots their bonnets as a sign of thanks. The enthusiasm was extraordinary.

The launches were hoisted back to their sea stations, and then brought back to their combat stations. The merchants left. They also made their little patriotic manifestation when their skiffs left, shouting at the tops of their voices "*Vive l'amiral!*" and "*Vive le Formidable!*" Soon, all the ships were signaling that the admiral's orders had been carried out—which meant that the boilers were under pressure, the moorings were ready to be reeled in, and that they were only waiting for the signal to depart.

At noon precisely the signal goes up to the top of the mast, and immediately the traditional cry is repeated in the batteries: "Every many to his post to set sail" Henceforth, my post is on the bridge or in the blockhouse—which is to say, in the redoubt, a few meters square, from which the commandant makes the Leviathan confided to his care maneuver as he wishes. I make a rapid inspection of the *Formidable*'s blockhouse, which is at the foot of the mizzenmast. I convey a few instructions to the helmsman who mans the wheel commanding the rudder, and take up a position near the quartermaster-sergeants who have to use loudhailers or mechanical devices to relay order to the ship's interior. "Release the moorings!" shouts the commandant—to which the first mate immediately replies: "Moorings released!" The engines begin to turn. The first beats of the propellers shake the *Formidable*'s stern. We're off!

Immediately, the musicians on the poop deck strike up the *Marseillaise*. As soon as the first notes are heard, everyone shuts up and looks at one another. We can guess what the admiral's thinking in having the national anthem played as we draw away from French soil. It's like a war cry, like a last farewell to the fatherland thrown into the air. Oh, that music at such a moment! I don't think I'll ever forget the emotion it caused me— me, who can't hear a joyful regimental hymn without feeling a frisson. But here, at that solemn moment, moved almost to tears, and I can see around me that the unexpected *Marseillaise* is making every heart beat in unison with mine.

The admiral, standing on the aft bridge, surrounded by his general staff and aides-de-camp, listened to the *Marseillaise* while looking at his squadron with a thoughtful expression I haven't seen before. What was he thinking? Some dream of glory, no doubt, which evoked the dazzling names of the past: Suffren, Linois, Courbet—all the glorious dead who made the flag illustrious. Then he suddenly snapped out of his reverie to give an order.

While we moved off slowly, the torpedo boats slid past at top speed, to get out of the bay as rapidly as possible. As they went past us, their captains saluted the admiral, who raised his cap. Now we've arrived between the dykes that close the entrance to Toulon. All the ships are under way. Already the line is beginning to form. I notice that fewer signals than usual are being displayed. Have the verbal orders given to the commanders been explicit?

Ten minutes later the entire fleet is clear of the jetties. It's followed closely by the *Suchet* and the three auxiliary steamships. The admiral signals to them to "Set sail for your destination" and then signals to the reserve squadron "Liberty of maneuver."

The latter separates from us. While we head eastwards toward the Hyères, it heads southwards. The separation intrigues me. I draw nearer to the commandant, who is talking to the first mate, and learn that only the active squadron is to take part in the "operation," without being able to grasp what the operation is, and that the reserve squadron is to remain close to the coast of Provence to ward off enemy attacks and maintain the defense. As for the *Suchet* and the steamers, they're going to cruise off Gibraltar in order to close the route to the steamers and sailing ships of the Triplice.[24] They're resuming the antique warfare of privateering, which is so suited to the temperament of our race, and which once won so many brilliant successes at sea. I envy those aboard them...but I'm wrong to complain. Our part is even better, since we're going to take the offensive.

The call to battle stations goes out. All the matelots run to their posts; the guns are put in battery, the loading and aiming apparatus is checked. The guns are loaded; the medium and small artillery are provisioned. The torpedoes are disposed and the launch tubes prepared. The bulkhead doors are closed. The pumps that will come into action if we take on water are tested. For several minutes, there's an unusual movement throughout the ship, but the movement isn't accompanied by any noise or confusion. Everyone does the work assigned to him, methodically.

The gunnery officer who'll be in charge of estimating and setting distances during combat has just taken his place next to the commandant in the blockhouse. He observes—which he already knows—that the blockhouse isn't a good place from which to appreciate distances; the openings in its armor not large enough to give a sufficiently wide view of the horizon. He talks to me, then, about the troublesome necessity of modern

---

[24] This contraction of "Triple Alliance" was to be routinely used during the Great War to refer to the alliance between Germany, Austro-Hungary and Italy anticipated herein.

warfare that encloses the commandant in that narrow redoubt throughout the duration of the battle. He thinks, not without reason, that it's a strange and false conception that wants a commandant to fight without being able to see and without elbowroom. Shut in his redoubt, the commandant will only have limited communication with the officers and matelots who have to operate and maneuver the colossal battering ram of which he's the responsible master. He won't know whether they're dead or alive, valiant or fearful; he won't be able to animate them with his voice, his gestures or his example. He'll give them orders via the almost infantile intermediary of an acoustic tube. He'll correspond with his machines via a mechanical apparatus that the slightest accident might disable, at the risk of compromising everything. It's been forgotten that naval warfare is waged by human beings, and can't be reduced to a few more or less complicated questions of mechanics or clockwork.

We pass through the Hyères. At Porquerolles we see the armed forts. The red uniforms of the artillerymen stand out clearly in the ardent light of a dazzling sun. Two torpedo boats of the mobile defense are in the little harbor of Porquerolles. When we're north of the lighthouse on the Île du Levant, the last of the golden isles, we set a course North 68° East, and the speed is fixed at eleven knots. I hasten to consult a chart. A lieutenant has got in ahead of me; he's traced the route and measured the distance. It's toward Spezzia that we're headed, and we'll be there at about two a.m.

Scarcely have we pushed out of view of the Levant lighthouse than the admiral signals us to assume battle formation. The order is carried out immediately. From then on we proceed in the following fashion:

In the lead, ten miles ahead of us, the *Cecile*; to the right, at the same distance, the *Alger*, and to the left the *Davout*; at seven miles the *Watignies*, the *Lalande*, the *Cosmao*; at three miles the *Iberville*, the *Bombe* and the *Léger*. Those scouts frame the bulk of the squadron, which is moving in an indented line in the following order: *Formidable*, *Marceau* and *Redoubtable*, forming the first division; *Dévastation*, *Amiral Baudin* and *Neptune*, forming the second division; *Hoche*, *Amiral Duperré* and *Courbet*, forming the third. The ocean-going torpedo boats *Dragon*, *Kabyle*, *Grenadier*, *Chevalier*, *Corsaire*, *Mousquetaire*, *Lansquenet*, *Coureur* and *Éclair* accompany the battleships. During the night, six of them will go to join the large cruisers and sail alongside them.

The scouts and flankers have orders to attack without hesitation the enemy's similar ships, which will inevitably be encountered, whether at moorings off Corsica or before Spezzia, to try to sink them.

When the new formation is taken up, the commandant lets it be known that he's going to inspect the battle stations. I accompany him on that scrupulous tour. First we see the big 37cm cannons, whose carriages always have the cheerful, not at all murderous, appearance that their sleek polished steel accessories give them; then we go down to the battery of 14cm and 16cm cannons, which have a truly superb aspect, with their neatly-aligned guns and their correctly-grouped men.

We go along the false deck where the torpedo launch tubes are ready for attack, and seeing the matelots standing beside their engines of destruction and death, I experience a singular impression on stroking the bright clear steel of one of the torpedoes, so inoffensive where they are, but which might cause irreparable catastrophe tomorrow.

We reach the engines and the boilers, and then the ammunition bunkers. I think fearfully of all those who will remain in these depths, confined there while we confront the enemy. There's a society in each of these innumerable redoubts, which have metal partitions between them designed to limit the ravages of projectiles and leaks. Here are the heavers who transmit the coal to the boilers, here the stokers who throw the fuel into devouring mouths the furnaces, here the cannoneers who place the shells and the powder cartridges in the breaches to ignite the battle. All these brave men will see nothing and divine nothing of what is happening—and if they hear something, it will only be the detonation of shells or the plaints of the wounded and the dying. Passively subjected to mechanical functions, in the midst of the confused noise of an invisible cannonade, they won't even know whether we're going forward or beating a retreat, whether victory is probable or catastrophe certain. By the light of electric lamps that illuminate their hermetically sealed compartments night and day, they'll wonder in vain how the battle is going. Their anguish will be terrible. Combat in these black cavities lost in the bowels of an immense ship is nothing like combat in broad daylight, when one has a weapon in one's hand, when everyone is animated by a common ardor, when one can look the enemy in the face.

Finally, we arrive at the infirmary, installed on one of the decks situated beneath the waterline in order to be better shielded from enemy fire. Mattresses are lying on the floor. On a table covered with black oil cloth, the doctors have set out their medical kits and a few surgical instruments, the sight of which causes me a particular frisson, while the orderlies are arranging bottles, boxes and buckets of water in one corner. Cotton wool, slings, gauze and bandages are accumulated on a mobile trolley. Already, the unbearable odor of iodoform is invading this entire section of the ship. The squadron chaplain is there, ready to fulfill his holy ministry with regard to the dying who will be brought to him.

We finally return to the open air and sunlight on the deck, and I experience a kind of relief.

The commandant gathers all the officers and midshipmen in the wardroom and gives them definitive orders for combat. The captain's isolation at the height of the battle, his distance from the batteries, the turrets, the engines and the corridors, and the possibility of damage to the means of transmitting orders, impose an obligation on him to tell us in advance how he wants to conduct the battle. He observes with regret that he can only furnish general indications, for the various circumstances of an encounter are impossible to anticipate, and the action will have to be modified according to circumstances, so he is forced to leave much of the initiative to the wisdom and composure of his subordinates. He does, however, specify certain conventions for opening and ceasing fire. That done, he sends word to the admiral that the *Formidable* is ready to honor her flag.

24 April

Victory! Oh, the great word, how well it resonates in French ears! Spezzia has been violated. One of the Italian squadrons has been defeated. The tricolor flag had been covered in glory. It's a glorious day. *Vive la France!*

We've sunk the *Sicilia*, one of the largest ships in the Italian fleet. We've damaged two other battleships similarly anchored at Spezzia, and a large cruiser. We saw one crippled cruiser disappear. We've only lost one torpedo boat, the *Mousquetaire*; our other ships have sustained slight damage but none is disabled except for the *Neptune*, which emerged badly bruised from its raking assault on the flanks of the *Sicilia*. She can be repaired, though. Two of our battleships weren't hit at all, and are thus entirely intact.

My joy would be greater if I didn't have to mourn the death of one of my best and dearest comrades. He was in the next bunk on the *Borda*.[25] We formed a rapid and permanent bond, and kept in touch. We had the same tastes and the same sentiments about many things. I found a sure and devoted affection in him.

Poor good and dear friend! He was killed in the *Formidable*'s battery by a shell burst that tore through his chest. I'll write to his father and mother, to whom he was such a good son, and I'm already thinking about the blow that the news will deal them. Victory is made of mourning, glory is made of tears—of the morning and tears of mothers from whom war has stolen their children.

Here is the account of a day that will be famous henceforth.

At two a.m. the advance guard, sailing like the rest of the squadron with lights out, fell upon two Italian torpedo boats placed as sentinels fifteen miles from Spezzia. Not far away there was a torpedo corvette. The three small ships immediately took evasive action, sending up rockets to indicate our presence. At two-thirty, they were reached by the *Cécile*, the *Dragon* and the *Chevalier*. After launching two torpedoes at the *Cécile*,

---

[25] The *Borda* launched in 1864—one of several French naval vessels to have that name—was used in the early 1890s as a training ship by the École Navale.

unsuccessfully, the torpedo boats were forced to retreat. The *Cécile* tried in vain to capture and sink them, in accordance with orders from the admiral, which specified avoiding any engagement that would waste time. The torpedo corvette, also escaping our shots, drew away southwards at top speed.

It had scarcely disappeared into the night, which was still quite black, when our scouts sent up flares to indicate the presence of the enemy squadron. It was the mobile squadron from Spezzia, cruising in front of the entrance of the port in order to intercept us.

Immediately, a white flare and a red flare went up from the mainmast of the *Formidable*, indicating that the commander-in-chief had decided to follow one of the plans outlined in advance at Toulon. As soon as the signal was perceived by the squadron, the first division veered to starboard in the direction of the Italian squadron and the second to port, drawing away from us, except for the Neptune, which joined us in order to fight, while the third division and its cruisers continued on course, without deviation, directly toward Spezzia.

The admiral's plan is as follows: since the mobile squadron is outside, he is heading toward it, but as it only has three battleships—which can be clearly made out—he is limiting the attack to four of his battleships. The second division—which is to say, the *Dévastation* and the *Amiral Baudin*, with its cruisers—will be held in reserve, at a distance, out of range of projectiles that might damage it. It will thus be spared and remain intact if the combat goes in our favor; in the contrary case, it will come to the rescue and help us crush the enemy. As for the third division; it will penetrate into the harbor through one of the entrances and exit through the other, destroying everything it encounters with torpedoes and cannon fire, and will then go to join up with the second division. We shall also remain out of range of the cannons on the Italian coast.

The plan might go awry if the Italian admiral, refusing combat with our first division, allows the third to enter the harbor and then blockades the entrances in order to close its exits. In that case we'd be constrained to lend assistance to that division, which would bring us within range of the coastal batteries, whose fire would combine with that of the squadron. But will the enemy realize immediately what the objective of the third division is? Will they believe in the audacity of only entering a third of our forces into the harbor, so renowned for the strength of its defenses? Everything suggested that they wouldn't.

So it proved.

At four a.m., as daybreak was beginning to display its first light over the horizon, the Italian squadron came to meet us, leaving the *Hoche*, the *Courbet* and the *Duperré* to head straight for the shore. Its scouts separated from it, imitating our maneuvers, which had already abandoned the cruisers and had rallied in a group in the open sea.

At four-thirty, very boldly, the three frontline ships, the *Italia*, carrying the admiral's flag, the *Sardegna* and the *Sicilia* attacked our four battleships, *Formidable*, *Marceau*, *Neptune* and *Redoubtable*. The French and Italians were moving in single file. It was to port that we were going to fire.

At four forty-five the small display, which consists of a single national flag at the top of each mast, was hoisted on all our ships, and immediately, the first cannon shot was fired from the *Formidable*. At the same moment, we heard the artillery of the third division rumbling in the distance, engaged with the batteries of the forts.

Suddenly, the cannonade commenced in all directions with a terrifying frequency and intensity. At first it was only the medium cannon that fired, for the big guns are reserved for the minute when one is broadside onto the enemy. A shell burst behind the blockhouse, a few meters away from me. I heard loud screams; I leaned out, trying to see, anxious and emotional. A second shell burst on the armor of the middle turret and shattered a section of the gangway, with such a racket of splintering wood and fragments of metal raining down that one might have believed that everything around us had been destroyed. Then a third and a fourth shell...I was no longer counting. The small projectiles of the Italian Nordenfelt cannons were whistling stridently through the air. Many of them burst, sending shrapnel flying.

Now the big guns are thundering. Our first armor-piercing 37cm shell strikes the hull of the *Italia*, which is a thousand meters away. We can't make out the damage we've inflicted very clearly, but it must be serious, because the blow was very well aimed.

The commandant, calm and admirably composed, but who hasn't yet unclenched his teeth, cries "Bravo!" Then he adds, as a sort of aside, as if to himself and in a low voice: "It's frightful..."

The mate supervising the helm is more loquacious. At every blow we receive, he murmurs in a low voice: "Oh my God!"

The two lieutenants who are with us say nothing; the one at the helm is lending a hand the helmsman, and the one in charge of the gunnery is absorbed by his distance estimates.

It's the turn of the *Sardegna* to come into our sights. I have sufficient freedom of thought to perceive her superb appearance, and I feel proud. The three funnels surrounding her single mast seem enormous. For a debutant, receiving his baptism of fire, it must be a good sign to be noticing details of naval architecture! Her fire is better equipped than the *Italia*'s. Her fine battery of 15cm cannon is vomiting a torrent of fire at us. Our mizzenmast is hit. The topmast cannons can no longer be animated by the interior breaches.

In the battery, the 15cm shells are causing havoc, because noises of breakage and cries of agony are reaching us from below, which cause the mate to repeat his eternal "Oh my God!" Then a terrible, frightful shock shakes the entire ship.

We look at one another mutely. "That's a 34 shell," says the commandant to me. "Go take a look."

I go down from the blockhouse via the interior ladder. On the false deck an officer and a few men give me the relevant information. I'm shown the place where the shell has struck, where the broken cornices and dislocated bolts testify to the enormous impact we've received, but the armor plating has done its job; the damage isn't serious.

When I go back to my post I see the mate in charge of the helm being taken down to the infirmary with a head wound from which blood is flowing abundantly. The poor man is no longer talking, and it's me, in my turn, who wants to cry out: "Oh my God!" The lieutenant has replaced him at the helm. I give my report to the commandant, who says: "Good!" The *Sicilia* has come abreast while I was on the false deck, and we've already begun to circle in order to catch up with the enemy and fight again.

That movement allows us to see that the line of our vessels is still holding firm. They present the appearance of being almost intact, externally at least, except for the *Marceau*, which has lost one of her masts, fallen sideways onto her deck. Our last two cruisers are directly abeam; they fire at the three Italians without disabling any of them.

Suddenly, however, the *Redoubtable* quits the line. We're gripped by anguish. If her rudder is damaged, if she can no longer steer, she's lost. An Italian will find a means of delivering a mortal blow. And indeed, the *Sicilia*, which is level with her, immediately steers toward her, while she increases speed—but she can no longer steer. She comes round in a sort of semicircle, and signals: *Serious damage to rudder.*

We fire at the *Sicilia*; our shots strike home, but she pursues her rapid and audacious course. Alas, we know that she has an advantage of speed of at least three knots over the *Redoubtable*, and we dread the outcome of the duel. Oh, if only one of ours could cut her off! But we're too far away.

She's getting visibly closer to the poor *Redoubtable*. She's going to ram her with her powerful spur...when an immense jet of water covers her and lifts her up. A torpedo from the *Redoubtable* has struck her. She's still going, though...but her course has deviated; she's no longer threatening the *Redoubtable* head on; she's coming alongside. She finally reaches her—but the impact we feared is reduced to a simple glancing impact.

The two adversaries incline in opposite directions, and then rapidly disengage, firing at almost point-blank range with their small and medium artillery.

The *Neptune*, which is following us in the line, receives the order to go after the *Sicilia* and the *Redoubta-*

ble. She therefore veers in that direction while we go on to meet the *Italia* and the *Sardegna*, which are mounting a new offensive.

We pass them at five hundred meters this time. Shells rake us furiously, and them too. A rain of small projectiles covers the deck; it's hell. The commandant wants to use the spur. He asks for orders from the admiral, who replies in the affirmative, against the *Sardegna*.

A huge shell from the *Italia* has just burst against the 37cm of our middle turret. The cannon has broken, its barrel falling onto the deck with a terrible din. We head toward the Sardegna in order to attack her with our spur.

We miss, and as we pass her stern she launches a torpedo at us—which, fortunately, is deflected by the eddies of our propellers and doesn't hit us. The shells continue raining down. The commandant, who leaves the blockhouse at that moment in order to get a better view of the situation, receives a wound in the arm that tears the flesh. Stoically, he comes back into the blockhouse and contents himself with stemming the blood flow with a handkerchief.

His lack of success against the *Sardegna* has rendered him irritable, and his ignorance of what is happening down below, in the entrails of his ship, is visibly weighing upon him. He has the officers in charge of the batteries questioned incessantly via the loudhailers, but the latter, fully occupied, only reply with monosyllables that don't satisfy our chief's perfectly natural curiosity. He becomes impatient with the quartermaster-sergeant, who ought to be in loudhailer contact with the battery and is no longer saying anything. He thinks that our cannons aren't firing rapidly enough, even though their shots are incessant and the sounds of their detonations are deafening me.

He sends me to stimulate the fire. On the way, I'm to instruct the quartermaster-sergeant at the loudhailer to keep us better informed. I obtain an explanation for his silence; the poor man has been killed and is lying on the floor, inanimate.

When I get back to the blockhouse I learn that the *Sardegna* has just been hit by a torpedo from the *Marceau*. She's listing badly to starboard. Water must have invaded a compartment of her keel. She's not losing speed, though, and is sustaining her fire.

In the meantime, the *Neptune* has been pursuing the *Sicilia*, which, seriously torpedoed, gives the impression of a bird with a broken wing, releasing abundant smoke through her funnels, drawing away and no longer seeking to return to the conflict. The *Neptune*, judging that she must be seriously compromised, has launched after her and returned the thrust of the spur that she delivered so awkwardly to the *Redoubtable* a short while before. She's been struck directly amidships, level with her engine room, in the place where the watertight partitions are most widely spaced, with the result that she's taken on water very rapidly. Indeed, it doesn't take long for her boilers to explode with an abominable din.

Our gazes, attracted to the location of the tragic scene by that sinister sound, contemplated the engulfment of that beautiful 122-meter ironclad, which was doing battle a little while ago with so much pride and impetuosity. Soon, we saw boats set out from the *Neptune* to pick up the survivors of the disaster, and a few moments later, there was nothing but a few pieces of floating debris to indicate the place where the unfortunate but valiant *Sicilia* had disappeared forever.

The Italian admiral made the decision at that moment to head for Spezzia. Doubtless the *Sardegna*, which had been covered in signals for several minutes, had made it known that she was no longer in a fit state to undergo a further assault. Confronted with the disproportion of forces, the best thing for the enemy to do was to abandon a battle whose outcome could only be fatal to their flag. In any case, their admiral could do himself the justice of having largely saved honor in the conflict. As he was faster than us, with his ships having a considerable superiority of overall speed, he was assured, given a start, of not being overtaken by us. He was, however, risking a collision with the third division, which would not take long in rejoining us, having completed its raid.

His situation was critical, but, fortunately for him, the third division, enveloped until then by a bank of morning mist, had just appeared some distance away from the route he had to follow. He was able to run to the coast safely and find the refuge he needed there, as his cruisers had done.

It was six-thirty. From then on we were masters of the battlefield. We drew closer to the *Redoubtable*, which had succeeded in repairing the damage to her rudder, and signaled to us that she was able to follow the squadron. Her bow had been badly damaged on the port side, staved in and ripped—a consequence of her collision with the *Sicilia*—but all in all, she was not seriously damaged.

The situation was quite different aboard the *Neptune*, which had just signaled to us that the blow she had struck the *Sicilia* had disrupted all the interior consolidations of her bow. Several of the armor plates at her waterline had been detached and had fallen into the sea; the wooden mattress sustaining them had been cracked, thus letting in water, which the pumps were having great difficulty expelling. In brief, the bold maneuver undertaken by the commandant of the *Neptune*, which had won him a brilliant success, since it had sunk one of the most powerful enemy ships, had also inflicted a wound on his own vessel that risked being dangerous, and perhaps mortal.

As we passed through the midst of the ships in order to resume our formation, we were able to take account of the damage caused by the enemy artillery. The holes could be counted in their hundreds—or, rather, could not be counted. The *Marceau* has an enormous breach near the stern that forms a gash seven or eight meters long. Her blockhouse has collapsed completely, her gangway no longer exists and her mast has fallen onto her deck, thus presenting a lamentable appearance. The enormous superstructure of the *Neptune* is holed, with the cannons mounted on it out of commission. Like the *Marceau*, moreover, she bears the visible traces of several large caliber shots in the vicinity of her waterline. Their armor plating has been broken and stripped away in several places, but in the main, their encircling armor has protected them. And to think that there were people who criticized the complete armor that we provided for our battleships!

As for the *Formidable*, she's badly battered, fore, aft and amidships. Our deck and our batteries look like demolition yards: so much debris of every sort is piled up everywhere in an inextricable tangle. In sum, although we've won the victory, we've suffered a great deal and have paid dearly for our success. That's the way of modern naval warfare; it disposes of such impressive means of destruction that it inflicts considerable losses on both of the adversaries involved.

The dead and the wounded, alas, are numerous. On the *Formidable*, the infirmary established in the hold was insufficient, which might have been anticipated. The false deck is cluttered with mattresses or rolls of sailcloth, on which fifty-seven men said to be seriously wounded are lying, and we already have twenty-one dead. If each of the four battleships has as many victims, the losses will be considerable.

And we're the victors! Oh, war, terrible war, the frightful devourer of men!

We have been joined alongside by the *Dévastation* and the *Amiral Baudin*, which remain simple spectators of the battle since their collaboration would not have been useful. Their officers are studying us through binoculars. And soon after them, here comes the third division, catching up with us. Its ships are in the same state as us: the sheet metal of their hulls staved in, their masts broken, their funnels punctured. The conflict back there at Spezzia must have been tremendous.

When the *Hoche* reaches our vicinity the vice-admiral of the third division comes alongside in a launch in order to give a report on his battle to the commander-in-chief. We go to set our boarding ladder in place to permit him to come aboard, but we find that the ladder no longer exists. It has been shattered into smithereens by a shell. The vice-admiral hoists himself aboard as best he can.

"Complete success," he says, as he sets foot on deck. He is surrounded and interrogated. He asks questions in his turn. He goes down to the commander-in-chief's quarters. Then I go to talk to the midshipman who has accompanied him. He tells us the story of their entry into Spezzia.

The three torpedo boats, the *Davout*, the *Wattignies* and the *Léger*, engaged resolutely into the western passage to Spezzia, hugging the shore as closely as possible to shield themselves from the batteries. Two scouts placed in the inlet of Portovenere had been held in respect and prudently set aside.

The Italians' surprise was complete. Their ships only had incomplete crews, which could not arm all the guns; none of them had their fires lit; only their electric searchlights were functioning, showing their whereabouts very clearly. A confused cannonade commenced, uncertain in the darkness. The Hotchkisses and musketry of our ships covered with bullets the enemy decks, which became uninhabitable. By contrast, the Italian Nordenfelts only had a slight effect on ships traveling at eighteen to twenty knots. The *Duilio* and the *Dandolo* had been struck by Whitehead torpedoes, and their captain took them into the depths of the bay to run them aground.

The battleships entered at that moment. The *Hoche* headed for the *Marco Polo* and bombarded her vigorously. The *Stromboli* received from the *Courbet*, almost at point-blank range, a shot from a 34cm that disemboweled her completely. As for the *Amiral Duperré*, she attacked the line of medium cruisers and torpedo corvettes with unparalleled violence, pouring a hail of small caliber fire over therm.

When that work was complete, the battleships filed behind the cruisers through the eastern passage and emerged from the bay at top speed. It was necessary, in fact, not to compromise that triumph by any delay, giving the Italians time to recover from their surprise.

In any case, the daylight would soon permit the artillery of the forts to rectify their targeting, thus far uncertain.

At the moment of emergence, a torpedo or a cluster of torpedoes exploded against the bow of the *Duperré*, but not enough to cause her to take on water dangerously. The observers, troubled or ill served by their machines, has made an error of a few meters. The armored Umberto I Tower on the island of Palmaria, commanding the western entrance of the gulf, was more fortunate. Its 40cm Krupp cannons had just opened fire; one of their shells struck the *Duperré* at the waterline, fortunately in the middle of the armor plate, and another blasted the *Courbet*, smashing the barrel of the fore 27cm cannon.

The losses of men had been fairly considerable, especially on the cruisers, which had suffered a great deal from the Hotchkiss and Nordenfelt guns. The commandant of the *Courbet*, one of our finest leaders, had been cut in two by a shell. The commandant of the *Davout* had been mortally wounded, and three officers had been killed aboard the *Wattignies*.

The leader of the light squadron, the commandant of the *Cécile*, has just come aboard. He, too, announced a success. He had taken his cruisers to attack the Italian cruisers as soon as he saw them separate from the main body of the squadron before the action. He had given chase to them. In the course of that pursuit, one cruiser—the *Elba*, it was believed—had suffered a breakdown of her engine or her boiler that had forced her to slow down. The other enemy cruisers, not wanting to abandon her, had reduced their own speed. Combat had been engaged immediately.

The *Cosmao* had almost collided with the *Dogali*; a superb maneuver by her captain had saved her. As for the *Partenope*, a shell had burst her boilers. Her crew had been evacuated and the *Dogali* had sunk her, firing at her in order to prevent her from falling into our hands. Unfortunately, our torpedo boat, the *Mousquetaire*, had been sunk by cannon fire from the rapid and powerful *Umbria*, which the *Alger* had engaged in fierce combat. It appears that the ultra-rapid-fire 37mm Maxim guns, mounted aboard the *Cécile* and the *Alger*, had performed marvelously. The Italian torpedo boats seemed terrified by the incredible rain of bullets that the little cannons vomited from the poops of our two large cruisers.

While the commander-in-chief is talking to the two subordinate commandants, a signal is prepared on the telegraph. The frame goes up and down along the halyards of the wheelhouse and the translators interpret the signal as: *The admiral expresses his entire satisfaction with the squadron. He is proud to have such skillful captains and such valiant crews under his orders. This morning's success is the portent of further victories, for which it is now necessary to prepare. Vive la France!*

Another signal succeeds that one: *Double rations for the crews.* The brave men have certainly earned the double ration, that small recompense so prized on board. Oh, if it were not for all those dead and wounded so close to us, what joyful and enthusiastic hurrahs we would have the right to utter! Everyone has done his duty nobly. What will people say in France when they learn about this victory? As long as everything has gone well in the North! As long as our armies have had the same good fortune as us, and they, too, have carried the day in their first encounters with the enemy! Our French character needs victory at the start of the game; otherwise, discouragement grips us and our ardor weakens. I'm judging this by myself, based on what I hear around me. It seems to me that if we had suffered a check this morning, we might not have the courage to believe in a possible revenge, while now we no longer believe in anything but victory!

In the emotion of the first moment that followed the battle, we had forgotten that the passenger pigeons that were brought aboard to inform Toulon about enemy movements could carry the great news very rapidly. We soon realize that; the matelot who is looking after the poor beasts catches four of them—with a great deal of difficulty, because the cannonade has terrified them. He finally succeeds in attaching a little tube to each of them in the usual place, containing a dispatch from the admiral. Then he releases them. They rise up, circle, search, seemingly lost, and finally take flight in the direction of France.

The admiral asks for a count of the men no longer capable of fighting, and instructs each ship to get ready to evacuate the wounded onto the *Mytho*, which is in sight, with the cross of Geneva on its flags.

This is the lugubrious enumeration that the helmsmen transmit: *Formidable*, 21 dead, 57 wounded; *Marceau*, 27 dead, 61 wounded; *Redoubtable*, 30 dead, 48 wounded; *Neptune*, 29 dead, 31 wounded; *Hoche*, 16 dead, 35 wounded; *Duperré*, 25 dead, 31 wounded; *Courbet*, 17 dead, 29 wounded; *Davout*, 8 dead, 23 wounded; *Wattignies*, 10 dead, 14 wounded; *Léger*, 7 dead, 9 wounded; *Cécile*, 9 dead, 11 wounded; *Lalande*, 4 dead, 11 wounded; *Herbville*, 8 dead, 8 wounded; *Alger*, 9 dead, 15 wounded; *Cosmao*, 10 dead, 17 wounded; *Bombe*, 6 dead, 8 wounded; torpedo boats, 15 dead, 6 wounded. Total, 248 dead and 439 wounded, out of 6,880 officers and matelots taking part in the battle.

The *Redoubtable* informs us that she has picked up 37 men from the *Sicilia*, and the *Neptune* 250, including three officers and the first mate; orders have been given for them to be sent to the *Mytho*.

The transshipment of the wounded begins immediately. All their wounds are serious and many will not survive. Nothing is as heart-rending as the departure of those poor mutilated men, who are lowered into the launches. Their bandages are impregnated with blood; their gazes betray the secret anguish that grips them. Unfortunately, the breeze is getting up and the sea is choppy; the launches are shaken, and the unfortunates utter cries of pain at every movement as the boat carries them.

When the *Mytho* has received the whole of her consignment, it sets off directly for Toulon, while we get under way, still in battle formation, except for the pretty *Mousquetaire*, which has disappeared.

"What will be done with the dead?" someone asks.

The response is not long in coming. They'll be buried at sea.

The thing is done very simply, but that simplicity gives the funeral ceremony a grandeur that moves us to our utmost depths. The crewmen are recalled from their inspection posts. The admiral, the commandants, the officers and the midshipmen gather in the stern, heads bare. The squadron chaplain, in a stole and surplice, come up on deck preceded by two matelots, one of whom is carrying the cross, the other the holy water sump. And there, facing aft, very emotional, very troubled, the abbé recites the prayers for the dead; then he gives absolution with a broad circular gesture that seems to embrace all the ships. Then the admiral advances to stand beside the abbé, and in a deep, slightly gruff voice he pronounces this sentence, whose words are still resonating in my ears:

"To all those who have just died so nobly for the defense and the glory of the fatherland, I give the adieux of the squadron and the salute of France."

Then, one by one, the poor dead men, horribly mutilated, are brought up from the false deck and the battery. A heavy lump of lead is attached to their feet, their arms are tied to their bodies, and a cloth is attached to cover their faces. They are taken to a gap in the bulwark where they are laid one by one on a plank covered by the tricolor flag. One end of the plank is lifted up; the body slides off and falls into the sea, which opens up and closes again immediately.

Our poor comrade is the last of all to depart. It is the midshipmen who have gone to fetch him from the false deck and have carried him to the plank from which he has been thrown into the abyss in order to sleep his final slumber. A glorious death, people will say. Well, no doubt—but it's death all the same, pitiless death, which cuts earthly ties; and our hearts are gripped so cruelly as we think about the friend that we shall never see again...

While those lugubrious scenes unfold on our ships, we're under way, at top speed. Oh, human misery! In the truly terrible moments we endure, which cause us to pass through terrible but great emotions, it's necessary that we think of "the beast," as the other puts it. We have a devouring hunger. The time has come for our habitual lunch, and our stomachs take responsibility for reminding us of that fact. As we sit down at the table, however, we learn from the chief of the mess that the galley has been destroyed—demolished and utterly wrecked by enemy shells—so that we are eating cold rations. What does it matter, after all?

The officers' mess, which is aft of the false deck, is in a pitiful state. The shells have done enormous damage there. The midshipmen's quarters, on the other hand, have not suffered much. We are able to sit down around an almost-intact table. There are three empty places, alas, among us; in addition to our dead comrade, two wounded midshipmen are not there. The *Mytho* has collected them.

Naturally, we talk about the morning's events; we tell one another what we have seen; we question one another, for in such a combat and on such ships everyone only sees a very restricted part of the general action. Those of us who were employed in shell supply, and only heard the cannonade, are eager for information. In exchange, they tell us what was happening in their vicinity, in the infirmary, and the details they give us communicate a frisson.

In spite of everything the ardor is extreme, and we all feel strong enough to go into combat again. One curious thing is all the praise of our superiors. Youth, ordinarily so prompt to criticize, doesn't criticize anyone today. We all agree in thinking that the affair has been well-directed and well-executed.

Three o'clock

We're changing course and heading southwards. What are we going to do now? Where is the squadron going? Although victorious, it's in a very poor state. In fact, the ships have just been instructed by signal to provide a summary account of their damage, and the list is long. The number of medium and small caliber cannons that have been hit and their carriages demolished is incredible. The Italian's excellent 15cm cannons, devastating the unarmored parts of the battleships and cruisers, have inflicted frightful material damage. On every ship there is at least one big cannon disabled in consequence of damage to the hydraulic machinery used in aiming or loading. The *Courbet*'s portside pumps are unusable. Demolished Hotchkiss guns are innumerable, and shattered electric searchlights are also very numerous. Fortunately, the engines save the situation. They have hardly suffered at all, although the funnels are so battered and broken that the draw of the boilers is diminished.

Thus, the squadron is distinctly lame. It's incapable of sustaining another battle, of accomplishing a longer cruise. Its return to Toulon is imperatively necessary.

5.30

We're still continuing to travel southwards, but while keeping away from the Italian coast. Are we going to Maddalena? In the state we're in, that would be singularly reckless.

Seven o'clock

No, we're not going to attack Maddalena, unless events force us to do so. We're returning to Toulon, passing by the mouths of Bonifacio. Why are we taking the schoolboy route? The officer of my watch has told me. The admiral has adhered to the following reasoning: the Maddalena squadron must have been alerted this morning by telegraph of our attack of Spezzia and are setting a northward course. The person in command must have assumed that after a battle of squadrons, our situation will require a rapid return to port, and must be trying to cut off our retreat to Toulon, sailing along a direct line between Cap Corse and Porto Maurizzio, in order to try and attack us with his fresh and intact ships. Thus, the admiral has decided to go via Bonifacio; we'll leave the enemy to languish north of Corsica.

There's no doubt that we'll reach Toulon; we'll leave our most damaged ships there, replacing them with intact ships from the independent division, and thus reconstituted with renewed force, we'll soon get under way again to do battle with the Maddalena squadron. We owe it to ourselves to inflict the same fate on them as on the Spezzia squadron.

All that is perfectly planned...if the Italian admiral takes his squadron north. But what if he stays at Maddalena? What if he's waiting there for us? We'll be constrained to fight, because we can't cross the mouths without being seen by him, and there are only the poor defenses of Bonifacio that can lend us any effective help.

Then again, there's another danger. If the Italians have sent a land force to disembark at Bonifacio, and if they've succeeded—which wouldn't have been very difficult for them—in occupying that port and the southern part of Corsica, we'll be caught between two fires in passing through the straight, and our situation will be extremely delicate. But the admiral is full of confidence in his lucky star. He says that he's certain that Bonifacio is sill ours, and that the Italian squadron is waiting for us in the north.

25 April

Let's give thanks to the God of Armies who protects audacious leaders in war! We came through the strait of Bonifacio at six-thirty this morning, and the Italian squadron wasn't there. The land of Corsica is still French territory. A torpedo boat of the mobile defense came to meet us; it passed by our stern in order that its captain could communicate with the admiral, who was standing on his balcony. He told us that the enemy ships left Maddalena yesterday at ten a.m., heading northwards to the west of Corsica. The admiral was radiant, it seems, on receiving that communication, which removed all his worries and proved him a good prophet. All his anticipations have, in fact, been realized.

Immediately, we set a course directly for Toulon, taking up a new battle formation and maintaining our speed of thirteen knots, in such a way as to cover the 186 miles that separate us from port in 14 hours. We'll be in sight of the coast before nightfall.

10 o'clock

The mistral, which was weak this morning, is increasing by the minute. The sea is choppy, our speed is dropping sensibly, and we can't, unfortunately, increase the speed of the engines because the *Dévastation* is doing all she can. The big waves are rising up along out flanks, and water is getting in through numerous gaps in our hulls. We're pitching steeply, but we have to keep going.

Noon

It's a real squall that we're suffering. The *Neptune* has just signaled that the pitching movements are causing her enormous stress. Her framework, already badly shaken by her terrible collision with the *Sicilia*, is being severely tested by the shocks that it's receiving as she falls into the hollows of the waves. Her fore compartment is full of water—and, indeed, she's visibly taking nosedives. Her watertight bulkheads have held thus far, but are giving rise to anxieties.

In brief, her commandant is asking for permission to slow down.

The admiral anticipated the problem half an hour ago; he hasn't ceased to aim his binoculars at the *Neptune*, sensing that her battle against the excessively powerful sea might end badly. At first he considered releasing the battleship and sending her to Ajaccio, but finally decided to keep her with us, at the expense of diminishing our traveling speed. In any case, there's doubtless no danger from the Italian squadron today. The weather isn't favorable for combat.

The *Neptune* has notified us that she's suffering less since we've been moving less rapidly. We are, in fact, making no more than eight miles an hour, so we won't arrive in Toulon until three a.m.

26 April, Two o'clock

We reached Toulon at half past midnight. Faithful to its habit, the mistral dropped at sunset; the sea calmed down, and, at the same time, we were able to put on speed toward evening without any danger of the *Neptune* being serious damaged.

But what an unfortunate adventure preceded our entry into the harbor!

The night was very dark. We were sailing with the lights out. At ten o'clock our scouts were spotted by the scouts of the reserve squadron, which was cruising outside Toulon. Our ships immediately sent recognition signals to advertise our presence and declare: *Have no fear, we're friends*. Were the signals poorly seen, poorly interpreted or poorly sent? We don't know as yet. At any rate, the *Vautour*, of the reserve squadron, thought that she was in the presence of the enemy. She mistook our recognition signals from the *Davout* for some signal made at hazard by an Italian, as a ruse of war, and she fired on the unfortunate *Davout*, while launching signals into the air saying: *Enemy discovered.*

The *Davout*'s cannoneers wanted to respond, and the commandant had a great deal of difficulty preventing them from doing so. He immediately had the recognition signals repeated, and this time, the *Vautour* ended up comprehending. Fortunately, there were only a dozen wounded on the *Davout* and a certain amount of material damage that isn't very grave. Without the composure of the cruiser's commandant, fire might have been opened on our side and the two vessels at odds would have caused one another more serious damage. Even so, the *Bombe*, on seeing the *Vautour* fire, mistook her for an enemy and raced toward her in order to attack her with torpedoes. She was almost within firing range when the *Vautour*, finally repeating the recognition signal, announced that she was in fact a French cruiser.

We were profoundly disturbed by that adventure. That kind of mistake is particularly regrettable. Unfortunately, it's rather frequent with such rapid modern ships, which can fall upon one another almost unexpectedly on dark nights. If the men on watch or the officers are a little nervous, they sometimes believe that they're in the presence of the enemy. The conclusion is that it's necessary to have simple recognition signals aboard, easy to send—and coolheaded mariners.

The city is decked with flags, after having been illuminated yesterday evening. It's a brave pigeon that brought the news of our victory on the evening of the twenty-fourth. We've taken our usual moorings in the bay; only the *Neptune* has gone into the harbor in order to go into dry dock and have her damage repaired. We're going to take on coal immediately in order to be ready to take to sea more rapidly, and we'll replace the powder and shells expended the day before yesterday without delay. Crews of workers from the arsenal have come aboard the ship in order to proceed with summary repairs and to patch up our innumerable wounds.

There's a replacement 37cm cannon in the arsenal. We are, therefore, going into dock at Castigneau shortly, and we'll moor there under the big crane, which will remove the stump of the cannon from our middle turret and deposit the new cannon in its place.

The activity in the port is marvelous. In three hours we've completed the movement necessitated by the replacement of the cannon. An hour after going into port we came out again, at four o'clock, to resume our mooring in the bay.

Small boats have brought out at least half the population of Toulon, avid to see us at close range and observe our victorious ships. The shell holes in our armor plating are so numerous that exclamations of surprise emanate from all the vessels at once: "Oh, look at that one!" "Look, there's another!" "Oh, that one's so big!"—all accompanied by the nasal tones that the Provencal tongue licenses.

The officers in service ashore and those of the independent division come aboard and make us recount the story of the forty-eight-hour voyage, which seemed as long as a week to us, so precipitate and tragic were the events crammed into it. In their turn, they bring us up to date with what has happened in our absence. The *Petit Marseillais* has primed us. There's no news of the northern squadron. There's rumor of a striking success in the vicinity of Metz. Nothing decisive yet in the Alps. News of the battle of Spezzia reached Paris yesterday evening

228

at ten o'clock; the newspapers published special editions that were snapped up. The boulevards were invaded by an enormous crowd that went to the Naval Ministry on the Place de la Concorde shouting acclaim for the navy and the fleet. The Ministry has been illuminated, like the majority of public edifices. That success was necessary to calm the excitement caused in the morning by the false news of the bombardment of *Marseilles*. There was no bombardment there; the truth is that two Italian cruisers were signaled by the semaphores. The reserve squadron was in the vicinity of Cannes and Nice. The *Océan*, escorted by two torpedo boats, set a course to intercept them, but the cruisers had disappeared.

What is more serious, however, is that during the hunt, six torpedo boats at *Marseilles* had remained in port, on the orders of the commandant of the *Océan*, who had good reasons for acting thus. The *Marseillais* did not find that to their taste and a few "patriots" have come along the quays where our torpedo boats are stationed in order to shout abuse at the captains and reproach them for their inaction. They were mostly youths of sixteen or seventeen, but there were a few graybeards among them—the only ones one still encounters in the streets of cities, since all the back beards and blond beards are in the regiments. Far from preventing the young hooligans from vociferating, those old inhabitants of the Cannebière encouraged them.

If the population starts abusing our officers when their attitude doesn't suit street corner tacticians and strategists, we'll see some fine things!

27 April

I've received my letters: one from Maman, who seems very sad, although she doesn't want to let it show.

She's filled her four pages, as usual, and then added a postscript—three very simple, almost insignificant words, although I've been repeating them incessantly since this morning because they express in a touching fashion all the alarms of which her heart is full. "Be very careful," she tells me. Careful of what? Poor dear Maman—of the shells, you mean? The bullets? The machine guns? You want him to be spared, your son, who means at least as much to you as to the fatherland, but you dare not confess it, and content yourself with writing a phrase that isn't too compromising, for which no one can reproach you, but which will relieve, slightly, the weight that is oppressing your maternal tenderness. Don't worry—I'll be "very careful," since you want me to...

The disaster at Spezzia has astounded the Italians. The surprise attack on the squadron in the harbor has made them indignant. The king, it's said, has asked for the navy minister's advice on what measures to take. The commanders at Spezzia were immediately dismissed.

The blow we delivered has struck Italy in the heart. She was so proud of her fleet that she thought it invulnerable. Will people be proud of ours now, in the beautiful land of France, where self-denigration passes as the commencement of wisdom? The government is satisfied, to judge by the eulogistic telegram that has been sent to the admiral and the squadron, but are our compatriots? One can suppose so, for the newspapers are covering us with flowers—their rarest flowers. They're all publishing flattering articles about the admiral or the captains of the squadron, accompanying their prose with biographical notes—which aren't always accurate, but what does it matter? The intention is there, and it's excellent.

The illustrated papers have sent several artists to make sketches. All old and all gray, the artists and reporters of "times of war"! It's the veterans of the pencil and the pen who are working now, because the young ones have all gone. The inevitable photographer has been "snapping" too; he came to aim his lens at our valiant *Formidable*, all covered in wounds, and he departed triumphantly with his box well-furnished with "authentic documents."

Grave news reached us this morning. The Italians have disembarked in Corsica. They've taken possession of the beautiful bay of Santa Manza, in spite of a defense force of torpedo boats supported by the poor armored gunboat *Mitraille*, which was woefully insufficient to repel an attack by a squadron and has been sunk. They've put some 5,000 troops ashore, infantry and artillery, brought by four transport ships escorted by the Maddalena squadron—the one we tricked by leaving them to the north of Corsica and which, after missing us, went to Civita Vecchia in order to take the disembarkation convoy under its protection.

According to the telegram received, the Italian admiral left one of his battleships and a few cruisers to guard Santa Manza, and then went with the other battleships to attack Bonifacio. The latest news is that the enemy troops are already occupying the crests of the Massif du Corbo, which dominates the south of Corsica; they'll doubtless set up bombardment batteries there, with the result that Bonifacio, caught between two fires, will be rapidly devastated. In any case, the enemy wouldn't have taken long to cover the few kilometers separating Santa Manza from Bonifacio.

So French soil has been violated! It's now necessary to take back that corner of land, which has been stolen from us. Oh, how bitterly our government must regret not having provided Corsica with better means of defense. For years, all the naval writers, all the mariners and many officers on land have criticized the deplorable neglect in which our great Mediterranean island has been left. The bay of Santa Manza had been identified as an excellent base of operations, where it was appropriate to carry out defensive works; the hills of the Corbo had been designated to receive batteries so as to transform Bonifacio, at very little expense, into a retrenched camp that would have rendered us masters of the strait. That would have been the logical, indispensable, obligatory response to the works carried out on the opposite side, toward Sardinia, on the island of Maddalena, in the vicinity of which, a hundred years ago, Nelson sheltered his ships while he blockaded our Provencal coast. But nothing was done, and this evening, or tomorrow, we'll doubtless learn that Bonifacio has been captured.

Fortunately, by way of compensation, we have a small success to record. Three torpedo boats from Villefranche have attempted, during the last few nights, to destroy the Italian railway that runs along the coast beyond Savone. On the night before last they could not complete their mission, having been disturbed by Italian ships. Last night they finally succeeded, by using subterfuge. A fishing boat was hired in Menton, which was manned by an ensign and two matelots disguised as fishermen and immediately sent to the vicinity of Savone, to an agreed location, where it awaited the arrival of the torpedo boats. When the latter reached the rendezvous, the fishing boat went to the shore alone and silently; the ensign and his men were disembarked, and deposited dynamite petards along the track, designed to explode when trains passed. Then they returned to the torpedo boats, one of which took the fishing boat in tow, to return to Villefranche as rapidly as possible. At present, the petards must have exploded and the resulting derailments have doubtless already hindered troop movements in the Alps.

We should, according to shipboard gossip, have been setting forth at midday to go in pursuit of the Maddalena squadron. The business at Santa Manza has suspended our departure. It's now said that we're going to begin by escorting a brigade of reinforcements intended to strengthen the Corsican troops as far as Ajaccio. What gives credence to the rumor is the entry into the harbor of four big steamers from Marseilles.

4 o'clock

The troops of the brigade in question are arriving on the improvised jetties where the four steamers are moored. The trucks are bringing them all the way to the bottom of the ladder that gives access to the ships. The landing stages are marvelous for that purpose. The troop movement is being executed with a surprising rapidity and order. It appears that the whole brigade will be embarked by ten o'clock this evening.

7 o'clock

Bonifacio has capitulated. But that anticipated news has had little impact on us, because by the time it reached us, we had learned about the great victory won by our army near the same village of Reichshoffen where we suffered our first great defeat in 1870. Oh, who could flatter themselves on being able to describe the intoxication that such a victory causes? A little while ago, as we read the telegram that the commander came to hand to the officer of the watch and me, our hearts were beating as if to burst. I ran to the midshipmen's quarters, into which I delivered the news with a cry of joy. On hearing me, everyone fell silent, gripped by surprise, and also with dread...if, by chance, the news were false, or simply exaggerated, we would greatly regret having indulged in flights of delight. But I gave all the precise details that the telegraph had transmitted, and our losses, those of the Germans, and the name of the prince who had been taken prisoner. Then the enthusiasm overflowed. Three of ours immediately went ashore, hoping to find more ample information.

The crew has been in a state of extraordinary excitement since we heard about the victory. All over the ship, in spite of the late hour, there are animated conversations and discussions. In passing through so many mouths, the facts have already been distorted, the details have been multiplied, the losses exaggerated, the results magnified. It's no longer four army corps that we've defeated, but six, and it isn't a simple German prince that has been taken prisoner, but the Emperor himself. The pride and joy of the great success has caused imagination to run free.

8 o'clock

We're sailing at midnight. The shipboard gossip, the thousand rumors born around "the wick" where the matelots go to light their cigarettes, has nothing inexact about it this time. We're taking the reinforcement brigade to Corsica and then going in search of the Italian squadron.

9 o'clock

Our comrades have come back from the shore. They don't know any more than we learned from the official telegram, because the battle was this morning. They've informed us, however, about a rather disagreeable event at sea. Two Italian cruisers—it's assumed that they're the same ones seen from Marseilles the other day—bombarded Algiers this morning. The coastal batteries returned fire vigorously. The *Vauban*, with the *La Pérouse* and four torpedo boats set out to give chase to the cruisers.

An artillery battle was immediately engaged, and our ships suffered considerably. The fifteen 14cm canons on the *La Pérouse* must have heaped heavy fire upon the Italians, but that cruiser, entirely made of wood, overplayed her hand. Italian shells started a fire on board. The blaze propagated rapidly, with smoke so thick that the commandant was obliged to draw away from the battle and return his ship to port in a pitiful state.

In sum, Algiers, the incomparable Algiers, appears to have suffered some considerable damage. The gracious mosque, whose arched cupola makes such a picturesque white patch in the center of the city, has been hit by shells. Several houses of the boulevard have been damaged. The Italian cruisers headed out to sea again as soon as their demonstration was complete. Where have they gone? Are they going to abuse all our commercial ports in turn? We must fear so—not that these attacks, generally brief and conducted from a distance, have very serious effects on the cities themselves, but they frighten and alarm the populations, and the mental consequences are more lasting than one might think.

28 April

We sailed at midnight for the gulf of Valinco, which opens in the west of Corsica about half way between Ajaccio and Bonifacio. We're traveling at high speed, and will arrive at our mooring at about one p.m.

The squadron consists of the battleships *Formidable, Dévastation, Baudin, Duperré, Magenta* and *Brennus*; the cruisers *Alger, Lalande, Davout, Forbin, D'Iberville* and *Dague*; and six torpedo boats. Of the battleships that participated in the battle of Spezzia, only the *Formidable* and the *Duperré* have taken to sea again; they are, in fact, the ones whose damage, although perhaps the most widespread, is the least serious, and none of their essential organs having been afflicted. The other battleships accompanying us are absolutely intact and ready to deliver brilliant combat. As for the cruisers, there are three going out for the first time: the *Forbin*, the *D'Iberville* and the *Dague*.

As soon as we left Toulon we took up battle formation. The cruisers and torpedo boats are operating as scouts, as usual, but the battleships have been arranged in two parallel columns, in single file, in such a way as to frame the four ferries between them. The captains of those ships have express orders to rally to the cruisers in case of an encounter with the enemy. They've been ordered to have their pumps and all means of expulsion ready to function, as well as tarpaulins, in case they take on water.

The general of the reinforcement brigade has come aboard the *Formidable* with the officers of his staff, in order to organize the details of the disembarkation, which will take place in the vicinity of Propriano in the depths of the gulf of Valinco.

The cruiser *Cécile* from our squadron and the cruiser *Tage* from the reserve squadron left Toulon at the same time as us. They're going to carry out demonstrations analogous to those the Italians have attempted against Marseilles and Algiers in open view of the cities of the Italian coast. Why haven't we been using that means of intimidation already, in the last four days? That's what it's difficult to explain within the squadron. The French government repudiates methods of war that it judges quasi-barbaric, and it only decided to send out the *Cécile* and the *Tage* in reprisal for the attacks of the two Italian cruisers. That's all well and good, but isn't that restriction excessive? Our enemies haven't shown as much restraint as us, and no one had criticized them.

Whatever one says or does, war is an appeal to brute force. Its ultimate end, its *raison d'être*, if one might express it this way, is to harm the enemy by any means possible. In consequence, anything that might cause damage or prejudice, anything that might afflict its wealth, its prosperity or its grandeur is authorized, and the bombardment of prosperous ports built on its shore is a perfectly legitimate enterprise. If one thought otherwise, it would be necessary to respect private property at sea—which is to say, to renounce privateering, the warfare that sets out to capture or destroy merchant vessels belonging to individuals. No one thinks that.

On the day of the declaration of war, we sent the Suchet and three support vessels to Gibraltar. The next day, the *Sfax* and another steamer set out to patrol the coast of Malta and pursue German, Italian and Austrian merchant vessels, while the Milan went to the coast of Tunis and Bizerte, with the same objective. The telegraph has already signaled the capture of three steamers, one of which belongs to the Austrian equivalent of

Lloyd's and the other to large Italian companies. Those ships have been taken to Tunis, and two more to Algiers. They're good prizes—as are, moreover, the two French cargo vessels that enemy cruisers have succeeded in capturing and taking to Tarente.

9 o'clock

The brigade that we're taking to Corsica is composed for the most part of territorial contingents; it lacks mountain artillery. In consequence we're going to compile three batteries of 65mm cannons from the battleships and cruisers and add them to the disembarking troops. Each battery will include a lieutenant, an ensign and a midshipman. The officers who will command these small cannon have just been appointed; I'll be the midshipman with the first battery. God knows that I've attracted envy and jealousy! When we heard about the provision of these batteries this morning, every midshipman was ardent wishing that he'd be lucky enough to be selected.

It's to the commandant that I owe the honor of the designation. Since this is a private journal I can report things that flatter me. The commandant was very pleased with me on the day of the Spezzia affair, when I was at his side in the blockhouse. He thought me very bold, and said so, letting me know that he wouldn't neglect an opportunity to put in for an accommodation for me. So, when he had to choose a midshipman for the 65mms, he thought of me. I thanked him enthusiastically, and he shook my hand like an old friend.

Here I am, then, transformed into an artillery lieutenant. I'm delighted. I realize in consequence that one sometimes experiences some pleasure in doing things outside one's habits—some might say outside one's aptitudes—thinking about Rossini only having pretentions for his cooking or Ingres, who wanted to be a virtuoso on the violin. My new métier delights me. I've just carried out an inspection of my gunners. They, too, seem quite content with their fate.

I don't need to be a profound psychologist—that is, I think, the correct term—to analyze the minds of those excellent and brave matelots. On the one hand, the thought that they're going to play the role of a gunner on land seduces them with its charm—there's a child even in grown-up men—and on the other hand, they're delighted to be quitting for a few days or weeks the life on board to which they're accustomed. Once again, the truth is that everyone has an innate love of change.

While I'm in an analytical vein, I've noticed something very characteristic. The crews and the officers, even the admiral and the big chiefs, no longer have the grave, almost meditative attitude that they had a few days ago during our first sortie. On the way to Spezzia, people only talked in low voices and only said the things that were strictly indispensable; today the voices are louder and people are exchanging banal remarks about everyday matters.

I certainly don't mean that our crews are less conscious of the great duty that they have to fulfill, but it seems to me that they're bearing the responsibilities of those great duties in a different way, and more lightly. They're as correct and serious as they ought to be, but they're less oppressed and less restrained than before.

The difference I've observed is only a nuance, but it's tangible, and it's easily explained. We've been emboldened by our first success; we've been given confidence by the victory won on land in the plains of Alsace; and finally, we no longer have that cruel apprehension of

the unknown, since we've met the enemy face to face—
and that renders us more alert, leaving our minds better
balanced...not to mention that those among us who have
every right to be frightened by the dangers of modern
naval conflict are less anxious now, since they know that
one sometimes survives them...

10 o'clock

We're in sight of the coast of Corsica. It would be
useful to know whether, as we suppose, the Italian
squadron is blockading the southern coast of the island.
The admiral is therefore sending up a captive balloon
that was embarked on the *Magenta*. An officer is going
to take his place in the basket; as the weather is very
clear, his view will extend a long way, and he'll be able
to see whether there are any plumes of smoke at the limit
of his horizon.

The balloon doesn't take long to rise up before us,
its envelope taking on a golden gleam in the sunlight
illuminating an ideally pure blue sky. The officer in-
spects the horizon and uses the telephone to inform the
boat to which he's attached that he can't see any suspect
ships. We won't encounter the Italian squadron, then.
The Admiral doesn't want to head directly for the bay of
Valinco, though. We set a course for the Iles
Sanguinaires, which extend out to sea from the Ajaccio
peninsula, the semaphores of which will inform us about
military operations already undertaken and the possibility of effecting a disembarkation at Propriano. It's necessary, in fact, not to risk going into a gulf occupied by
the enemy, where our troops would be running real danger at the ever-delicate moment of landing.

Noon

The semaphore on the Iles Sanguinaires signals that communications with Sartène are open and that the enemy has not yet appeared. Thus, the gulf of Valinco isn't occupied yet. It also tells us that further Italian transports landed in Santa Manza this morning. Numerous skirmishes have already taken place. The situation is getting complicated, if one can be forgiven a pun in such circumstances.[26]

We ask the semaphore-operator for news of the Italian squadron. He can't give us any, having not seen it. It would doubtless have served as an escort yesterday for the new transports from Livorno or Civita Vecchia.

The squadron won't go into the gulf of Valinco. It will remain outside. Only the transport vessels will go to moor at Propriano. The mariners making up the 65mm batteries will embark in launches at the entrance to the bay and will be escorted to land by torpedo corvettes, one of which will carry the general and his officers.

At one o'clock, in superb weather I disposed the components of my two small cannon on the deck of the *Formidable*. The commandant came to pass us in review. He addressed a few well-chosen words to our gunners, instructing them to set an example everywhere and always of the discipline and military spirit that are the habitual virtue of the navy. Then we took our places in the two launches that ferried us to the *D'Iberville*. My comrades "escorted" me to the bulwark, as did most of the officers. The admiral shouted "Good luck!" to us from the height of his balcony as we passed astern of the

---

[26] It is a pun in French because *se corse* [getting complicated] echoes *Corse* [Corsica}.

ship. On the deck of the *D'Iberville* I introduced myself to the captain of my battery, who belongs to the *Baudin*. His welcome was perfect, as cordial as I could have wished. I think that we'll get on well together.

We didn't waste any time setting out for the depths of the bay, where the ferries were already dropping anchor. Scarcely had they moored when they received orders relative to the disembarkment, which had been elaborated during the morning by the general and the admiral's senior aide-de-camp. The latter, whose rank is that of frigate-captain, came aboard the *D'Iberville* with us, having received orders to supervise the disembarkation operations.

The operations have been executed efficiently. The sea, it must be said, was admirably cooperative, being "oiled," as they say in Provence. Each steamer had taken aboard four large metal-hulled barges at Toulon, which shuttled back and forth between the ships and the shore from two o'clock until seven in the evening. The lighters were able to reach the shore directly and disembark their foot soldiers there, while the vehicles and baggage were landed behind the little jetty that encloses the embryonic harbor of Propriano. As for us, the artillerymen, we went ashore in the launches of the torpedo corvettes. Everything proceeded in a very orderly fashion, so at seven p.m. the ferries were completely unloaded and able to return to Toulon at top speed, leaving the squadron free in its movement henceforth.

My battery, which disembarked early, was immediately designated to form part of the advance guard. We went to take up position on the road to Sartène, while awaiting marching orders. That delay permitted me to make the acquaintance of the Corsicans more amply. Their martial ardor is boundless. Already, in Propriano, I had noticed the attitude of the Maire and his administrators, who made every effort to facilitate the disembarkation, but on the road, chatting with the local women, I was amazed by their enthusiasm.

The violation of their island by the Italians has exasperated them. They understand that the defenders of Bonifacio have only succumbed to the weight of numbers. What delights them is that the commandant of the place had sunk all the breeches of the cannon in his batteries in the middle of the harbor so that the enemy could not use the pieces. So far as they're concerned, only the government is guilty. They accuse it not of incapacity but of neglect and even of treason. They scourge it in energetic terms for its incredible indifference to the island. They swear death to it—and on the classical land of the vendetta, they know what that word means. I wouldn't advise any of our ministers to come here to reanimate patriotism; they'd be lynched.

All the shepherds familiar with the wild areas and too young to be incorporated into the army and all the aged mountain men have already set off to take potshots at the invaders. "Let them do as they please," one old woman told me, "shouldering their rifles as they like, setting ambushes at bends in the road, behind bushes, moving along paths that only they know, and they'll soon have killed all the enemy officers and chiefs. They only ask for two things: bread and bullets. One Corsican is worth ten Italians!"

The worthy old lady came to offer my gunners "a drop." She was accompanied by her granddaughter, a pretty brunette of eighteen with an olive complexion and dark eyes, who also praised the ardor of her compatriots in proud and definite terms. I thought her even more eloquent than her grandmother and took, I confess, a great deal of pleasure in listening to her. I regretted the bugle call that interrupted our charming conversation...but it wasn't the time to sketch out a romance, and I gave my little Corsican a short letter for Maman, written in pencil, asking her to put it in the post.

29 April, Sartène

During the night, we've traveled the four leagues separating Propriano from Sartène, where the governor general of Corsica set up his headquarters yesterday. This morning, when we woke up, we received some bad news. The bulk of the Italian force has attacked Bastia and took possession of it during the evening, while a big ship which one assumes to be a battleship, accompanied by two cruisers, protected the disembarkation of a strong continent on infantry and cavalry in the bay of Porto Vecchio. The semaphore on the Chiappa promontory, at the entrance to the bay, has been destroyed.

With no battery or earthwork defending the superb position of Porto Vecchio, the enemy vessels reached the bottleneck that forms a kind of initial harbor in advance of the one where the troops were disembarked without a shot being fired. The elevation of the seabed prevented the big ship from going any further, so only one cruiser accompanied the two transports.

Our troops, who had gathered in the south via the road to the west, had been warned of the disembarkation in time. They distributed some two thousand men over the wooded hills surrounding Porto Vecchio and succeeded in holding off the ships that were about to land the Italian soldiers. At the same time, moreover, the cruiser was recalled by signals from the big ship, and the transports swiftly returned to open water; the disembarkation had failed.

We have no details of the occupation of Bastia. According to what's being said, five or six torpedo boats must have been there with the cruiser *Rolland*. What could they do against a force coming in broad daylight to attack a town almost devoid of defenses, whose picturesque old forts are virtually useless and which had only one battery, that of Toga, capable of offering any resistance?

These simultaneous attacks at multiple points in Corsica had been anticipated. Since the island was neglected, the enemy was bound to attempt to establish itself there. The lieutenant in command of my battery doesn't envisage the occupation of Corsica like everyone else, including me. He deplores it, but isn't indignant about it. He doesn't think that the Italians are any stronger for having captured this corner of our territory. He says that they have no need of a new base of operations against us, since they have Maddalena and Spezzia. Corsica would be very useful to the English if they were at war with us, but it's almost useless to the Italians. In his opinion, the damage we'll sustain by virtue of the occupation of Bastia is purely a matter of morale. If we took Cagliari, would we be any further forward? No. That's so obvious that no one in France has thought about occupying southern Sardinia, although it would be an easy expedition to undertake.

According to him, what we might have done, as soon as the war began, was to mount an attack on Maddalena and try to take possession of it; the Italians wouldn't have attempted anything against Corsica then, and we'd have caused them real material and moral discouragement. But an operation against Maddalena would have been difficult and long; public opinion wouldn't have had the patience to await its outcome without denouncing the inertia of the navy. So the government ordered as a matter of priority the attack on Spezzia, whose execution demanded rapidity and audacity, and could furnish a striking success on the day after the declaration of war, albeit less decisive than an attack on powerful Maddalena.

We set out on our march early and have taken the road to Bonifacio. There's no doubt that we'll encounter the enemy today. Our matelots are full of enthusiasm; they're making the best impression on all the officers. I have more confidence than ever in their resilience under fire.

Midnight, Convent of the Trinity, near Saffa

Machine gun bullets definitely don't like me. We were in action today from one o'clock until eight in the evening. My battery was constantly in the thick of the battle, but I don't have the slightest scratch.

Unfortunately, the combat was far from being a success. We were forced to retreat from our positions twice, and it was with great difficulty that we were holding on when dusk arrived to put an end to the engagement.

At midday, after having covered twenty kilometers on a road whose picturesque aspect we admired in spite of the circumstances and preoccupations of another sort that were assailing us, we saw the first enemy battalions ahead of us in a rich and extensively cultivated plain. Rifle fire was soon exchanged between our advance guard and the forward enemy oppositions.

My battery was immediately sent to a small rise in the ground, from which we launched our first shells 1,500 or 1,600 meters. The restricted width of the valley in which battle was joined didn't permit us to deploy over a considerable front, with the result that the initial attacks were only made by small contingents, but the fusillade was no less lively. The decided attitude of our soldiers was a pleasure to behold; they launched themselves at the enemy with a bold resolution. The latter, much weaker in numbers, did not take long to retreat, but we were evidently only dealing with a troop sent on reconnaissance, which hastily fell back before our much superior forces.

We continued to advance, firing from time to time. Finally, at three o'clock, on a more extensive plateau, we ran into the main body of the enemy, which opposed us with a line a kilometer long to either side of the road. We estimated that we had between seven and eight thousand men in front of us. We were almost equal in numbers, because we'd been joined in Sartène with contingents sent from Ajaccio to reoccupy the south of Corsica.

The Italian artillery was entrenched behind earthworks constructed during the previous days. It launched a sustained and murderous fire. The 65mm cannons of the squadron had been joined by a few mountain cannons from the land army in order to attack the enemy artillery, but it took a long time to set up our earthworks, and machine gun fire decimated the front ranks of our battalions, which had to fall back several times. At about six o'clock an offensive surge of our battle forces regained us a few lost positions and we were able to take possession once again of the Convent of the Trinity, which was close at hand when the battle began.

Our mariners have been superb in their audacity and ingenuity. They dug like true sappers in order to entrench us, and yet things were very hot around us. I've lost three men and I have four wounded in my section.

Our light and agile guns have rendered the finest service; we've established them at several positions behind the walls, which we've pierced with "gunports," from which our gunners have peppered the mass of our adversaries vigorously. As dusk approached we carried three of them onto the terrace of an Italian-style house, from which we were able to mount downward fire, which was more devastating for the enemy.

In sum, I think I've fought well and made a good fist of it—a merit that isn't indifferent for an improvised artilleryman. In truth, though, how much simpler it is to fight on land than at sea! I certainly don't mean that the merit of a military tactician is less than that of a naval tactician. I'm only talking about individual courage, and I think that it's easier to have a valiant heart in broad daylight on the battlefield than in the depths or the remote redoubts of a modern ship.

On land, one senses that one is fighting, one defends oneself, one battles. One can see the target, one wants to reach it, and courage then becomes an intoxication that carries everyone away, which people communicate to one another and which drives one forward almost in spite of oneself. One doesn't experience anything similar aboard ship. Whether one is distant from the enemy or nearby, one is generally unaware of it. One is only an infinitesimal cog in an enormous machine operated by the commandant alone. Immobilized at one's combat station, one awaits the outcome of the conflict. The courage one deploys then is made of reflection. Is that not the true courage?

30 April

The Italians were finally forced back this morning. Two battalions of reinforcements arrived from Ajaccio during the night, took the lead in the attack and succeeded in dislodging the enemy from a very strong position, which it had occupied since the previous day. Our other troops, in spite of their fatigue, followed the two fresh and hearty battalions. Once the momentum was built up no one stopped, and we pursued the Italian regiments all the way to Bonifacio with our swords at their backs.

The rout happened very quickly—so quickly that we were unable to understand at first how soldiers that had resisted our assaults heroically the previous day could concede ground today so easily without showing the valiant courage that had caused us a real and sincere admiration.

We divined without difficulty that something serious and unexpected must have happened in the enemy camp to modify the attitude of Corsica's invaders in that fashion. At eleven o'clock our supposition became a certainty when we learned that an officer had approached our advance posts and asked to speak to the general. Rumor of an Italian surrender spread rapidly.

We soon learned that our enemies had suffered a defeat yesterday on the road to the east, level with Porto Nuovo, and that, driven into the corner of a triangle formed by the line connecting Bonifacio and Santa Manza, it was absolutely impossible for them to receive help by sea, as our squadron was blockading the south of Corsica and barring the route to any Italian vessel that attempted to replenish their food supplies.

Thus, the Italian corps has been taken prisoner; more than ten thousand men have fallen into our hands. The conditions of the capitulation were settled a short while ago. They are very honorable, for the enemy showed much valor having watched the best of its men perish so bravely.

The rumors circulating on the subject of Bastia are completely contradictory. It's said, on the one hand, that the city has been evacuated after a fierce battle, and claimed, on the other hand, that the Italians have brought in strong contingents there, that they've occupied St. Florent on the western slope, and that they hold the whole of the long slender peninsula that terminates Corsica to the north. The truth is that we don't know anything, any more about Corsica than about France, in fact. The rumor has spread among the prisoners that we've entered Turin after a brilliant victory—but is it reliable?

The prisoners had a few newspapers on them, including a copy of the *Tribuna*, which contained an article that was the object of much comment on our part. It's a very violent attack on the inertia of the Italian navy. It's reproached for allowing itself to be taken by surprise at Spezzia, of not having vigorously taken the offensive at Toulon, and of not having carried out the attack on Corsica at the beginning of hostilities on the day that war as declared. It was not to have such a defensive navy, said the newspaper, pointing out that Italy had sacrificed so much money over ten or fifteen years that it had got into such heavy debt.

The superb navy that paraded so proudly in the ports of the peninsula had been the object of the highest hopes of all Italians, because other rival nations were pleased to cite it as an almost inimitable model, but those ships had not so far attempted anything against an insolent enemy. That fleet carried the destiny of the fatherland and ought to have been placed in a decisive role. Instead, the Admiralty had fragmented the naval forces, separating them into two squadrons, rather than recognizing that by constituting a single concentrated and homogeneous squadron that would have been intimidating, it would certainly have crushed the French fleet.

Why, in any case, had better preparations for war not been made? It had only been possible to assemble the troops intended to occupy Corsica twenty-four hours after the opening of hostilities, because the mobilization plan caused all the regiments and railway trains to converge on the north, toward the Alps, and no one had dared to alter anything in the program settled in advance. No Italian would admit such an excuse, and the nation would hold to account those who had not been able to rise to the occasion.

The article concludes with an energetic demand to the immediate assembly of all the available forces into a single naval army, which, ceasing to play hide-and-seek with the enemy fleet, ought to take advantage of its speed and catch up with it without delay and engage it in battle. It is now a matter of saving Italian honor, which was gravely afflicted.

The same newspaper announces that there have been tumultuous scenes in Spezzia, where the population has manifested its discontent with the mariners. It added that Germany is very aware of the maritime disaster that has just struck its ally, and is exasperated by the laxity of her fleet.

What is going to become of us—the squadron's artillerymen—now? We're ducks in the midst of chickens here. Our mission is complete, since Corsica, or the southern part of the island, at least, has become French again. We can now be sent back to our ships, all the more so as mountain batteries have been sent from France and are ready to replace us in the ranks as the troops of occupation.

1 May

The reoccupation of Bonifacio is proceeding actively, along with the reinstallation of the coastal batteries, whose guns will be provided with new breeches unless the ones sunk in the harbor on the day the town was taken can be fished up again and rendered usable.

The Italian soldiers have handed over their weapons. The officers have been authorized to keep their swords. Everything has been done correctly and appropriately; the victors have been generous to the vanquished; but the general, who seems certain of being able to control his troops and who is counting on their good will to avoid any disagreement, is less reassured concerning the sentiments of the Corsican population with regard to our enemies. It would be as well to make the exchange of prisoners with the garrison of Bonifacio—which was taken to Civita Vecchia a few days ago—as quickly as possible. That would be the wisest thing to do.

The wounded are numerous. Field hospitals have been set up in various places and are overflowing. The Italians have sustained great losses—as have we have, in fact. During the march from Sappa to Bonifacio we passed over ground strewn with cadavers, and even wounded men that the enemy had not had time to pick up during the night. Our own stretcher-bearers were obliged to collect those unfortunates and take them away with ours.

10 o'clock

We've received orders to return to the squadron with our 65mms. The cruiser *Forbin* has just come into port at Bonifacio to pick us up and take us back to our respective ships.

While we're making preparations to depart, the rumor is going around that the squadron has been involved in combat with the second Italian squadron, that we came out on top, but that the success was more dearly bought than the previous one, and that the *Formidable* has been sunk. This news, brought to us by the men of the *Forbin*'s launch, is causing us a keen anxiety. We hastened to seek enlightenment, but the cruiser's commandant, who came ashore to discuss the matter of our repatriation with the general, had already returned to his ship, and we haven't been able to obtain fuller details than those we already had, nor more precise details—for in passing from mouth to mouth, the original news has been so completely disfigured that it's impossible to orient oneself amid everything that's been said.

Nothing is as astonishing as the ease with which one's imagination that is supposedly limited can embroider any subject whatsoever. The old people of Bonifacio stop us in the street to give us a complete and detailed account of the naval battle that took place the day before yesterday, in the morning or the evening— they don't know exactly; they affirm that the *Formidable* has been hurled into the air like a mere cork and that five Italians have been sunk. This evening, they'll doubtless be relating that the entire Italian fleet has gone to the bottom. By dint of repeating it, they'll become convinced. It's so easy to believe what one desires. At any rate, we'll soon know the truth.

Our life as artillerymen is coming to an end. It will have been short. For my part, I'm glad to have been chosen to lead it. I think it's good to experience everything. Even so, I regret that the rapid mission has deprived me of witnessing the great naval battle of which rumor has just reached us. All in all, though, I haven't remained inactive. While my comrades in the squadron were going up against the enemy, I was fighting, too, and while having fought against battalions instead of braving the fire of a fleet, I've done my duty nonetheless.

Noon

We reassembled in a small square. Appeals had been sounded; a lieutenant-colonel in the artillery has inspected us; he gathered the captains of our batteries and shook their hands. Then—with neither trumpets nor drums, it must be said—we went down to the dock where the *Forbin*'s launches were waiting for us.

The poor *Forbin* is bearing visible traces of the battle. Her mizzenmast is broken two meters above the deck; her hull is holed in many places and her rear funnel had been smashed.

We've found places as best we can on the cruiser, which is a little small to carry all of us, and soon set out for the Mouths, where the squadron is, blockading both the south of Corsica and the north of Sardinia—for it's now a matter of attacking Maddalena.

The squadron is, alas, much reduced. It's really true that the *Formidable* has been sunk, along with the cruiser *Lalande* and the torpedo boat *Kabyle*, in the great battle that took place the evening before last, on 29 April, in the vicinity of the islet of Pianosa, between Elba and Monte Cristo. Victory went to us, since victory consists of remaining on the battlefield and seeing the enemy draw away, but with what losses we have paid for that success!

The Italians have also suffered considerable losses. Their battleship *Duilio* has been sunk, as well as the cruisers *Aretusa* and *Goito*. As for their *Andrea Doria*, it has been so maltreated that people are wondering how it is still afloat. At any rate, they were pursued by us after the battle and fell back to Maddalena, where they're now narrowly blockaded.

I've asked with poignant anxiety about the end of the *Formidable*. I'm told that she sank in a matter of minutes after a blow from the spur of the *Lepanto*, that the greater part of the crew has been rescued, but that the commandant has disappeared as well as several officers and midshipmen.

The commandant's death causes me a cruel emotion. That excellent man had always testified in my regard, especially in recent times, an interest by which I've been profoundly touched. He was greatly loved by those he commanded, and his brilliant qualities as a leader had earned him an esteem on our part that went as far as infatuation. He was married and leaves three young children, pretty little girls who often came aboard during our sojourns in Toulon.

Poor *Formidable!* The tears come to my eyes as I think about her end. She looked so beautiful when I left her the other day outside Propriano in order to disembark in Corsica. During the year I'd been living aboard her, I'd become very attached to her, as one becomes attached to a cherished house where one has spent happy days. The thought that I shall never see her again saddens me. It seems to me that a page from the book of my life has been ripped out forever.

As one never loses sight of oneself even in the gravest and most dolorous conjectures, I think with an infinite sadness that in the precipitate shipwreck of the *Formidable* I've lost all the intimate memories that I guarded so piously since I left the maternal hearth to go to the *Borda*: birthday presents, cherished letters, pictures of dead loved ones. I was so very fond of looking at those little, almost sacred things in my moments of reverie and solitude. They evoked the past and the absent so sweetly! What will I do now that I no longer have them? We mariners, who are perpetual exiles, have a greater reverence for souvenirs than anyone else.

A second preoccupation haunts me. What will become of me, since my *Formidable* no longer exists? Where will I be assigned? What will be done with me and my gunners? The *Forbin*'s first mate, whom I questioned on that subject, was unable to give me a reply. The general staff haven't mentioned us. The *Forbin* has only been ordered to make a tour of the squadron and to return to each vessel its 65mms along with their personnel. When we pass close to the *Magenta*, on the mast of which the admiral's flag is flying, the senior staff will be asked what destination is intended for us.

The admiral had left the *Formidable* before the battle and had been transported to the *Davout*; thus, he escaped he catastrophe. Since this morning, he's been on the *Brennus*, on which he intends to organize the Maddalena affair.

3 o'clock

My fate is decided. I'm embarking on the *Duperré*, whose crew has been one of the most depleted, and which needs my gunners to replace a number of hers, which have been killed.

I arrived on the *Duperré* at four o'clock. I already had friends there; I've found in addition two colleagues from the *Formidable* who were embarked here after the shipwreck. After being introduced to the commandant, who gave me a very good welcome, I came down to the midshipmen's quarters in order to hear the story of the naval battle. Everything that's been said increases my regrets at not having seen that gigantic collision.

It was not, in fact, only the squadron of three battleships that had been designated to us by the name of the Maddalena squadron that was engaged in the battle, but everything that was still available and genuinely strong in the Italian arsenal. Public opinion, of which the article in the *Tribuna* was only the echo, had demanded with such insistence the abandonment of the practice of fragmenting the kingdom's naval forces, that the minister had constituted without delay a squadron of six battleships, ten cruisers and ten torpedo boats, capable of measuring up to us with equal armaments.

As all those ships had a veritable superiority of speed over us, it would have been possible for them to give us the slip, but they had, on the contrary, resolutely sought the combat, wanting to engage us in a decisive battle.

According to what has been discovered from the officers and matelots picked up by our ships after the sinking of the *Duilio* and the *Goito*, the squadron was originally intended to launch forth at top speed for the coast of Provence in order to try to catch and defeat our reserve squadron there. With the occupation of north Corsica, however, which is definitely an accomplished fact, having taken longer and proved more difficult than anticipated, the Italians had been obliged to reinforce their expeditionary forces, and had thought that they could spare a few hours for their squadron to ensure communications between Bastia and Livorno or Civitta Vecchia. It was that mission that had led to the encounter with our active squadron.

In fact, the Italian ships had been sailing between the islands of Pianosa and Carpajo when they were spotted on the morning of the twenty-ninth, traveling at great speed, by our squadron which was sailing northwards along the coast of Corsica, after having crossed Bonifacio on the night that followed the disembarkation at Propriano. Our admiral, warned by his scouts, immediately veered eastwards, with the objective of cutting the enemy off from the Italian coast. He therefore left the island of Monte Cristo to port and headed in the direction of Poimbino. Having traveled twenty miles on that new route, he turned abruptly to port, passed between Elba and Pianosa, and discovered the enemy squadrons at about three o'clock in the afternoon, to the northwest.

Immediately, he signaled the cruisers and the torpedo boats to rally to the battleships, which were traveling in single file, and to form a second line some 2,000 meters to port. Then he embarked on the *Davout*, which was displaying his flag.

When they got closer to the Italians they saw distinctly that they were aligned in four parallel columns, of which the first two were each formed by three battleships and the latter two by five cruisers.

We headed straight for that compact group, which opened fire at 3,000 meters. We riposted immediately, and a few minutes later we veered to port, at right angles to the direction they were following, in such a fashion that all of our ships could fire in succession at the three leading battleships. Thanks to that maneuver and the formation they had adopted, the ships of the second, third and fourth enemy lines found it almost impossible to make use of their artillery, hindered as they were by the battleships in the first line.

When our squadron had passed the front of the Italian columns, it turned at a right angle in the direction opposed to the enemy and formed a line abreast, thus presenting the rear and, in consequence, a position of retreat.

The ships of the Italian frontline, after having sustained the broadside fire of our six battleships, thus found themselves exposed to their fire as they retreated. They formed a single file then, but our well-directed fire directed at their lead ship, the *Ruggiero di Lauria*, covered that valiant vessel with innumerable projectiles.

Meanwhile, the Italian squadron is gaining ground rapidly and coming closer. We form a single file in our turn and the two adversaries ran parallel, a hundred meters apart, traveling in the same direction. The *Duperré*, which is the rearmost, closing the column, receives almost all the effort of the enemy battleships. But the *Re Umberto* leaves the line abruptly; a damaged engine has doubtless obliged her to abandon the battle; two cruisers and a torpedo boat join her to form a bodyguard.

A quarter of an hour goes by of violent cannonade, with missiles of every caliber traversing the space and inflicting terrible ravages in both camps. Nevertheless, the enemy fire appears to slow down. It has one fewer battleship than us in any case, and its big guns are only thundering now at rare intervals. Has the machine-gun fire that our small pieces were vomiting rendered its turrets untenable? Perhaps. At any rate, in the artillery combat we have obtained a real tactical advantage and are able to engage in action at closer range.

The *Davout* therefore gives the signal to cut the enemy line. Immediately, all the French battleships pivot at a right angle and launch themselves at the enemy perpendicularly. The *Formidable* passes behind the *Doria*, which is the third in her line; she bombards her furiously, and almost completes the job, but a torpedo from the other ship hits her amidships and another strikes her aft

259

and doubtless breaks her starboard propeller, for she lurches badly. The *Lepanto*, which is following the *Doria*, sends a large caliber shell at the *Formidable* that smashes her helm and breaks the stem of the tiller. Incapable henceforth of steering, the French battleship is doomed to certain destruction. In any case, she is visibly sinking; her pumps cannot succeed in expelling the water that is invading her hold through the two breaches made by the torpedoes. Her fires are soon extinguished and the unfortunate paralyzed ship receives the mortal blow from the *Lepanto*'s spur.

At least the final discharge of the rear 37cm cannon, skillfully directed, pierces the decks of the *Doria* and explodes in a powder bunker, provoking an explosion that forces the crippled Italian battleship to withdraw from the battle.

At the same time—almost at the same second—a fate similar to that of the *Formidable* is reserved for the *Duilio*, which the *Amiral Baudin* has encountered in front of her and whose flank she has opened with a thrust of her redoubtable spur.

From then on the Italian squadron is cut, separated into three fragments. On the one hand, her lead battleships can be seen continuing on their course and striving to bring assistance to the *Doria*, which seems cruelly afflicted. On the other hand, one can see all the Italian cruisers under the fire of our five battleships, which surround them and strike terrible blows on their light hulls. Finally, further to the rear, the disabled *Re Umberto* can be seen, with her three acolytes, which have not abandoned her.

The enemy battleships *Lepanto, Ruggiero* and *Morosini* immediately come about and head toward the group of our cruisers, but the latter take flight and come to join our vessels, near to which they form up, not without bombarding and launching torpedoes at the Italia cruisers as they pass by, which lose in a matter of minutes the *Goito* and the *Aretusa*, while we lose the torpedo boat *Kabyle*, sunk by a salvo from the *Piemonte*.

Meanwhile, the group surrounding the *Re Umberto* is targeted by our fire. We therefore set forth to engage with it. On drawing nearer, it is perceived that it has started moving again, the damage to the battleship having been repaired. The *Lalande* and the *Forbin* are sent forward to take on the two cruisers. They attack them head on, very resolutely. Unfortunately, the *Lalande* is torpedoed; her engine stops, and the *Forbin*, constrained to sustain her, has to cease the engagement. The Italian battleship and her cruisers, *Fulgore* and *Saetta* are bombarded ardently, but they put on maximum speed and rapidly succeed in putting so much distance between them and us that our cannon fire is no longer dangerous to them.

The admiral thinks about having them pursued by the five torpedo boats that are close to him, and he launches them forward; already, they are reaching the enemy at speed and are about to catch up with them when the Italian torpedo boats move to bar their route. A violent exchange of fire takes place between the little ships. One of ours suffers an explosion that forces it to stop. The *Davout* signals to the torpedo boats to abandon the pursuit.

Meanwhile, dusk is falling. It's half past seven. The battle has been raging for more than two hours. In spite of the loss of the *Formidable* and the *Kabyle*, the French squadron is still cable of continuing the battle against an enemy that is also drastically weakened. It is, moreover, well-grouped, for it has always been able to follow the signals from the *Davout*, which have been consistently clear and simple. By contrast, the enemy squadron is dispersed. It hastens to form up again before the darkness is complete. It makes repeated signals to the *Re Umberto*, which sets a course toward it. It soon becomes obvious that it has abandoned the conflict.

It's a matter of giving pursuit. The order is given when the *Lalande*, which has been crippled since being hit by the torpedo, sends out distress signals. Her pumps are no longer working, and her boilers have been reached by the water that is invading her hull. She is sinking slowly. The *Alger* is signaled to take her in tow. Futile effort; the wound in her flank is mortal. She disappears.

The *Alger* picks up her crew. Then we turn toward the enemy, which is heading southwards, and we give chase, launching our cruisers forward.

That chase lasts almost all night. At daybreak, the enemy re-enters Maddalena, where it has since been blockaded—or, rather, kept out of sight—by our ships...

Such is the story I've been told of that beautiful conflict, which I would dearly have liked to witness. I envy those of my comrades who had the chance to confront the fire of the enemy fleet for those two memorable hours. What memories they'll have! And what an honor for them to be among the heroes of Pianosa!

The losses of men have been enormous. There's talk of five hundred men killed and nine hundred wounded. Many officers are in that number. The hospital transports *Mytho* and *Shamrock* are hardly sufficient to transport the wounded. Serious wounds are numerous; mutilations can't be counted. The machine guns have claimed many victims, but it was shell bursts, most of all, whose projected shrapnel struck the men, carrying away limbs and ripping flesh atrociously.

The survivors of the *Lalande* were almost all picked up by the *Alger*. Of the two hundred men making up her crew, only fifteen were missing at roll call, and four or five of them had been killed during the artillery battle. Unfortunately, the poor mariners of the *Formidable* fared less well. The catastrophe occurred for them at the height of the action, when the conflict was furious, and no one could think of anything but oneself. No launch went to the aid of those unfortunates, who had only been able to put to sea two of their boats intended to receive the wounded—or, rather, some of the wounded. It appears, however, that the greatest order never ceased to reign over the disemboweled ship, lying on her side, ready to be swallowed up forever.

Until the end, the commandant remained on his bridge, giving his orders as calmly as if he had been directing an exercise, and succeeded in preventing panic. When he saw that all hope was lost, he ordered the crew onto the deck and sent the officers to make rounds to ensure that the lower decks had been evacuated. If the launches had come, I was told, we would only have to deplore the loss of an insignificant number of mariners.

But the launches could not come and did not come. The torpedo boats, sent in all haste by the admiral, arrived when the catastrophe was already complete; they only picked up those who knew how to swim or had been able to cling to some piece of wood that could help them remain afloat. The others had disappeared, many of them dragged down by the enormous whirlpool caused by the sinking of the ship.

The commandant and two officers were in that number; faithful to discipline, they had not wanted to quit the ship until the last moment, and had paid with their lives for the accomplishment of that duty.

The material damage is frightful. And yet today, as at Spezzia, we're the victors! With the new weapons of modern fleets, the ravages surpass anything that the imagination can conceive. The hulls of the ships are pierced like colanders. The masts and the funnels are broken, split or torn to shreds.

The *Dévastation*'s blockhouse no longer exists. As for the various machines and apparatus that clutter the ships of today, they are all, or almost all, smashed. The *Brennus*, some of whose medium caliber guns were in armored shelters, was able to make use of its artillery until the last moment, but the other ships have had many of their cannons put out of action, their carriages broken or their loading mechanisms disabled. The elevators of the big guns have suffered a great deal on the *Duperré*, where they had too little protection, with the result that by the end of the combat the battleship only had one big cannon that was functional. On the *Magenta* there has been similar damage to the same components. It's only too true that, as has often been repeated, these precision systems, admirable in peacetime, are too delicate and too clever for service in war.

The adversaries of redoubts will be triumphant, because a single projectile has virtually disabled two of the four cannons accumulated in that narrow citadel of sorts. A terrible accident occurred on the *Baudin*. In order to ensure the rapidity of fire, our new ships have been provided with bucket hoists to bring the necessary ammunition up from the stores, but the hoists are insufficient in themselves, so veritable projectile piles are created on the deck near the guns, whose servants can take the charges that they need at intervals. Present day ammunition consists of eminently explosive machines.

One such parking bay had been prepared on the *Baudin*, which contained a pile of some forty charges. An enemy shell struck that cluster of ammunition and the whole thing exploded with a frightful bang. The deck was staved in over a length of three or four meters, the wall was split, the two cannons nearest the park were put out of action, and debris of every sort encumbered the battery for several minutes, which prevented firing until it had been cleared. As for the unfortunate gunners manning the battery, I leave the calculation of the number of deaths caused among them by that terrible explosion to the imagination.

An analogous, but less serious, accident afflicted the *Alger*. On one of the torpedo boats several 37cm projectile exploded simultaneously. Finally, on another of the small ships—the *Corsaire*, it's said—the compressed air reservoir of a loaded torpedo ready for launch was hit by a shell; the steel wall of the torpedo was immediately ripped open with an extraordinary violence; a fragment of that wall was projected at another torpedo, which exploded in its turn, causing as much serious damage as the first.

Oh, this modern naval warfare is truly terrible. Progress—for that's the name given to the forward march in the art of destruction—has put devices in the hands of mariners that are evidently incomparable instruments of devastation and death. By a singular irony, however, those instruments, improved and complicated and marvelous—if the word is not excessive—are equally as dangerous even to those who employ them. It is not enough to have to fear the enemy's weapons; one is henceforth exposed to being gravely struck by one's own.

In spite of the terrifying consequences of the new machines, in spite of the sickening spectacles that they have before their eyes, the crews have been superb, and their enthusiasm has not relented. The men kept in reserve in the depths of ships are burning with desire to replace those of their comrades who had fallen under the hail of fire.

I've been given accounts of courage, tenacity and heroism that are magnificent, but it's too late for me to recount them here today. I've forgotten that time is marching on, as I was experiencing so much pleasure and pride in retracing in this notebook the exciting phases of that second victory. It's time to get some sleep, and truly, I have the right, for my day has been very full. This morning, I woke up in Bonifacio, still being a land artilleryman, and here I am this evening a midshipman again, aboard the *Duperré*, on watch off the Bocca Sorocco, one of the "mouths" that lead southwards to the harbor of Maddalena.

My installation aboard this new ship has been made with an exceptional rapidity, since I no longer have anything of my own except the clothes I'm wearing and a few spare items that I crammed into a little bag for my Corsican expedition. It's very painful, this situation of being deprived of everything after a shipwreck. Only people who have seen everything they possess perish in a fire—all their property and all their memories—can experience a similar bitterness.

My comrades have charitably put at my disposal shirts, handkerchiefs and sheets, so I won't be reduced to the awful extremity of continuing the tour of duty without being able to change my underclothes. Not to mention that I'll incur heavy expenses replacing everything! The State, ever parsimonious, allows midshipmen an almost ridiculous indemnity of 388 francs.

I ask you, O legislators, what can one do with a sum like that? Even going to fifth-rate suppliers, that compensation wouldn't permit me to re-equip myself. I've already had to pay out 100 francs to buy new shoulder knots. Fortunately, dear Maman will come to my aid when she hears of my distress.

2 May

Six coastguard torpedo boats have just arrived from Toulon, at the admiral's request, to reinforce the blockade, which is very narrowly maintained. The various ships of the squadron have been distributed at the three principal exits by means of which one can emerge from Maddalena. Last night, the electric projectors never ceased functioning, in order to illuminate the passes. On our side there were a few alerts; there were possible sightings of torpedo boats on several occasions. The agitation of the men of the *Duperré* is very considerable, their nervousness quite singular. On the basis of information received, the rumor has spread through the crew that the Italians have the submarines *Audace* and *Pullina* at Maddalena. Hence their emotion: the dread of being torpedoed unexpectedly, so to speak, has caused them to lose their composure. The officers have had a great deal of difficulty reassuring them, calming them down and containing them. It's certain that the two submarines carried out satisfactory trials some time ago, but are they instruments of war that can undertake underwater maneuvers? That's somewhat doubtful.

It appears that the admiral wants to establish in haste a kind of port of refuge and resupply in the gulf of

Santa Manza, which will become the base of operations in the south of Corsica demanded in vain by so many mariners. He's decided to close the entrance to the gulf by barges of chains and beams that are being sent from Toulon; he's going to defend the access to the bay with batteries of small cannons that will at least be useful against torpedo boats. Finally, he's requested that a hospital transport be sent to the new center to receive the squadron's casualties, and two cargo vessels laden with coal in order to reconstitute the squadron's supplies, which are running low.

Change of front. The *Duperré* is in too poor a state to be of any great help to the squadron in the present circumstances. She needs repairs sufficiently considerable for the admiral to have decided to send her back to Toulon, along with the *Dévastation* and the *Alger*, and one of the torpedo boats that's equally badly damaged. We're leaving in a few hours. We'll be replaced here, in the Maddalena blockade, by the second reserve division: *Trident, Indomptable, Caiman, Sfax, Vautour* and *Lévrier*, with three ocean-going torpedo boats—nine ships that have not yet seen action, and will, in consequence be able to make a useful contribution to the offensive.

I hope that I won't remain inactive in Toulon. I'm counting on my lucky star to obtain another berth, which won't immobilize me. I have the sacred fire. War intoxicates me; I'm thirsty for combats in which I can expend all the ardor that animates me.

Everyone aboard, I ought to say, is in a similar state of mind. This morning, at breakfast, we discussed the question of what would be done with us when we arrive in Toulon. As we all fear being tied to the fate of the

Duperré during repairs that might take a long time, we had the idea of making representations to the commandant to the effect of staying here with the squadron and being distributed to the other ships, where there are gaps in the personnel.

I was of the opinion that we ought to attempt that step, which is in no way contrary to discipline and could only be honorable for us, but my neighbor, who is a reflective type, not a hothead like me, demonstrated to me eloquently that down here it's necessary to be meekly fatalistic, that, given our ignorance of events, we can't know whether it's preferable to be here or there, and that it's appropriate, today more than ever, not to oppose our destiny. I yielded to his reasoning, and all the midshipmen did likewise.

Why did I give in so quickly to those reasons? Because since yesterday evening, I haven't stopped telling myself that if I hadn't been in service in the blockhouse of the *Formidable* that day at Spezzia, I wouldn't have been picked to disembark in Corsica with the 65s, and that if I hadn't disembarked, I'd have been aboard the *Formidable* when she sank, and perhaps I wouldn't be here to philosophize about the chances given to us by war, hazard…or Providence.

So, we're going to Toulon to follow our fate—but each of us has said prayers to be employed very rapidly on ships that have a role to play. War is cruel, it's true; it's sickening, it's horrible, and it brings with it an entire cortege of gloom and sadness; but it's holy, it lifts up the souls and ennobles the sentiments of those who participate.

Oh, how far one is in hours like those that we're lived through, from the pettiness of banal life and the paltriness of everyday routines! The heart truly beats more powerfully and thoughts are more elevated. One exalts oneself for an idea—the sublime idea of the fatherland—with as much enthusiasm as persecuted martyrs for their faith. All hopes and aspirations melt into one, and it is so superior to immediate interest that everyone feels himself becoming better.

That's what I thought this morning on seeing all my comrades, all those midshipmen, usually so cheerful, so insouciant even of their duty, so ardent for pleasure, no longer possessed by anything but one unique dream: that of going into battle again. Doubtless they sometimes have a sad presentiment, but they forget the horrors of the death that threatens them in order to see nothing but the halo of glory that will crown their heads. Their sacrifice is made in advance, until death, because that's how it's necessary to love one's fatherland: until death.

3 May

We left Maddalena yesterday in the afternoon, and this morning, while I was standing watch from four a.m. to eight, we perceived the heights of Sicié ahead of us. We reached Toulon at about nine o'clock. Not the slightest sighting of the enemy last night—so much the better, for the little group of cripples that we form would not have been in a brilliant position if we'd been attacked, either by the two phantom cruisers that are roaming the seas without anyone being able to find them, or by the Austrian squadron whose appearance in our waters has been announced by vague rumors.

3 May will be a fine and great day for me; I've been decorated!

The commandant, on coming back from the maritime prefecture, where he'd gone to put himself at the orders of the port authority, brought back a list of recompenses, decorations and promotions conferred on the squadron for the battle of Spezzia. Now, I figure on that list, which contains some twenty names. My joy is unparalleled, almost feverish, so I feel incapable of writing much longer this evening in this notebook, the confidant of my secret thoughts. All that I might say can be reduced to this: I'm delighted, I'm enchanted, I'm in seventh heaven. And as the news of the war is good, the intimate satisfaction I feel can be manifested externally.

4 May

It's still and always my decoration that I've been thinking about for twenty-four hours. The thought had never occurred me for an instant that I might have earned that medal, so what a surprise, what a shock I had! It's to the poor commandant of the *Formidable* that I owe the recompense. He told me the other day that he had "thought about me," but I didn't understand. I was a hundred leagues away from supposing the fashion in which he had worked for his blockhouse midshipman. He too had a number of recompenses; he was promoted to Commander...on the very day that he was killed in the second battle. At least his relatives will have that supreme but impotent consolation.

Another midshipman on the *Duperré* has been decorated. I'm delighted for him...and for me. It seems to me that I would have been slightly embarrassed to be the only one decorated, and that I'll generate less envy by sharing the honors of the day with someone else. For I'm not under any illusion: I have no more merit than one or other of my colleagues, and doubtless many other comrades have done their duty as I have, or even better than me, who have not been rewarded today. But luck dictated that I would be closer to my chief than the other midshipmen, and I've been placed among the elect. My neighbor at my table is right: destiny plays a great role in human affairs.

Good and tender letters have reached me. Maman is so happy, her joy so intense that she has lost all anxiety in my regard. She says that she would like to see me with my medal. Yes, I've thought, like her, the one who is no more would have been so proud of his son on seeing him with the little red ribbon that flatters fathers and mothers at least as much as children. How happy he would also have been! When I was very small I talked about becoming a mariner; he had a custom of repeating, in order to overcome Maman's resistance, and perhaps appease his own: "It's a fine métier; one is decorated young!" His prophecy has been realized, even sooner than he thought—but without his being able to enjoy it, alas.

The aunts have written to me, and a few friends too. Madeleine was able to fill the six pages of her missive with closely-packed and overlapping lines that are utterly persuasive. The red ribbon exercises a fascination on young women of her age that I didn't suspect. She's sent me scarlet knots to ornament my buttonhole and doesn't want me to wear any but hers, which she has twisted with her own cousinly fingers. As she has a friend whose uncle writes for the obscure newspaper of our petty province, she hopes that the honest *litterateur* in question might consecrate a few lines of his prose to my humble person, in order that she might read with her own eyes and enable her friends to read that her cousin has been decorated at twenty-one. Poor Madeleine! I seem to be making fun of her, and that's ingratitude; her letter gave me very great pleasure, and even something more than pleasure.

As for news of the war, it's flowing in quantity. First of all, we learned with the most intense joy of our brilliant successes both along the Rhine and in Italy. Of course, we had confidence in the valor of our soldiers and the science of their leaders; we thought that our generals would reap the fruits of so much effort accomplished since "the terrible year," to edify our revival. But we had been so cruelly struck then that some doubt and dread remained in our minds, and, in spite of everything, we dared not hope too much. Well, we were wrong; we shall see once again the stunning march of an army that sends its enemies tumbling before it, incessantly, without ever suffering defeat, but it's no longer us who are the eternal losers! Our new successes are avenging us for the repeated disasters of 1870, and returning to France the old renown as a great military nation that she had lost.

The eclipse of our ancient renown is over. The revenge has finally come for which our bloodied hearts yearned so desperately. The victory that had reverted to us has returned the smile to our flags. Glory follows our soldiers on the battlefields, and the sad defeats of the past are forgotten henceforth.

The mariners are very glad that the navy has been worthy of the army. The Northern squadron marches in the footsteps of the Southern, and it, too, has served the fatherland well, for it has inflicted a serious defeat on a German division. I've received a letter from a midshipman who has written from Dunkerque, giving me a few details that I'll summarize.

The squadron left Cherbourg the day after the declaration of war with the mission of blockading the narrow entrance to the Jahde and keeping watch on the mouths of the Weser and the Elbe as well as the head of the Eider canal, and finally, to monitor the Skagerrack. To fulfill that demanding mission, it remained composed of six battleships, but also received two armored cruisers, *Dupuy-de-Lôme* and *Latouche-Tréville*, which had just finished their trials. Its operations were linked to sending to the German coast an expeditionary army that was to create a diversion and retain a considerable fraction of the German troops a long way from the Rhine. Such a diversion had been planned in 1870, but our first defeats, unfortunately, had required the expeditionary troops to be diverted to the eastern frontier, and the plan had to be abandoned. This time it will be different.

The expeditionary army is made up of corps of marine artillery and infantry, a division of the 10th territorial army corps and a cavalry brigade. All those troops were embarked on a fleet of small transport vessels, steamers of mediocre tonnage, tugs and large steam launches. On receiving the order to take the offensive against the German coasts, the squadron was to protect the armaments and the landing preparations—it was, in modern parlance, a covering squadron.

When it set forth for North Sea, a division formed by coastguard vessels able to play an offensive role went to take up stations in the strait of Calais, like a second echelon. The purely defensive coastguard vessels were concentrated at Cherbourg, ready to defend that arsenal and the Channel ports. Finally, two cruisers and two auxiliary steamers were sent as soon as hostilities began to the Channel moorings in order to cut off the route of German steamers from Hamburg, capture them, and, if necessary, destroy them.

On 25 April the squadron met an enemy division emerging from the passes of Wangeroog, which lead to the Jahde and the great port of Wilhelmshaven. A battle took place, which ended to our advantage; two enemy battleships were badly damaged and the Germans were forced to return to port. The blockade of the Jahde ought to be maintained at present by the coastguards originally assemble in the strait of Calais, in order that the squadron can go around Denmark and reach the Baltic in order to engage another German squadron in battle. In conclusion, we're attempting to defeat our enemy in both the seas that bathe its empire. When that is done, the expeditionary force will leave Cherbourg and land at the chosen point. Until now, everything has gone well, everything proceeding according to plan.

The two cruisers sent to patrol the route of the transatlantic steamers are the *Isly* and the *Jean Bart*. Each of them has captured a German steamer. The *Jean Bart* was discovered by two German cruisers, said to be the *Irene* and the *Princess Wilhelm*, which are assumed to have come from the entrance to the Channel after going around England and Scotland, as our ships in the strait of Calais didn't see them. Confronted by those two powerful and rapid adversaries, our cruiser was obliged to retreat and take refuge in Brest. She arrived under the protection of the coastal forts just in time, at the very moment when a breakdown in one of its engines obliged it to proceed with only one propeller. The *Isly* was similarly pursued by two ships and forced to run to Cherbourg. In consequence they were ordered not to split up again and always to sail together in order to be able to fight the Germans when they only had the same number of ships.

We've had news of our cruisers isolated in the Mediterranean, *Cécile* and *Tage*, which have done good work. They haven't had any captures to effect, since all the Italian merchant ships are now in port and are no longer emerging, which is very wise and well inspired, but they've carried out a demonstration against Livorno, another against Gaete and a third at Tarente. Unfortunately, they haven't been able to catch up with their Italian equivalents, which are the *Bausan* and the *Vesuvio*.

Those two cruisers have attempted a bold strike at Tunis, which was successful. They've blocked the canal between Goulette and Tunis by taking a large tartan laden with stones into it the middle of the night and sinking it in mid-channel. The only ships there to riposte were the *Milan* and two torpedo boats, which they kept at a respectful distance with cannon fire until the operation was completed. The affair won't have very grave consequences for us since it will only take a few days to clear the channel, but it demonstrates that the captains of the two ships have acted with a singular audacity, and that proves that our Tunisian coasts have been abandoned to the mercy of the enemy.

That abandonment of our young and rich colony is very regrettable. Why have we not made it to Bizerte, which lends itself so marvelously as a maritime and military center that could have commanded the sea of Sicily, the passage of Malta and the route to Port Said and India? It is claimed that England would be opposed to it, but by what right? In any case, have we even tried in order to make sure of the opposition of our rivals? Admiral Aube has not spared his warning regarding the importance of Bizerte. As well as him, a number of officers and maritime writers have preached in favor of that splendid position, placed in the depths of a large gulf, dominating the entrance to an interior harbor in which the most numerous and imposing fleets could lie at ease.

Those clear-sighted individuals were preaching in the wilderness! We have limited ourselves to making Bizerte a commercial port and have timidly, almost shamefully, organized a mobile defense of one or two torpedo boats. What could those minuscule adversaries do if they were attacked? That error—or, rather, that weakness—will cost us dear if the war is prolonged. When the Italians have acquired the certainty that we're poorly defended in Tunisia, they'll prepare an expedition to occupy that vast territory, as they've done in Corsica, to the northern part of which they're holding on, in spite of everything.

There, in fact, things are only going half as well. We've been obliged to send further reinforcements to dislodge our enemies. Numerous engagements have taken place already, but without success. Even so, the reserve squadron is sailing in the vicinity of Cap Corse, baring the route to any ships that Italy might send to assist its expeditionary corps, whose capitulation is only a matter of time. The Corsican affair is a disagreeable and inconvenient thorn in our side.

Persistent rumors are going round about the entrance into the line of the Austrian squadron. It's affirmed that it has penetrated into the western basin of the Mediterranean. A few officers are convinced, in spite of our victories at Spezzia and Maddalena, that we're far from being masters of the situation. Either that squadron will leave us undisturbed to blockade the north of Corsica and Sardinia, and will be free either to attack various points on our coast or to hinder communications with Algeria, or it will attack the squadron that is guarding Maddalena, and by concerning its maneuvers with a sortie by the Italian forces, will catch up between two fires.

In either of those hypotheses, it could cause us real embarrassment.

The possibility of the imminent irruption of Austrian ships is the subject of all conversations. A few officers seem very pessimistic in that regard, and all of them are unanimous in recognizing that we do not have enough ships, since all our combat units are presently employed and we're bound to face further complications.

The pessimists also think that the blockade of north Corsica is bad, because it immobilizes a squadron to no great profit—a second line squadron, it's true, but imposing nevertheless, and which, in the present circumstances, might play a decisive role. Their opinion is that it will be necessary to abandon the island to its unfortunate fate, for its occupation, at least of the northern part, only causes us a moral prejudice, and in war, that kind of prejudice ought not to count for anything.

I've even heard officers, in that regard, calling into doubt the efficacy of our naval forces on the high seas. We've defeated the Italian fleet twice they say, inflicted serious losses on them and deprived them of their best ships, but what advantage have we gained from it? What weight will our two victories have in regulating the conditions of the peace treaty when the day comes for it to be signed? The disappearance of the most magnificent and most powerful battleship will be reduced to the few millions that it cost. A wound in the pocket isn't mortal. The Italians have been injured most of all in their self-esteem. If they're victorious on land, if they expel us from Italy, they'll be able, in spite of their lost ships, to impose a harsh peace on us.

Let's assume, they also say, that the Austrian squadron will soon be crushed, that our northern forces keep the German forces narrowly blockaded and that we truly become masters of the Mediterranean. What advantage, other than the moral advantage, will we obtain from that?

It seems to me, in my humble midshipman's judgment, that that's very poor reasoning. If we're the masters of the sea, we can, almost without risk, impose contributions of war on the major Italian or Austrian ports, while we avoid that disagreeable prospect for our coastal cities. If the hostilities do go on for some time, the enemy's commerce will end up being paralyzed, because the ship owners, knowing that the sea is ours, won't dare to send their cargo vessels to sea. Our adversaries' finances will suffer. It's true that wounds in the pocket aren't mortal, but as they also say, money is the sinew of war.

Five o'clock

Great news! Five midshipmen from the *Duperré* have been taken off their ship, which is going to go into port to be repaired. I'm one of them. I'm embarking in the capacity of a midshipman serving the functions of an ensign on the ocean-going torpedo boat *Tourmente*. And as the said torpedo boat has, in total, only two officers, a lieutenant and an ensign, I am the first mate—pardon me, the second in command—of the *Tourmente*. I'm an important individual; I'm going to be "someone" on a ship, no longer the thirtieth or thirty-fifth wheel on a cart, like a vulgar midshipman; I'll have some initiative to take, some authority to exercise.

I shall inform Madeleine of this important event right away. The poor thing! What will she say? A decorated cousin second in command of an ocean-going torpedo boat, which can travel at 25 knots, which is 42 meters long and 5 meters broad, and has a crew of twenty-seven...

I'm joking in writing that nonsense, but deep down, I'm very proud, and I find it charming to make war...war, which procures, at the moment when one least expects it, such enviable situations!

Ten o'clock

I've been ashore to buy and order uniforms and other items or bits of clothing of which I'm deprived. I've only got the indispensable, but I owe it to the truth to declare that the first acquisition I made, after having set foot on the quay at Toulon, was a red ribbon, with which I immediately ornamented my buttonhole. How many times have I tilted my head to the left in order to see the effect of that ribbon on my breast? I refuse to say. It seemed to me that the passers-by looked at me a great deal after that and studied me; I thought I saw the shopkeepers treating me with more consideration, and I felt that might credit to me unusual proportions.

Then I went to introduce myself to the commandant of the *Tourmente*. He was charming, and complimented me very nicely on my medal. He showed me to my cabin and gave me a very detailed tour of his vessel. He gave me all my instructions with regard to maneuvers, navigation and combat, so fully that I was with him for a long time. I won't begin my service with him until tomorrow; in consequence, I've come back to sleep one last time in a hammock aboard the *Duperré*, as if I were still a simple midshipman and not the second in command of the *Tourmente*.

But what is the *Tourmente* going to do? Not knowing that yet is tormenting me (!) So many erroneous things are said about operations to come—and even about operations past and accomplished—that I daren't put any credence in what I hear.

The "well-informed" gentleman who knows everything and has seen everything is a running sore in peacetime, but he becomes a calamity in time of war, because one is always so eager for news that one feels obliged to hear him out. He's always and invariably met the aide-de-camp of some admiral that very morning, who has shown him an official telegram, which has communicated the thoughts at the back of his chief's head to him, which he advances as more than certain...

5 May

The *Tourmente*, which received me this morning with arms and baggage, has set off for Cap Corse with the battleship *Terrible* and two other ocean-going torpedo boats. We're going to join the reserve squadron, which will soon lift the blockade and go in search of the Austrian squadron. On that subject, we're assured that the Austrian admirals don't have the slightest intention of placing themselves under the orders of their Italian colleagues. The Austrians, in any case, want to be the allies, not the friends or the subjects of King Humbert. They still remember that they were the victors at Lissa and they only have a moderate confidence in the professional worth of the vanquished of 1866. It is to that state of mind, it appears, that we owe the fact that we do not have a combined Austro-Italian fleet against us.

We've left in the bay of Toulon the battleships *Courbet, Marceau* and *Redoubtable*, the principal damage to which, inflicted at Spezzia, has almost been repaired, and which will eventually be able to face up to the enemy in case of an attack on Toulon.

I've proceeded lovingly with the arrangement of my cabin. It's so good to have a corner to oneself on a ship, to oneself alone, where one can isolate oneself at leisure. Midshipmen, who only have a locker and a hammock, and live in the uncomfortable promiscuity of a common station, truly have much of which to complain.

I can walk proudly on the deck of the *Tourmente*, giving orders that I don't receive from anyone. I've even been the sole master on board while my commandant went to the prefecture to take care of some business. Now, here I am on the way to Corsica. It's the third time in a fortnight that I've left France to go to meet the enemy. I ought to be used to that sort of emotion, but nothing of the sort. I felt my heart beating faster when I saw the heights above Toulon disappearing into the mist, as on the day when I left with the *Formidable* for the attack on Spezzia.

My torpedo boat is in perfect condition. Her engine is solid, her boilers new, the men are well-trained and seem full of ardor. They'll be easy to manage and won't give me too many headaches while I'm in charge of their discipline. In brief, I'm delighted with my fate. May it please God that we have fine things to accomplish!

6 May

We found ourselves yesterday evening in the first division of the reserve squadron sailing in the vicinity of Cap Corse, level with Macinaggio, the second division having already departed to reinforce the active squadron outside Maddalena. The commandant of the *Terrible* immediately went aboard the *Richelieu*, which is carrying the vice-admiral's flag. He gave the latter the instructions that he's brought from Toulon. And this morning, about four o'clock, at daybreak, we headed southeast. The adjunction of the *Terrible* to the first division of the reserve brings to four the number of battleships we're accompanying; they're the *Richelieu*, the *Friedland*, the *Colbert* and the *Terrible*, to which are added the cruisers *Sfax, Troude* and *Dragonne* and six ocean-going torpedo boats.

The *Tourmente* is at her station as a scout, not far from the *Sfax*, which is in advance of our group exploring the horizon. My commandant assumes that we'll be going to establish ourselves at the exit from the Strait of Messina. We're traveling at a speed of ten knots, which isn't excessive, although the waves are continually covering our deck from fore to aft, because the sea, lifted up by a strong east wind, is becoming increasingly agitated as we head away from land. The rain is falling frequently, and the sky is covered with large black clouds.

Must I admit that I have some anxiety about seasickness? We're so shaken on this little torpedo boat that I can confess without shame to that troublesome malaise. I'm resisting it sufficiently to put on a brave face and not to lose my prestige in the eyes of the crew, but I dare not hope to emerge victorious from the struggle, so I'm in haste to leave my cabin to go and get some air on deck, in spite of the rain and the wind. There, at least, I'll be able to breathe more freely...

The open air has done me good. I've only been "indisposed," and not *ill*—an essential difference. I didn't have the courage to go down to the wardroom for lunch, though. I was only moderately hungry, and the mere thought of shutting myself up for half an hour in a narrow and close cabin chilled me with terror. The commandant divined my anguish; he went through the same thing, he told me, when he started out on the torpedo boats, and he sent a few slices of cold meat up to me on deck, which I scarcely touched. Fortunately, I feel better this evening, even though the sea is still heavy and the pitching and rolling haven't diminished. I'm getting acclimatized.

The sky is still covered. It's the first sunless day since the beginning of the war. I'm experiencing a painful impression in consequence; dull weather has always depressed me, and today's is giving me lugubrious ideas. It's making me see the war in its cruel and sickening aspect. Why these racial hatreds, these national rivalries, which end in all this human slaughter, this atrocious butchery? Humankind isn't made for these fratricidal conflicts; it ought to know nothing but community, concord and love. What, after all, in the infinity of the world and the sequence of the centuries, is the supremacy of one people over its neighbors? What is more fragile, more ephemeral, than that supremacy? What is more monstrous than the bloody battles fought for the sake of conquest?

Thus, because of a storm rumbling in the sky, I curse the war. But come tomorrow, a ray of sunlight will fill the air with light and gaiety, and I'll find, as I did yesterday, that war is holy and that there's no higher task down here than to fight for the glory and honor of one's fatherland.

7 May

I've become accustomed to the disorderly bouncing of the torpedo boat. My stomach is quite solid. I'm no longer thinking about seasickness; the proof is that I experienced a little while ago the desire to smoke a cigarette. In addition, the weather is a little less poor.

I'm getting on very well with my commandant, who is affable and full of concern for me. He's initiating me, with a care for which I owe him gratitude, into my service as first mate, which doubtless isn't very complicated on such a small ship with a crew full of good will, but it means a great deal to me to know that I have the necessary advice and help. Twice, he's had long conversations with me regarding the *Tourmente*'s engine and boilers. The lesson wasn't unnecessary, because the motive apparatus of torpedo boats is so delicate and so various that one needs to make a special study of every one.

The squadron spent the whole night traveling south. The ships weren't very far apart, because it was important not to get lost and it was difficult to see in the darkness, the night being very gloomy. We haven't seen any suspect ships.

This morning, at daybreak, we broadened out our front as much as possible, in order to embrace a greater horizon, and at the same time we changed course, inclining westwards. At midday we were on the line that extends from the south of Sardinia to the western extremity of Sicily—which is to say, between Spartivent and Marsala. But we didn't take long to veer a long way eastwards, in such a fashion as to pass to the north of Sicily in the direction of the Lipari Islands.

By nightfall, the weather was getting better and better. The easterly wind had disappeared completely. And still no enemy in sight.

I must say that in spite of all my energy and all my determination to be valiant, I feel fatigue gaining on me. It's one thing to make a long and eventful tour of duty on a big ship where one is almost comfortable, and watches only come around at widely-spaced intervals. It's quite another to do the same on a torpedo boat, on which one is narrowly confided, where the trepidation of the engines makes the nervous system vibrate, where one is "eaten by the sea" and, in consequence, always soaked to the skin, where the pitching and rolling are abrupt and incessant, and where the number of officers is reduced to two, without ceasing to be obliged to be on deck day and night. One needs to be robust to support such a hard regime without fatigue, or, at least, it's necessary to have acquired by practice an endurance that I don't yet have.

8 May

We had a sharp alert last night. It's understood that any ship that sights the enemy has to launch a green flare. About midnight, the torpedo corvette *Dragonne*, which was in our vicinity, launched a rocket of that color. The *Tourmente* immediately moved toward her.

"Ships in sight to the north!" someone shouted to us.

My commandant seemed surprised by such a categorical affirmation, because the night was as black as ink, but it wasn't the moment to argue, and, as his role in such a case is to serve as a rapid courier, he took us at top speed toward the main body of the squadron in order to pass on the *Dragonne*'s signal. We transmitted the information to the torpedo boats *Audacieux* and *Agile*, which repeated it to the nearest of ships in our line. An hour later we met up with the *Dragonne* again and headed northwards, with all beacon lights extinct and all lamps carefully masked, while the men on watch strained their eyes in the attempt to perceive the suspect ships—but in vain.

When dawn broke, the horizon was perfectly clear, and we hadn't seen the slightest trace of any warship.

There was nothing within sight but a few sparse sailing ships, one of which was a small Greek brig, which the *Troude* visited and which, having shown papers in good order, was judged to be inoffensive. The *Dragonne* had put us on a false trail! We cursed her, but in truth, her mistake is one that is frequent on expeditions like the one that we're undertaking at present. One goes in search of the enemy, striving to discover it; everyone interrogates the horizon and lends himself to that task all the more intently if the night is dark; the eyes get tired, one thinks that one can see suspect masses in the distance; one communicates one's hesitations to one's neighbor, who replies: "Perhaps...it seems to me, too..." As soon as two people have glimpsed something, all doubt vanishes, in the dread of letting the enemy escape, and one fires the green flare. It doesn't require any more to mislead a squadron.

As the weather was fine again, the sea calm and the wind gentle, the admiral ordered the battleships to transfer a little coal to the torpedo boats, whose supplies were running low. Launches brought us the extra fuel. The operation went without a hitch. When it was concluded we resumed our cruising formation, and now we're at the extreme limit of visibility from one another. We've taken a course that is bringing us in the direction of Naples at low speed.

10 o'clock

The *Sfax*, after having stopped a balancelle and communicated with her, has rallied to the *Richelieu* in all haste. She'll take the balancelle in tow. What's going on?

Noon

We're changing course and heading west, drawing away from the coast. It's obvious that the *Sfax* has obtained important information from the Neapolitans in the balancelle, and that, in order that the latter won't be able to announce our presence to their compatriots this evening, the cruiser's commandant has thought it wise to keep the fishermen in view. All that intrigues us greatly.

5 o'clock

Having arrived 50 miles south on the islands Ponza and Ventotene, which are themselves situated 30 miles from Gaete, we received orders to rally in battle formation.

As soon as we had grouped, the admiral summoned all his captains to his ship. He told them that the Austrian squadron is at Gaete, that he wants to attack it at its moorings by night, and he's acquainted them with his battle plan.

The commandant came back from the *Richelieu* quivering with impatience. He senses that a major role in this affair will naturally devolve to the torpedo boats, and that excites his ardor and his enthusiasm.

At six o'clock we'll set out en route for Gaete at a speed of 12 knots, which should bring us within sight of the city at about midnight.

9 May

Yes, it's to Gaete that we went, and it's there that we were to suffer our first defeat. For me, the bitterness of that defeat is doubled by an eternal regret. My commandant was killed by my side during the attack. I heard the whistle of a bullet, and then, immediately afterwards, a cry. I turned round; my chief had fallen into the bottom of his blockhouse, motionless. Blood was coming out of his mouth and nostrils. I immediately took over the direction of the maneuver, ordering a matelot to wash the unfortunate officer's wound.

When our attack was concluded, I was able to go see him. He was still inanimate, but was breathing. The bullet, having entered behind the right ear, had gone through the nasal fossa and the left cheek. A quarter of an hour later, as I held him up in order to give him a few drops of brandy, he died in my arms, without suffering. And it was beside his inert body, while lay bloodily at my feet, that I continued to give orders and direct the *Tourmente* during that unhappy night.

On arriving at Gaete we had not taken long to perceive that we were expected and to convince ourselves that the Austrian squadron had found a good refuge there, as the Neapolitans had said. Electric beams departed from several ships moored in the port or cruising at sea. Two vessels in particular were directing the beams of their searchlights in fixed and immutable directions, which led us to think that a barge had closed the entrance to the port, leaving two passes at its extremities, which the searchlights were illuminating.

The *Sfax* and the *Troude*, which were ahead of us, did not take long to come under fire from the shore batteries, which did not do the any great harm, given the uncertainties of nocturnal fire, but they were chases by seven or eight torpedo boats, which drew them out to sea. Seeing—or rather divining—that, the *Tourmente* and the *Audacieux* headed for the supposed barge in order to reconnoiter it. On returning from that reconnaissance, we found two torpedo boats in our path. We took fire from cannons and rifles at close range, but that didn't prevent us from reaching the *Richelieu*—after having searched for some time in the darkness—and informing the admiral of the existence of the inconvenient barge.

The admiral signaled an order to the squadron to imitate his maneuver, which consisted of heading for the southern pass in order to force an entrance to the port. The headlights that it was necessary to illuminate in order to send the signals gave away the precise position of the ships, which then became the target of a heavy cannonade. Meanwhile, steering by means of the "rat-trap"—the minuscule box placed at the extreme stern of a ship, which contains two tiny red and green lights, our battleships succeeded in forming a line in single file behind the *Richelieu.*

Unfortunately, the enemy searchlights had discovered us, and the Austrian squadron, taking advantage of our groping and slowness in coming into formation, emerged from port at the same moment and succeeded in reaching open water, thanks to the heavy fire from the forts the shore and the menace of the torpedoes that were launched against us. It was during that exchange of fire that my commandant was mortally hit, along with two of our mariners.

I am recounting all this rapidly and summarizing the action to such an extent that the action might seem simple and clear. Alas, it was nothing of the sort, for what I haven't said and which it is necessary to relate is the abominable confusion that reigned in our line, the uncertainty of our movements and, finally, worst of all, the debilitating and obsessive apprehension that gripped our hearts at firing on our own ships.

Let no one speak to us again of night combats, or at least moonless night combats! The one that we have just fought has taken away the taste forever. It's madness to suppose that one can orchestrate the movements of a squadron in the darkness. The plans and maneuvers indicated in advance are bound to be disrupted by the incidents of the battle, but it's almost impossible to signal to one another and have orders carried out. It's only an isolated ship, free to act on its own initiative that can bring a night battle to a successful conclusion.

So, it was necessary to renounce our entrance in force. Our attempt to surprise the Austrians at their moorings had failed, and as for attacking them on the move, it was necessary not to think of that either. In fact, our ships, engaged for some time in the direction of the southern pass through the barge, had their backs to the Austrian fleet, and could only watch its flight, revealed by its illuminated searchlights. The difficulties of grouping ourselves and launching ourselves in pursuit in a new direction were insurmountable in the middle of the night.

Then again, to say everything, we had such an inferiority of speed relative to the Austrians that pursuing them would have been futile and crazy. The battleships *Rudolf* and *Stephanie* travel two knots faster than ours; the cruisers *Franz Josef* and *Elisabeth* can make nineteen knots. We were materially incapable of catching them. Ah, speed! How is it that mariners have been able to deny its absolute necessity and affirm that for squadrons of big ships it's of only secondary importance? If we'd had faster ships yesterday evening, we could have set off on the heels of our enemies, overtaken them and crushed them, whereas today, we're reduced to beating a sad retreat, after having suffered serious losses and grave damage—and all for nothing, since the Austrian squadron has escaped us!

Fatality has made me commandant of the *Tourmente*. In other circumstances, how proud and happy I would be! But today, beside the poor dead commandant, whom we have just laid on his bed, I don't have the heart to rejoice. It required all the violent desire to obtain revenge that I have in order for me to overcome and master my emotion.

10 o'clock

Is the hour of revenge sounding already? I hope so. Just as I was trying to get a little rest, a signal from the admiral summoned the captains of the squadron. I therefore went to the *Richelieu*. Before the conference, I approached the admiral in order to explain the reason for my presence. He listened sadly to the account I gave him of my captain's death, and said to me: "You'll keep the command that you've exercised so well after the death of your chief until further notice."

Tears rose to my eyes when I heard praises lavished on my conduct by so many officers gathered together.

The admiral asked me in this way: "Is the *Tourmente* in good condition?"

"Yes, Admiral," I replied.

"In that case," he said, "you can make good use of it."

We were sitting around a table on which there was a map of Gaete. In a few words, the admiral made various criticisms of the previous night's combat, and then added that having arrived off Gaete, he wanted to attempt to destroy the barge and the improvised defenses. He developed his plan of attack very methodically, assigned each of us a precise role, and concluded by saying to us that he was counting on the vigor and intrepidity of us all.

He can certainly count on me. I feel ready for any audacity. I'm in haste to justify the confidence that he's testified toward me. Poor Maman, poor Madeleine, who are already so proud of me—what will you say when you know that I've commanded an ocean-going torpedo boat and guided her under fire? I'm thinking of you from afar, and I want you to know that I shall do my duty well.

Now the die is cast, and all my preparations for combat are made, all my orders given. I'm only waiting for the signal to move forward. The *Tourmente*, guided by me alone, will try to cover herself with glory. May God protect her and watch over me.

[Here the war journal entrusted to us for publication by pious hands concludes. Those lines are, in fact, the last ones in the notebook, and also the last of the young officer who wrote them. It will be remembered that, in that final attack against the defenses of Gaete, the French torpedo boats had to confront terrible fire from a flotilla of steamships moored broadside behind the barge. The *Tourmente* boldly led in the heart of the action, and suffered a great deal from enemy machine gun fire. A bullet struck the young commander in the middle of the forehead; he fell stone dead, without uttering a word.

The poor fellow did not live long enough to learn that the previous night's defeat, which had affected him so keenly, had been partly repaired. That success would have pleased him, as someone who, in setting forth for that last battle, was only dreaming of the glory of conquest.

Those who have read his journal and who have been able to see therein by what noble and ardent patriotism he was animated, will have no difficulty divining that he would have learned with a very vivid joy of the striking triumph of our arms and the fortunate outcome of that great war, which has been the decisive revenge for 1870. He died too soon to savor that supreme satisfaction.

If his existence was brief, however, it was well-filled and crowned by a beautiful conclusion, since he fell bravely, confronting the enemy, giving his blood for his country, which he loved too much not to have made the sacrifice of his life in advance.]

SF & FANTASY

Adolphe Alhaiza. *Cybele*

Alphonse Allais. *The Adventures of Captain Cap*

Henri Allorge. *The Great Cataclysm*

Guy d'Armen. *Doc Ardan: The City of Gold and Lepers*

G.-J. Arnaud. *The Ice Company*

Charles Asselineau. *The Double Life*

Henri Austruy. *The Eupantophone; The Olotelepan; The Petitpaon Era*

Cyprien Bérard. *The Vampire Lord Ruthwen*

S. Henry Berthoud. *Martyrs of Science*

Aloysius Bertrand. *Gaspard de la Nuit*

Richard Bessière. *The Gardens of the Apocalypse; The Masters of Silence*

Albert Bleunard. *Ever Smaller*

Félix Bodin. *The Novel of the Future*

Louis Boussenard. *Monsieur Synthesis*

Alphonse Brown. *City of Glass; The Conquest of the Air*

Emile Calvet. *In a Thousand Years*

André Caroff. *The Terror of Madame Atomos; Miss Atomos; The Return of Madame Atomos; The Mistake of Madame Atomos; The Monsters of Madame Atomos; The Revenge of Madame Atomos; The Resurrection of Madame Atomos; The Mark of Madame Atomos; The Spheres of Madame Atomos*

Félicien Champsaur. *The Human Arrow; Ouha, King of the Apes; Pharaoh's Wife*

Didier de Chousy. *Ignis*

Jules Clarétie. *Obsession*

Michel Corday. *The Eternal Flame*

André Couvreur. *The Necessary Evil*; *Caresco, Superman; The Exploits of Professor Tornada* (3 vols.)

Captain Danrit. *Undersea Odyssey*

C. I. Defontenay. *Star (Psi Cassiopeia)*

Charles Derennes. *The People of the Pole*

Georges Dodds (anthologist). *The Missing Link*

Charles Dodeman. *The Silent Bomb*

Harry Dickson. *The Heir of Dracula; Harry Dickson vs. The Spider*

Jules Dornay. *Lord Ruthven Begins*

Alfred Driou. *The Adventures of a Parisian Aeronaut*

Sâr Dubnotal *vs. Jack the Ripper*
Alexandre Dumas. *The Return of Lord Ruthven*
Renée Dunan. *Baal*
J.-C. Dunyach. *The Night Orchid; The Thieves of Silence*
Henri Duvernois. *The Man Who Found Himself*
Achille Eyraud. *Voyage to Venus*
Henri Falk. *The Age of Lead*
Paul Féval. *Anne of the Isles; Knightshade; Revenants; Vampire City; The Vampire Countess; The Wandering Jew's Daughter*
Paul Féval, *fils. Felifax, the Tiger-Man*
Charles de Fieux. *Lamékis*
Louis Forest. *Someone is Stealing Children in Paris*
Arnould Galopin. *Doctor Omega; Doctor Omega and the Shadowmen* (anthology)
Judith Gautier. *Isoline and the Serpent-Flower*
H. Gayar. *The Marvelous Adventures of Serge Myrandhal on Mars*
Léon Gozlan. *The Vampire of the Val-de-Grâce*
G.L. Gick. *Harry Dickson and the Werewolf of Rutherford Grange*
Edmond Haraucourt. *Illusions of Immortality*
Nathalie Henneberg. *The Green Gods*
V. Hugo, P. Foucher & P. Meurice. *The Hunchback of Notre-Dame*
Romain d'Huissier. *Hexagon: Dark Matter*
Jules Janin. *The Magnetized Corpse*
Michel Jeury. *Chronolysis*
Gustave Kahn. *The Tale of Gold and Silence*
Gérard Klein. *The Mote in Time's Eye*
Fernand Kolney. *Love in 5000 Years*
Paul Lacroix. *Danse Macabre*
Louis-Guillaume de La Follie. *The Unpretentious Philosopher*
Jean de La Hire. *Enter the Nyctalope; The Nyctalope on Mars; The Nyctalope vs. Lucifer; The Nyctalope Steps In; Night of the Nyctalope; Return of the Nyctalope; The Fiery Wheel*
Etienne-Léon de Lamothe-Langon. *The Virgin Vampire*
André Laurie. *Spiridon*
Gabriel de Lautrec. *The Vengeance of the Oval Portrait*
Alain le Drimeur. *The Future City*
Georges Le Faure & Henri de Graffigny. *The Extraordinary Adventures of a Russian Scientist Across the Solar System* (2 vols.)
Gustave Le Rouge. *The Mysterious Doctor Cornelius* (3 vols.); *The Vampires of Mars; The Dominion of the World* (w/Gustave Guitton) (4 vols.)

Jules Lermina. *Mysteryville; Panic in Paris; To-Ho and the Gold Destroyers; The Secret of Zippeliu; The Battle of Strasbourg*
André Lichtenberger. *The Centaurs; The Children of the Crab*
Jean-Marc & Randy Lofficier. *Edgar Allan Poe on Mars; The Katrina Protocol; Pacifica; Robonocchio; Return of the Nyctalope;* (anthologists) *Tales of the Shadowmen 1-10*
Xavier Mauméjean. *The League of Heroes*
Joseph Méry. *The Tower of Destiny*
Hippolyte Mettais. *The Year 5865; Paris Before the Deluge*
Louise Michel. *The Human Microbes; The New World*
Tony Moilin. *Paris in the Year 2000*
José Moselli. *Illa's End*
John-Antoine Nau. *Enemy Force*
Marie Nizet. *Captain Vampire*
C. Nodier, A. Beraud & Toussaint-Merle. *Frankenstein*
Henri de Parville. *An Inhabitant of the Planet Mars*
Gaston de Pawlowski. *Journey to the Land of the 4th Dimension*
Georges Pellerin. *The World in 2000 Years*
Ernest Pérochon. *The Frenetic People*
Pierre Pelot. *The Child Who Walked on the Sky*
J. Polidori, C. Nodier, E. Scribe. *Lord Ruthven the Vampire*
P.-A. Ponson du Terrail. *The Vampire and the Devil's Son; The Immortal Woman*
Edgar Quinet. *Ahasuerus; The Enchanter Merlin*
Henri de Régnier. *A Surfeit of Mirrors*
Maurice Renard. *The Blue Peril; Doctor Lerne; The Doctored Man; A Man Among the Microbes; The Master of Light*
Jean Richepin. *The Wing; The Crazy Corner*
Albert Robida. *The Adventures of Saturnin Farandoul; The Clock of the Centuries; Chalet in the Sky; The Electric Life*
J.-H. Rosny Aîné. *Helgvor of the Blue River; The Givreuse Enigma; The Mysterious Force; The Navigators of Space; Vamireh; The World of the Variants; The Young Vampire*
Marcel Rouff. *Journey to the Inverted World*
Han Ryner. *The Superhumans; The Human Ant*
Pierre de Selenes: *An Unknown World*
Angelo de Sorr. *The Vampires of London*
Brian Stableford. *The New Faust at the Tragicomique;The Empire of the Necromancers (The Shadow of Frankenstein; Frankenstein and the Vampire Countess; Frankenstein in London); Sherlock Holmes & The Vampires of Eternity; The Stones of Camelot; The Wayward*

Muse. (anthologist) *News from the Moon; The Germans on Venus; The Supreme Progress; The World Above the World; Nemoville; Investigations of the Future; The Conqueror of Death*
Jacques Spitz. *The Eye of Purgatory*
Kurt Steiner. *Ortog*
Eugène Thébault. *Radio-Terror*
C.-F. Tiphaigne de La Roche. *Amilec*
Louis Ulbach. *Prince Bonifacio*
Théo Varlet. *The Golden Rock. The Xenobiotic Invasion; The Castaways of Eros; Timeslip Troopers* (w/André Blandin); *The Martian Epic* (w/Octave Joncquel)
Paul Vibert. *The Mysterious Fluid*
Villiers de l'Isle-Adam. *The Scaffold; The Vampire Soul*
Philippe Ward. *Artahe ; The Song of Montségur* (w/Sylvie Miller) *Manhattan Ghost* (w/Mickael Laguerre)

MYSTERIES & THRILLERS

M. Allain & P. Souvestre. *The Daughter of Fantômas*
A. Anicet-Bourgeois, Lucien Dabril. *Rocambole*
A. Bernède. *Belphegor; Judex* (w/Louis Feuillade); *The Return of Judex* (w/Louis Feuillade); *The Shadow of Judex*
A. Bisson & G. Livet. *Nick Carter vs. Fantômas*
V. Darlay & H. de Gorsse. *Arsène Lupin vs. Sherlock Holmes: The Stage Play*
Séamas Duffy. *Sherlock Holmes in Paris*
Paul Féval. *Gentlemen of the Night; John Devil; The Black Coats ('Salem Street; The Invisible Weapon; The Parisian Jungle; The Companions of the Treasure; Heart of Steel; The Cadet Gang; The Sword-Swallower)*
Emile Gaboriau. *Monsieur Lecoq*
Goron & Emile Gautier. *Spawn of the Penitentiary*
Rick Lai. *Shadows of the Opera: Retribution in Blood; Sisters of the Shadows: The Curse of Cagliostro*
Steve Leadley. *Sherlock Holmes: The Circle of Blood*
Maurice Leblanc. *Arsène Lupin vs. Countess Cagliostro; Arsène Lupin vs. Sherlock Holmes (The Blonde Phantom; The Hollow Needle); The Many Faces of Arsène Lupin*
Gaston Leroux. *Chéri-Bibi; The Phantom of the Opera; Rouletabille & the Mystery of the Yellow Room; Rouletabille at Krupp's*
Richard Marsh. *The Complete Adventures of Judith Lee*

William Patrick Maynard. *The Terror of Fu Manchu; The Destiny of Fu Manchu*
Frank J. Morlock. *Sherlock Holmes: The Grand Horizontals; Sherlock Holmes vs Jack the Ripper*
Jean Petithuguenin. *The Adventures of Ethel King*
Antonin Reschal. *The Adventures of Miss Boston*
P. de Wattyne & Y. Walter. *Sherlock Holmes vs. Fantômas*
David White. *Fantômas in America*
Pierre Yrondy. *The Adventures of Thérèse Arnaud*

SCREENPLAYS

Mike Baron. *The Iron Triangle*
Emma Bull & Will Shetterly. *Nightspeeder; War for the Oaks*
Gerry Conway & Roy Thomas. *Doc Dynamo*
Steve Englehart. *Majorca*
James Hudnall. *The Devastator*
Jean-Marc & Randy Lofficier. *Royal Flush*
J.-M. & R. Lofficier & Marc Agapit. *Despair*
J.-M. & R. Lofficier & Joël Houssin. *City*
Andrew Paquette. *Peripheral Vision*
Robert L. Robinson, Jr. *Judex*
R. Thomas, J. Hendler & L. Sprague de Camp. *Rivers of Time*

NON-FICTION

Stephen R. Bissette. *Blur 1-5. Green Mountain Cinema 1; Teen Angels*
Win Scott Eckert. *Crossovers* (2 vols.)
Jean-Marc & Randy Lofficier. *Shadowmen* (2 vols.)
Randy Lofficier. *Over Here*

ART BOOKS

J.-M. Lofficier & D. Taylor. *Tongue Lash*
Jean-Pierre Normand. *Science Fiction Illustrations*
Raven Okeefe. *Raven's L'il Critters; Rave's Faves*
Randy Lofficier & Raven Okeefe. *If Your Possum Go Daylight...*
Daniele Serra. *Illusions*